7-16

WD

LAIR OF THE LIZARD

ALSO BY E. C. AYRES

Hour of the Manatee
Night of the Panther
Eye of the Gator

LAIR OF THE LIZARD

E. C. Ayres

THOMAS
DUNNE
BOOKS

ST. MARTIN'S PRESS ❧ NEW YORK

THOMAS DUNNE BOOKS.
An imprint of St. Martin's Press.

LAIR OF THE LIZARD. Copyright © 1998 by E. C. Ayres.
All rights reserved. Printed in the United States of America.
No part of this book may be used or reproduced in any manner
whatsoever without written permission except in the case of brief
quotations embodied in critical articles or reviews. For information,
address St. Martin's Press, 175 Fifth Avenue, New York, N.Y. 10010.

Joshua Croft characters by permission
of Walter Satterthwait.

Library of Congress Cataloging-in-Publication Data

Ayres, E. C.
    Lair of the lizard / E. C. Ayres. — 1st ed.
        p.   cm.
    "Thomas Dunne books."
    ISBN 0-312-19295-9
    I. Title.
PS3551.Y72L35   1998
813'.54—dc21   98-19405
                                    CIP

First Edition: November 1998

10 9 8 7 6 5 4 3 2 1

Acknowledgments

Thanks to Walter Satterthwait for the use of his Joshua Croft characters

LAIR OF THE LIZARD

1

PALM COAST HARBOR, FLORIDA
NOVEMBER 15, 3:00 P.M.

Ariel Schoenkopf-Lowell awakened in her bedroom in the big house overlooking the tony old-money resort harbor. She'd been taking an afternoon nap—a daily event of increasing frequency in her young life. She was tired a lot lately, as though some unseen spirit was sapping her strength. Her mother had started to worry, but Ariel had warded her off. "I'm fine," she'd insisted.

A stiff breeze rattled the venetian blinds, oddly reminding her of rattlesnakes. Shivering, she forced herself to get up and close the double French windows. Through them, she could see her grandfather's long pier, where the sudden gusts were rocking his beloved twelve-meter yacht *Wellington*. Distant thunder rumbled out over the Atlantic. But it wasn't the storm that had disturbed her sleep. A sudden fear gripped her heart, and she almost fell as she groped for the telephone . . .

ON MANATEE BAY
3:05 P.M.

Tony Lowell was stuck. He contemplated resuming work on the *Andromeda,* as he always did when he was upset. He didn't even know why he was upset, but somehow he sensed that something was wrong in the cosmos. Better to lose himself in work. And Lord knew, the venerable and leaky old schooner needed all the work he was willing to put into it, and then some. The brightwork needed its annual refinishing, and there was a lot of it. Six months of relentless sunshine had taken their toll on the varnish, despite the brave proclamations set forth on the product labels. It was late in the day, and the waters out on Manatee Bay were still and turbid.

He watched the horizon to the south as a small flock of white ibis scurried across the water toward what was left of the wetlands along Rattlesnake Key. Most of the migrating birds had already arrived from Yankee land—the latest, two flocks of plovers with their distinctive black bands had returned from New England, where they'd spent an enviable summer, probably prancing on the shores of Nantucket or the Vineyard. He wished he could do that some day. Sail the *Andromeda* up the intercoastal, maybe even risk an offshore run over to Bermuda. Get Perry to come along . . . he shook his head, knowing that was a pipe dream. Perry knew forty-seven ways to break bones without a sweat, but he couldn't swim. Not a good mate for a cruise. He thought about Caitlin off and on.

2

Now there would be a good mate. Then he remembered how it had been in confinement with her during that one road trip they'd taken together an inconceivable three decades ago, before the Admiral had caught up to them and—for all intents and purposes—seen Lowell off to 'Nam, hopefully for good.

The daily towering white thunderheads soared into the impossibly blue sky out over the Gulf. Hurricane season was nearly over, but sudden weather changes were commonplace along the Gulf Coast. Perry Garwood had been by earlier, like a knight to the rescue with a six-pack of Kirin's—sort of an apology for not having shown up a few days earlier, when Lowell had wanted to step the mast for revarnishing. Lowell had rented a big block and tackle for the job, so instead, he'd made use of it by undertaking a task he'd been postponing for about two decades: pulling out the long-since-shot V-8 from his old rust-bucket Impala.

For reasons not clearly understood by Newtonian science or automotive engineers, the car still insisted on going and going, sort of like the mythical pink bunny, and about as noisy.

He sighed and sat on the overturned dinghy to watch the sky and the birds, and to ruminate about lost loves and lost years. Not to mention lost money. He hadn't worked in two months, and that last case was a down-and-dirty pre-divorce investigation for a three-time loser up in St. Pete, resulting in absolute zilch. After which the displeased wannabe ex-hubby had stiffed him for the fee.

He still had three days' leftovers in the fridge, a fresh supply of beer, and a severe case of the blues. Plus a car that didn't run, but with nowhere to go anyway.

The thunderheads were beginning to turn ugly and making moves in the direction of Manatee Bay. When the phone rang up in the house, Lowell was ready to go inside.

"Daddy, it's me!" The familiar, long-missed young female voice seemed impossibly far away when he finally found the phone under a pile of cushions after about eight rings.

"Ariel!" he shouted. "How the hell are you, honey?"

"Good." She hesitated. "Sorta. Mostly."

He got it out of her gradually. He hadn't seen her since her visit the previous summer, when she'd come home from out west, gone New Age. She'd promised time and again to get back over to his side of the swamp to see him again, but she never seemed to find the time. He understood. He'd been young once too.

Ariel had seemed subdued last visit which made him wonder, but this time, he knew something was wrong.

"Dad, do you believe in premonitions?"

"Not usually. Why?"

"Please don't go anywhere," she begged him. "I'm coming over. I need to talk to you."

Lowell was always happy to see Ariel, of course. But he didn't like the tone of her voice. He didn't like it one bit. She, his beautiful young daughter, had sounded like the voice of doom.

Ariel made it across the state in three hours. It was just after six and nearly dark when she pulled into Tony Lowell's long oyster-shell-and-sand drive leading to the aging Queen Anne bungalow where he sat patiently waiting, fiddling with his venerable old Nikon. She waved it away. "No pictures, please. I look like a floor mop."

4

"You do not!" But he ushered her inside with a shrug.

"Dad," she told him tersely as she accepted a root beer, "I need your help. I want you to find my friend."

He blinked at her, startled. "What friend?"

"My friend in New Mexico," she exclaimed impatiently. "Alicia Sandoval. We met last year. She sent me an e-mail, then disappeared."

"Ariel, aren't you overreacting a little? I understand the importance of maintaining a friendship, but isn't this a bit extreme?"

"I'll pay you," she stated flatly.

That hurt. "Honey," he protested, "I'm always glad to help, but I just need a little more background here. Why is it so important you find this friend of yours? As opposed to, say, waiting to hear from her?"

"Because I'm afraid I won't hear from her." She jumped to her feet. "Dad, I think she's in danger." She told him about her dream. About how she'd seen her friend in a shimmering cloud that was trapped in a dark pit. Demonic figures lurked around the edges. One, the most terrible one, looked almost reptilian. He had her suspended, like an East Indian levitator, and Reptile Man laughed maniacally with a fiery breath, and Ariel had known he was going to devour her. And there had been something else. Jewels maybe, shimmering. Something about temptation, she'd felt. And evil.

"She's in danger, something very bad is going to happen. May have happened already." Ariel seemed confused, uncertain. "When I called the number I had, her phone had been disconnected. So I sent her a postcard and it was returned 'Addressee Unknown.' It doesn't set right, Dad. Something's definitely wrong."

5

Lowell didn't like the thought of his only daughter being involved with anything, or anyone, that even remotely suggested danger. If there was going to be danger, that was *his* job. But he was suspicious of things of which he had no experience or knowledge. He had never put much stock in mystical phenomena such as premonitions, not even when on a serious grass buzz. But he'd also never seen his daughter like this before.

"Sometimes people just up and move." He frowned. "What makes you so sure she's in danger?"

Ariel paced the studio in growing agitation. "Because when I was with her last year, we became like really close, you know? But she would never talk about her background at all, and I could tell she was afraid of something. I mean really afraid."

"How could you tell?"

"Dad, I'm not a moron. I can tell from people's vibes. Also, she was into some heavy processing at the seminar. And hers wasn't the past-life kind of stuff like most of us go for. It was present life, unresolved, serious heavy-karma kind of stuff."

"Whoa, slow down!" he exclaimed. "Where is she, or was she, last time you saw her, because I really don't want to run off to Arizona every time you lose something. Or someone."

"She's not in Arizona. She's in Santa Fe, Dad," said Ariel. "New Mexico."

He sighed, remembering. "Oh, yes. Santa Fe." Ariel told him the rest. About how she'd gone to Santa Fe last year with her boyfriend from Syracuse, whose whereabouts were presently unknown. About how, feeling low self-esteem, she

6

had heard about this great seminar on self-awareness—the Recovery Seminar, it was called—and had signed up, even though it cost a thousand dollars, which was all she had in the whole world. She'd met Alicia Sandoval there. A recently divorced young woman just a few years older than herself, from an old, established Santa Fe Hispanic family.

"Okay," he said, recapping. "So you and this Alicia got to be friends. And she was scared of something."

"Or someone. She wouldn't say. But I think it was someone from her past, or maybe even someone in her life right now."

He threw up his hands. "But you just . . . what, intuited this?"

"I have good intuitions, Dad," she insisted stubbornly.

"Of course. You're a woman!" he exclaimed. "Sorry, sorry," he recanted as she started to flare up at him. "Just kidding. All right, honey, I believe you. But to go to Santa Fe to find someone just because you were friends for what, a week?"

"Two weeks!"

"Fine, two weeks. Then she . . . what? Writes a few letters and you write a few letters, and suddenly she disappears. Is that the gist of it?"

"I know it doesn't sound like much." Ariel sighed again. "You probably think she just met some guy or something and, like, took off. But she wasn't like that. Not at all."

He shook his head. The worst of it was that he couldn't think of one single really good reason to turn her down. It wasn't as if he had a job or anything. And clients were nonexistent this time of year. As for his boat . . . well, it had waited

7

this long. But there was the matter of expenses. He couldn't take money from his daughter. Not even if she had a rich grandfather she sometimes lived with.

"If it'll help," she said with a thoughtful frown, as though reading his mind, "I just so happen to have a couple of round-trip tickets, courtesy of Gerald, may he rot in hell."

Lowell didn't quite know how to react; he was taken aback by her determined competence. "Gerald? Who's Gerald?"

"Gerry! My creepo ex-boyfriend of the last two years," she practically hissed. "Come *on*, Dad!"

"Oh. That Gerald."

"Yeah. We were like traveling from San Francisco down to San Diego last year and we got bumped and got these tickets, which are supposed to be transferable. Anyway, Gerry took off without them and good riddance, and now we can use them!"

Once again Lowell was left breathless by his daughter. "We?"

"Of course. I'm going too."

"That's out of the question, honey. You said yourself it might be dangerous, that your friend might be in real trouble."

"That's just theoretical. Dad, I'm a grown woman."

"No." He was adamant. "I don't want you getting involved in something like this—especially if there's danger. You could become the next target. There're too many things that could happen."

She was disappointed and considered fighting him about it, but finally she backed down. She wouldn't admit to her father, or to anyone, that she was afraid of Santa Fe. It had the highest rape rate in the nation, and most of the victims were young Anglo women. When she was there, the men had looked at her with a strange, predatory hostility, and she'd been glad she was with Gerald. Sure, she'd feel safer with her dad, but even so . . .

"Okay, okay, but will you call me regularly from there?"

She was talking as if it were a fait accompli, he realized. But he also recognized the concession. He was already formulating a plan. He'd been wanting to visit Santa Fe for a long time. He even had an old friend there, someone who might prove useful. But he wasn't about to capitulate too quickly. No way of knowing what she'd ask him to do next, otherwise. Marry her mother, or jump over the moon, or go find Gerald, or God knows what.

"So you don't have any address for her, anything like that?"

She shook her head. "Only the old one. I know she has family there, but . . . if her phone was disconnected . . ." She trailed off, her voice sounding small and uncertain. "I do have a photo, though, if that will help. She gave it to me after the seminar ended."

The photo was dog-eared and faded, but the image was unmistakable. Alicia Sandoval was a classic beauty by any standards, with long, black tresses, finer than Asian, with dark, impenetrable eyes that could easily be Native American—Perry had always insisted that the roots were the same, in any case. Lowell sighed, sensing trouble. But he couldn't say no to Ariel. Not when she looked at him like that . . .

2

Lowell was up before dawn. He had slept fitfully at best, struggling with unfamiliar emotions, trying to make sense of his feelings, of what Ariel had asked of him. He'd dreamed of ancient runes and ruins, of wise, wrinkled Pueblo chiefs sitting cross-legged like silent sentinels, of Spanish churches, and heavy, ornately carved wooden doors that slammed repeatedly in his face.

In his strange dream, he had pictured a woman's face that seemed very real to him, had felt her fear. It was the woman in the photograph Ariel had given him. He'd sensed there was something untouchable about her; still, he felt irresistibly drawn to her. And yet, in the dream, she'd been warning—or was it warding?—him off with a face twisted and distorted into a manifestation of sheer terror, holding her hands outward, arms stiff, palms turned upward. Her nails were painted with old, caked blood. Lowell had awakened with a yell, sweating.

He wondered if he still had the option to do the sensible thing, the prudent thing, to call Ariel—who'd insisted on driving home last night—and beg off, stay away, not get involved. What if Ariel was right, that her friend was in serious trouble? It wasn't really any of her business, of course. Or his. From what he gathered, it had been a casual friendship— one that hardly warranted a trip across the country on his part. Nor did he want to confess to mystical misgivings to his daughter; she'd just say "I told you so." But he couldn't deny a growing concern, which was not diminished with wakefulness—this uncanny feeling he couldn't explain, not to Ariel or anyone else, except maybe his Native American pal Perry—that someone, a woman in some inexplicable way connected to him, yet someone he did not know, was in serious danger and that for some reason, only he could—or was it would?—help her.

He also wondered and worried, without any basis, if it wasn't already too late. He could only surmise. He didn't have a clue as to why he should feel this way, other than it was how Ariel had felt, and now this dream. In any case, none of the possible reasons made him feel any better.

He went down to the kitchen and made some coffee in the little French one-cup coffeemaker that Ariel had sent him last spring for his birthday. He paced, went to the phone, and finally, braving the necessity of risking conversation with her mother—or worse, with her grandfather—he called Ariel.

"Well, have you decided?" she demanded at once.

He sighed. There was no way he could tell her about the

dream last night. "All right, all right, I'll go," he agreed. "But I'm going to need more information. Her nearest relations, friends, where she worked, that sort of thing."

"I told you, that's just what I don't know," Ariel lamented, sounding slightly peeved.

He sighed again.

"Are you okay, Dad? You sound strange."

"I'm fine. Are *you* all right?" He could feel the tension in her voice. There was a lot left unsaid between them.

"I'll be all right when you find her," she asserted.

He hesitated before continuing. "Ariel, have you considered contacting the FBI, or the police out there?"

She forced a laugh. "Dad, you have to understand. Alicia Sandoval comes from one of the most insular, protective societies in America. They don't talk to strangers, and neither do the police. As for the FBI, there's no evidence of kidnapping, and anyway, they'd have the same problems you will."

"So what good is my going there? They sure as hell won't want to talk to me."

"Dad," she pleaded. "You're my only hope. Maybe her only hope. You're a detective!"

"Part-time," he conceded.

"Dad, more than ever, I'm convinced there's something wrong. I think you should start with her ex-husband. The more I think about it, the more sure I am that she was involved in some kind of abusive domestic situation."

"You didn't mention an ex-husband before. You just said she was in danger. That could mean a lot of things."

"Dad! All right! I'm sorry, I meant to. She told me that much, that she'd been married to this really creepy guy. It was one time when we were in this trance."

"Trance?"

"At the seminar!" she exclaimed, as though that explained everything there was to know in the entire universe.

"Okay, whatever. I said I would go, but this domestic equation poses a whole new set of problems and scenarios. The more I know ahead of time, the better prepared I'll be."

Ariel took a deep breath and expelled it into the handset. "Dad, I'm sorry about all this. The more I think about it, the more I'm having second thoughts. I shouldn't have asked you to go out there. It was a stupid idea."

"No!" he heard himself saying. "Not at all. I told you I'd go look into it, and that's what I'm going to do."

"It's just that I didn't know what else to do. You're right, I probably should just call the police out there and let them handle it."

"Look," he said with another sigh. "If, like you said, they won't talk to you, that won't help either. What's the husband's name? Maybe I can start there."

"I don't *know!*" She sounded exasperated, as though it was his fault somehow. "I think it was Gomez, something like that. She wasn't using his name, and only mentioned it once."

"All right. Look, I'm already practically on my way. I've been meaning to check out this famous Santa Fe place anyway. I hear the food's great and that they have a nice local ale. So I'll make a few calls, then go on out there and look around. *No problema.*"

"Are you sure?"

"Sure I'm sure." He'd start with Bedrosian, he decided. And Joshua Croft, his old acquaintance. "I have a friend I've always wanted to look up out West anyway, and my schedule here is pretty clear. So consider it done. I'll go out there, have

13

a few laughs, see the sights, check up on your girlfriend, and be back in a few days. It'll be like a vacation. One can stand all these palm trees and pelicans for only so long, anyway."

"Sure," she said. "A vacation." There was a pause. "Well, thanks, Dad." They both knew it wasn't going to be that easy. Her laugh was hollow. There was another pause. "You really are a prince," she sighed. "But *please* be careful."

"Sure, honey. I will."

She hesitated. "Maybe I *should* go with you."

"Not a chance. We already discussed that."

"Just . . . be careful," she repeated. "And if it gets too heavy, you get out of there, okay?"

"Not to worry," he told her. "So it's settled, then—"

"Do you believe in astrology?" Ariel suddenly asked.

"Not really. Why?"

"Maybe I should get a reading on her. On you. I have a friend in Palm Beach Gardens who—"

"Honey, that's all right." Just because he was bound for the land of the stargazers, it didn't mean he had to join them. "I'm not much of a believer, I'm afraid. Astrology, channeling, or any of that."

"All I'm saying is that there are forces in the universe besides just you and me, with powers and knowledge we can't even imagine. And there are people who know how to tap into those forces."

He'd have to think about that later. "Okay," he acceded. "If I need my karma adjusted, I'll let you know."

"Don't be snide. All I'm saying is that you are going to the New Age capital of the world, and there are people who might be able to help you if you are open to them."

"How open?"

14

"Minded, for starters. Anyway, it's a small city," she added lamely. "It can't be that hard to find one woman."

"Right."

She thought for a moment. "There *is* someone I met there who you might want to talk to."

"A seer, or a channeler?"

"Do you want some leads or don't you?"

"Sorry. Go ahead."

"There was this artist, Thomas Royster. He hung out at the bars on Canyon Road. He'll probably be drunk and offer you a painting for a drink. His work is done with some kind of ink wash, very good. But he knows a lot of people. Also, you should try to find a woman named Christina Taylor. She's one of those Texas heiresses who live on the east side. She was our seminar facilitator in Denver and has a history with a violent husband." She gave him a phone number. "Better brush up on your Spanish, Dad," she added as an afterthought. "It's a mostly Hispanic city."

Lowell didn't have much Spanish. But Santa Fe was in New Mexico, which was part of the U.S.A., wasn't it? Surely English was the primary language. On the other hand, he'd been down in Miami enough times. And he knew enough history to know that the Spaniards had settled the southwest—like Florida, which they'd originally named the entire southeastern region of the New World—almost a hundred years before Plymouth Rock. It was probable that their descendants would still insist on speaking Spanish. People sure as hell did down on Calle Ocho.

"Don't worry," he reassured his daughter, who was sounding more and more worried. "I still know a few phrases. I'll find her."

15

She hoped he was right. "Good luck, and Godspeed," Ariel told him, "and call me as soon as you get there."

"I will, honey. I love you," he added haltingly, but she'd already hung up.

Lowell called his old friend and rival, Detective Lieutenant Lena Bedrosian, at Manatee City Police Headquarters and asked her to run a "Missing Person" past the New Mexico State Police. She grudgingly agreed after he reminded her of about ten years' worth of favors he did for her last year in Big Cypress Swamp.

"What is this, a shakedown?" she complained.

"Not at all," he said. "I just need a favor."

She muttered some more about blackmail, grumbled, and finally agreed. He paced his studio, still troubled by the intrusion of such intangibles as dreams and premonitions on what was supposed to be a highly empirical, scientific, logical, and fact-driven undertaking.

Bedrosian called back a half hour later.

"Sorry, there was nothing," she told him with an "I told you so" inflection in her voice. "You won't get any cooperation in New Mexico, as far as I can see."

Lowell thanked her and hung up. Digging through his files, he finally found an old, tattered business card: JOSHUA CROFT, THE MONDRAGON DETECTIVE AGENCY. With an address on Palace Avenue in Santa Fe. He called the number and got an answering machine. There were a lot of beeps, indicating a lot of unanswered calls. That worried him.

He would have to go it alone. As he always did.

He got on the phone to get flight information, then packed his gear, including his rarely used ski parka, picked up his Nikon camera case and six rolls of film for no certain purpose

16

other than admitting to himself that, being a retired photographer, he might still want to take some pictures. He was on his way to the airport within the hour. Compounding his anxiety, he missed his flight and the next one from Tampa wasn't until one in the afternoon. The only other possibility was to drive to Orlando—always a bad idea—and despite the sense of urgency he couldn't quite shake, he knew he wouldn't be able to save any time by going there. It would be a three-hour delay either way. He would have to wait.

Lowell bought the latest *Time* magazine and sat in the waiting room, but was unable to concentrate. He tried a women's magazine, attracted by its cover featuring an article on domestic violence, and found he still couldn't concentrate. He was bothered that he had no real knowledge about who or what he was dealing with.

He caught the American Airlines one-fifteen flight to Albuquerque, changing at Dallas. It was the best he could do, but the nagging feeling that had begun to work its way into his consciousness would not go away—the sense that time was of the essence.

Six hours and fifty minutes later, Tony Lowell sat forward in his coach seat on American Airlines Flight 1110 as the stewardess announced: "Ladies and gentlemen, we are now approaching Albuquerque International Airport. Please return to your seats and buckle your seat belts. We will be on the ground in approximately ten minutes, right on time. The temperature in Albuquerque, by the way, is forty-six. Have a nice evening, and thank you for flying American."

Lowell leaned over to the window and gazed down at the

17

sprawling city below, wishing there was more daylight left. A brilliant glow of pink and violet on the western horizon was set off by the dark outlines of incalculably distant mountain peaks. It was nearing dark, 7:51 P.M., Mountain Time. He reset his watch—an old Casio he'd found in the bay one time—two hours back.

Lowell spotted the parallel strips of lights outlining the runway as the Boeing 737 banked steeply to the right and dove for the ground. He closed his eyes, reflecting on having accepted a mission of which he had only the vaguest sense, other than its being of importance to his daughter. He still had no plan of action, had no clear idea of who Alicia Sandoval's alleged tormentor, or tormentors, might be, other than an alleged ex-husband—if, in fact, that was the problem—or of how he would deal with the woman's situation. The police were out of the question, according to both Ariel and Bedrosian. And he knew from past experience that there was little reason for the cops to listen to a stranger from out of town—from out of state, in any case. Especially in regard to the personal affairs of a local resident. Especially a native daughter. Especially involving what in so many places and cultures was still considered "a domestic dispute" and as such, nobody else's business.

A new wave of uncertainty crept over him. It was as though there was something else at work here as well. Some other force, some other need, driving him. Damn, he fretted to himself. He hoped this New Age crap wasn't contagious. He was entering strange territory. And very likely, hostile. New Mexico, once the hunting ground of the now-deified Billy the Kid (Pueblo mystics and New Agers aside), was still the

18

Wild West. Big oil and big cattle still ruled here in an uneasy truce with Native American and old Hispanic interests. As an "Anglo," as he knew he'd be called out here, he was well aware that Anglos were by tradition despised foreigners in New Mexico. Tony Lowell was not only an Anglo, but an Easterner to boot, even though most Floridians considered themselves Southerners.

Furthermore, he'd been west of the Mississippi only once since 'Nam, and that had been on a nonstop flight to San Francisco, tracking an insurance embezzler. Which meant he was also a greenhorn. It was going to take all his wits and resources to learn his way around the turf, to comprehend the people and their customs, to adapt, to survive. And to accomplish an uncertain mission.

A sign welcomed him to Albuquerque, New Mexico, population 420,000. Albuquerque was the only major metropolis serving the huge area stretching from the Mexican border to Denver, from Phoenix to Dallas. As he exited the tunnel and made his way into the airport proper, he warily took in the surroundings, an automatic response to his training to be ever the observer. He noted the palace-like, adobe-style halls of the actually very modern Albuquerque Airport. It was eerily empty. He half-expected to see a sleeping Indian or Mexican propped up against the wall—or against one of the huge columns that presumably held up the high, frescoed ceiling. He expunged the thought, knowing it to be racist in origin, conditioned in him by TV, films, and comics—and realized that he had no real knowledge whatsoever of the place he was going to visit. He had read the latest Tony Hillerman during the flight, hoping to glean some preparation from it for his journey. It hadn't offered much, other than to make it clear that Santa Fe was a long way from Florida, and so was the Pueblo Indian country that surrounded it.

No matter, he reasoned. He was a quick learner.

The terminal walls were brightly adorned with Native American designs. Anasazi, he'd heard somewhere. He began to feel he could like it here under different circumstances. Such as once he found Alicia Sandoval and could report to Ariel that she was safe. Then maybe he could relax a little and enjoy the sights.

He followed the signs to the luggage pickup area, a long left turn into the main building and lobbies. The floors were tiled, as were the wainscoted walls. There were huge, carved beams, called "corbels," which had once been giant trees— much revered, he knew, by Indians throughout the continent.

After retrieving his single bag and stepping through the automatic glass doors out into the transportation area, he felt the chill wind at once. A dry, frigid gale was ripping down from a now-invisible mountain pass—one over which he'd just flown. The feeling was long unfamiliar to him, and he had to stop a moment just to savor the experience.

The small crowd, mostly from Lowell's flight, zipped up their ski jackets or woolen Pendletons, leaned against the wind and hurriedly scrambled into waiting vehicles. He knew he would need a car, although there was a shuttle bus that ran every few hours to Santa Fe. An hour and a half away, he was told. There was a small airport there, but connections were few, and he was advised that he would arrive sooner by ground transport.

Night had already fallen by the time Lowell got onto the next Alamo shuttle and headed for the car-rental area. A tall mountain loomed up ahead, a pitch-black profile against the night sky, sharp and close. The van driver pointed to it.

"Sandia Peak," he announced in his pleasing southwestern Hispanic accent. "There're thick pine forests up there. We already have a foot of snow on top. You can see it from here. They're already skiing in some areas." Lowell looked up absently and nodded, his thoughts seventy miles farther north. The closeness of the mountain seemed ominous, a towering eleven thousand feet directly above the sprawling city.

Thirty minutes later, Lowell was driving a rented Buick LeSabre due north on Interstate 25, up the Rio Grande River Valley toward Santa Fe. He couldn't see the legendary river, a few miles west, but he knew it was there.

The Interstate continued to climb, a series of plateaus rising like stairs into the mountains. After an hour's drive through the coal-black night, he passed the Cochiti Lake Indian Reservation, to the west along the Rio Grande. As he crested the hill, a glow of city lights became visible dead ahead: Santa Fe, capital city of New Mexico. He could see the twelve-thousand-foot Sangre de Cristo Mountains soaring directly above the city—a dark, black profile against the night sky, dusted with snow. The entire vista was illuminated like a Vermeer painting when the full moon suddenly and majestically arose from behind another, smaller mountain range just to the east—the Ortiz Mountains.

Santa Fe lay before him now as he drove down the north slope of the plateau toward the mountains ahead. The city beckoned and glimmered like a jewel shining in the moonlight.

Lowell exited the Interstate on Cerillos Road, past an adobe-style shopping center—one of those new, so-called fac-

21

tory store outlet malls that served to remind him he was still in America. He drove the dismayingly familiar gauntlet of mini-malls, fast-food stands, gas stations, and motels of varying sizes and degrees of appeal—from Holiday Inn to Motel 6. Most of the businesses were closed at this hour. Some appeared, by their lighting, as though intended to be quaint. Most were not. He passed a Wal-Mart, then turned up St. Michael's Drive past a Kmart, along with the inevitable Pizza Hut, McDonald's, Taco Bell, Wendy's, on and on. Then north once more, on St. Francis Drive, literally feeling his way, wondering where all that famous charm was. He'd heard that Santa Fe prided itself in being the "City Different." So far, he saw no difference between this and virtually any other small American city he'd been to.

After a couple of miles of national chainstores and franchises, he found his way at last at the old center city and capitol district. This, at last, began to take on the aura of another time and place. "You might need a passport," the airport ticket agent had told him jokingly when he'd checked in with Ariel's tickets.

Lowell pulled into an empty parking lot near the round state capitol building and got out his map. It was close to midnight, and the city was quiet. Traffic was sparse, late-night workers or partyers scurrying home. The government buildings—mainly of Territorial or adobe design—were dark. Some teenagers in a low-rider Chevy cruised past. All had dark eyes and dark hair, he noted. They regarded him with open hostility and slowed down—all Fifties' mufflers and loud rap music rumbling from one of those infernal base boosters. Hip-hop, he noted. Not salsa. Not mariachi. They wore black jackets.

22

Lowell, aware of the image he projected in the rented Buick, wondered if he was an easy mark. In Florida, the state had had to remove the identifying numbers of the license plates that had alerted prowling predators the cars contained tourists. He pulled back onto Paseo de Peralta and drove on past the government center.

His apprehensions were instantly realized.

Halfway down the block, the Chevy suddenly braked to a halt, tires chirping, then spun right and screeched into the next parking-lot entrance, backed around, and burned rubber back in Lowell's direction. Lowell quickly calculated his options, the various possible scenarios about to unfold, their likely outcomes. He didn't much like any of them. He hit the gas and took off as the gang sped past in the opposite lane. He heard shouts of rage and derision, a squeal of brakes, and a big V-8 roar into action as the Chevy made a U-turn and came after him. It was no contest, he knew. Quickly, he pulled into the right lane and allowed the Chevy to overtake him on his left. Three young males leaned out the two side windows, shoving each other as they vied for space.

"Hey! Get the fuck out of town, gringo!" shouted one of the two heads wedged in the backseat right-side window. Lowell grinned at them and waved. Insults, he could handle. The kid in the front seat, though, clutching a Mac-10 automatic pistol, did worry him. Lowell slammed on the brakes and the other car surged ahead. Spinning into a one-eighty, he skidded across the center divider into the opposite-bound lane—thankful there was no traffic—and tore away just as a police cruiser pulled into the Paseo.

The pursuing Chevy spotted the cops, squealed into a side street and took off. The Hispanic cop in the passenger seat gave Lowell a look of some chagrin and apology as their cruiser whipped past the rental car and took off after the Chevy. Lowell let out a long sigh of relief and silently wished the officers luck. Welcome to Santa Fe, he thought.

He turned the Buick left onto Old Santa Fe Trail. According to the map, it would dead-end shortly at Water Street. On the right stood one of the bigger hotels in town: the Inn at Loretto, named for a small, ancient chapel with a "hanging staircase" that brought almost as many pilgrims as Mecca did. The hotel boasted all the features to be expected of Santa Fe—ersatz adobe architecture with tile-and-mosaic decor, and all modern conveniences. He had selected it on the basis of its location, although he was shocked to learn of the cost here: $125 and up for a room. Money was going to be an issue. He'd cashed out most of his remaining money-market and mutual-fund shares to make the trip, and his limited resources were not going to go far in this expensive jet-set city.

Lowell's hotel room was small but neat, with what he construed to be traditional Santa Fe furnishings: rustic, heavy, hand-painted pieces made of small logs, called *latillos,* usually in bright pastel colors, with splashes of design and a calculated worn and weathered look.

Still shaken by his reception earlier, he opened the window and gazed out at the sky. The night was cold and bright, the thin air dry, with a crispness that was clear and rare despite the storm clouds approaching from the north. At seven and a half thousand feet above sea level, this was one of the highest cities in the hemisphere. He felt light-headed and oddly disturbed by the knowledge that he was surrounded by hundreds of miles of mountains and desert in every direction. He was literally in the middle of nowhere. Accustomed as he was to the always-close proximity of water back home, Lowell found the vast, dry, empty landscape completely alien and disturbing.

He unpacked his bag. He didn't know how long he would be here, but sensed it might be for a while. Fumbling for his pocket organizer, he made a note to call Joshua Croft again, first thing in the morning. That would be a good place to start. Meanwhile, he could use a decent night's sleep.

He took a shower, crawled into the big oak bed and slept fitfully, his sleep disturbed by alien dreams, hostile natives, and the relentless sound of the wind. He woke up suddenly after a particularly virulent gust shook and rattled the window. He blinked for a moment, disoriented, for a moment not remembering where he was. The wind gusted again. Tony Lowell realized he did not like wind at all unless he was out sailing on Manatee Bay. It always foreshadowed foul weather and worse back home in Florida. Here, it was a mournful sound, chilling to his thin, subtropical blood. Lowell decided he was going to spend as little time in the Southwest as possible.

3

———

The wind began to subside around five A.M., diminished to an occasional hard, brief gust that briefly disturbed Lowell's restless sleep and then receded into the dark desert dreamscape. By dawn, the city was still, as though lying in wait.

He rose at eight, shaved, and put on a loose white cotton shirt, pale blue wool sweater, casual loafers, jeans, and a pair of almost-Western hiking boots he'd had since college. The wind was a faint nighttime memory, its sounds now replaced by the stirrings of traffic and early morning commerce outside. For a moment, as he looked out the window and caught his first daytime glimpse of the lovely old city, he almost forgot why he was there.

At nine he tried Joshua Croft's office again and got the same recording, so he left his hotel number and dug out the piece of paper on which he had written the names of Ariel's New Age contacts. He called Christina Taylor but there was no answer. As for the artist Thomas Royster, it was too early to begin searching the bars. Which made him worry about what, or why, Ariel would know about bars. He still had trouble adjusting to the idea that she was a bright and independent—albeit riskily, heartbreakingly beautiful—young woman, not the little girl he never got the chance to protect.

After taking the elevator down to the lobby, he nodded brusquely at the desk clerk and doorman and went out to seize the day. The weather was crisp and glorious. The air smelled of sage and burning wood. The skies were azure; there was new snow on the peaks above the city, and as evidence of the season's first wave of skiers, the streets were jammed with traffic, both foot and vehicular. Shiny sports-utility vehicles with skis on top and brightly bundled vacationers within competed for space on the narrow, cobbled streets with equally determined pedestrians. The store façades were self-conscious in their adobe stylishness, offering Zuni and Navajo arts and crafts for any budget, as long as there was one.

Around the plaza itself, the old Spanish-Indio adobe buildings, while renovated and elegant on the inside, were studiedly ancient and crumbling on the outside. The showpiece was the original sixteenth-century Palace of the Governors. Some of the newer buildings were Territorial—remnants of the nineteenth-century Anglo takeover—and a few modern edifices in the same de igueur style, such as the oversized new Hilton and El Dorado hotels, blocked the sunset views to the west. The plaza had white wrought-iron benches, crisscrossing pathways, and plenty of now-dormant flower beds, still-green grass and trees—cottonwoods, aspens, and numerous ornamental fruit trees.

Were it not for the urgency of his mission, Lowell would have enjoyed strolling about, perhaps even driving up to the ski basin for an overview of the city and valley. It was a stunning city and region, he had to admit. He'd always imagined that Santa Fe would be rustic and dusty, with some funk and charm but little substance to really hold onto someone. Now he began to wonder if it might not have some mystical power of its own, like Camelot. Certainly enough to captivate a wide-eyed young woman like Ariel.

As he walked around the small city center, Lowell observed that there was no shortage of dark-skinned, long-haired Hispanic women, not to mention more than a few Native American women with similar looks. But the Indians were generally somewhat withdrawn, keeping their heads down and tending to wear true traditional dress. He studied the local Anglos in their cowboy attire. Although they seemed more authentic than the growing crowds of Texans—vying with tourists from California, New York, and Europe—they still looked oddly out of place, as though they weren't sure of what they were doing here.

Lowell needed a plan. But the first thing would be to get some coffee, then try Croft again. He felt increasingly anxious to find the elusive woman, call Ariel to tell her that her friend was safe, and then get out of here. His strange apprehension would not go away, despite the brightness of the day and the extraordinary beauty of his surroundings.

He chose the La Fonda Hotel for breakfast. It was an old hostelry of the Mexican tradition, featuring frescoes and wall paintings reminiscent of José Orozco and Diego Rivera. He'd read in the airline magazine that there was an outdoor ter-raced patio bar on the roof. Maybe they served coffee in the morning, and he could check out the surroundings.

He was in luck: the rooftop bar was open. A Midwestern couple was just finishing coffee and croissants—croissants, in New Mexico! Lowell noted wryly—and an Hispanic head-waiter gestured Lowell to their vacated table, right at the cara-pace overlooking the city and plaza to the west.

The waiter was a twenty-something Anglo with long, blond hair worn in a tight bun and sporting a trim beard.

"Are you enjoying your stay, sir?" he asked, placing a large, ornate menu on the table. "I understand the skiing is getting pretty good for this time of year, if you're interested." He was apparently in no hurry. "You're too late for the aspens, though. But a lot of people come just to see the celebrities. Like Shirley Maclaine, she was here yesterday, signing her new book."

"She comes to see the celebrities?"

The waiter laughed. "Or vice versa. What can I get you?"

Lowell hated being pegged as a tourist; he had traveled fairly widely and knew enough that in places such as this, there was always an implicit snobbery on the part of the lo-cals—however transient—toward newcomers. But the waiter seemed genuinely pleasant.

Lowell pushed the menu aside. "Just coffee, thanks," he said. "Low-fat milk if you have it, and honey." The low-fat part was the latest wrinkle in his heretofore carefree cruise through life, a begrudging acknowledgment of the threat of middle-aged spread.

The waiter brought the coffee, along with a plate of steaming-hot, fluffy buns, a honey bear, and several pats of butter. Recognizing Lowell's puzzled reaction, the waiter grinned. "Sopapillas," he explained. "Sort of a local tradition. You put honey on them, they're really good. On the house," he added.

Lowell thanked him and tried one. It was delicious. So much for the low-fat diet, he thought wryly, digging into a second bun.

The waiter returned. "Will there be anything else?"

Lowell considered, remembering the names Ariel had given him. "You ever hear of an artist named Thomas Royster?"

The waiter laughed. "Sure, everybody knows Tom. He's a local institution. Paintings for drinks, and a long philosophical discourse on the subject of your choice for a chaser. You'll probably find him at El Farol, that's where he usually hangs."

"Would that be on Canyon Road?" Lowell asked, remembering Ariel's instructions.

"It would. About halfway to the top, on the right. Across from a big Chinese restaurant that looks like it belongs in L.A. You can't miss it, it's one of the so-called authentic old saloons in town."

Lowell smiled. "Thanks," he said. It didn't sound like Royster would be coherent enough to be much help. Still, he didn't want to leave any stone unturned. Drunks were sometimes good for extracting indiscretions, but they were rarely of much use in finding missing persons, unless personally involved in some way. Lowell wanted to talk to him, but it would have to wait.

A group of tourists in brand-new cowboy outfits emerged from the elevator. The waiter glanced in their direction. "Will there be anything else?" he asked again. "Some breakfast, maybe?"

"I think I just ate one," said Lowell, his mouth full of the last of the sopapillas. "But thanks anyway." They traded grins, and Lowell decided it was worth a try. "I'm here looking for someone, actually. I heard that Royster might be a lead, but he's not the one I'm looking for."

The waiter's eyebrows arched slightly. "This is a small town in a lot of ways, especially among the locals. Maybe I know him."

"Her." Lowell showed him the photograph.

The waiter looked and nodded appreciatively. "Nice. What's her name?"

"Alicia."

The waiter shook his head. "Sorry. I haven't seen her." He shrugged. "One thing about this town you gotta understand," he went on, "is that people come and go a lot. Everybody comes here with, like, a mission of some kind. Get their act together, get their crystals tuned, sell a painting, write a book, that kind of thing."

"She's from here, if that makes a difference."

The waiter's eyebrows rose a millimeter. "Really?" He shook his head. "Even so, it's a hard place to survive in. There're no jobs worth spit," he added, glancing again in the direction of the new arrivals. They were studying menus provided by the headwaiter. "Everybody who comes here's got ten college degrees and ten cents."

"Like you?"

"Absolutely. I have a masters in psychology from Berkeley. That and a quarter'll get you a phone call to Tusuque. People come here because they want to *be* here, and they'll do anything to stay. But the sad thing is that most of them don't make it. This place is expensive. All the new money coming

31

in, all the celebs and tourists who want to buy places, all the people ditching California—they've driven the prices for everything sky high. In case you haven't noticed," he added with a grin.

"I noticed."

"Like, you can't get breakfast or a burger for less than six bucks."

"I noticed," agreed Lowell again, thankful for the sopapillas.

"And a place to stay," the waiter went on, "you're talking a grand a week for a hotel, a grand a month for an apartment. Then you have to have a lease unless you want to crash with about four other people in one of the barrios, like I do. And the wages—the wages are real low, unless you're lucky and get to work on one of the film productions or something like that. As for the locals . . ." He just shrugged.

"So you don't know where I might find this woman?"

"Not offhand." The waiter frowned once more. "What's her name again?"

"Sandoval. Alicia Sandoval."

Two more customers entered—a middle-aged Texas couple dressed to the nines in silver and turquoise. "Sandoval," repeated the waiter in hushed tones and a nervous look over his shoulder. "She's Spanish?"

"Hispanic," Lowell affirmed.

"Sorry, I have to go, man. I wish you luck. You are on the *wrong* side of town."

The waiter hurried away, as though he'd been exposed to the plague.

Lowell finished his coffee and ventured out into the city once again, puzzled by the waiter's reaction. Alicia Sandoval was out there. He could feel her presence. The influence of her people was everywhere, the most dominant influence in Santa Fe. Not just because of the preponderance of churches and plazas. Most of the names, most of the traditions, were Spanish. But there was something else: an atmosphere, almost palpable, of ancient hostilities. He sensed this to be a place dependent upon and clinging to its history, both physical and metaphysical, caught in a continuing struggle between ideas and traditions at the same time terrible and enlightened.

This was Alicia's home. All of those complexities that surely existed in such a woman, all of those contradictions and fears, all that wonder and beauty that seemed to have captivated Ariel so—and that at secondhand, he had to admit to himself, had begun to capture him—all had come from here. It wasn't that big a town. She was here, somewhere, among the seventy thousand residents and ten-odd thousand visitors scattered among these winding streets and landscapes. Lowell would find her. Even if he didn't know much Spanish . . .

4

Lowell abandoned the plaza. He'd been drawn there initially, as were all visitors to Santa Fe. But he was searching for a "local," a resident, and it was obvious that locals tended to avoid the place as being overrun by tourists. His thoughts and feelings were dark and foreboding as the morning passed, and he found himself no closer to the object of his mission.

He'd already checked the directories without success—there were a hundred and fifteen Sandovals listed in the Santa Fe phone book, none of them as Alicia. He'd tried a couple of them at random from the hotel and gotten responses ranging from guarded to hostile. No one admitted knowledge of Alicia Sandoval or her family.

He'd then gone and spoken to the manager at her old address. He was met with a shrug of indifference, and was not aware that more than one pair of eyes remained fixed on his back when he left the premises.

His quest became aimless and frantic. Armed with the dog-eared photo Ariel had given him, he began searching along Guadalupe Street, showing the picture to anyone who would stop and look. Discouraged, he bought a mocha latte at a restored shopping plaza, called Sanbusco Place, and asked a couple of teenagers skateboarding around the parking lot if they had any suggestions about how he might find a local Hispanic resident.

"Try the unemployment office," sneered one with a long blond ponytail as he whizzed away, practicing jump turns.

"Ask at one of the bodegas down on Agua Fria," offered his friend, a boy with dark eyes and hair who looked as if he might be Native American. "If you know any Spanish, it might help, too."

Lowell had observed that this part of town was still mostly Anglo and tourist. He began to realize that a local woman wouldn't spend much time here if she could help it, unless she had a job in the vicinity. Still, how likely was it that she would turn up in any one part of town at the same moment as he? And would he recognize her if she did? The possibilities were remote, he had to admit. The city was small, but it was still a city. And if Ariel's premonitions were valid, it was not likely that Alicia Sandoval would be casually strolling the city streets. There was the grim possibility he had to face up to—that she might be dead. He pushed the thought into the dark corners of his mind where such unwelcome images dwelt and checked his watch. It was time to try Croft again.

The agency phone rang three times and he was about to hang up when a harried-sounding male voice answered. "Mondragon Detective Agency."

Lowell hesitated. It didn't sound like the Croft he remembered. It wasn't. It was somebody named Leroy. "Mr. Croft only works part-time these days," the voice informed him. "I'm just here to do some cleaning up. Anything I can help you with?"

Lowell masked his disappointment. "Is there any way I can reach him?"

"I can give him a message, sir. He'll probably get back to you. Can you tell me what it's about?"

The voice sounded bitter, Lowell thought. Something must have happened. "Tell him Tony Lowell is in town and is trying to reach him. I'm staying at the Inn at Loretto."

"I'll tell him," said Leroy and hung up.

Lowell stepped out of the phone booth and contemplated his options. It was still too early to look for Thomas Royster; the bars wouldn't be open yet. He tried Christina Taylor again, without success. But this time the phone was answered by a machine, so he left his name and hotel number.

Lowell didn't want to talk to the police until he had no other options left—especially not before he'd had a chance to talk to Croft. He made a decision. It was time to pay a visit to the barrios. He hoped his high-school Spanish would prove adequate. Returning to the hotel, he got into his rented Buick and checked the map one more time. As in most ancient cities, the small, narrow streets seemed to meander without rhyme or reason, and the traffic was appalling. But he found Agua Fria without difficulty, only a block from Sanbusco Place. Turning left at the Sanctuario de Guadalupe, a classic Spanish adobe basilica, he headed west. Agua Fria paralleled the diminutive Santa Fe River—more of a creek, really—which flowed directly west out of the mountains. The waters were essentially melted snowpack, hence the origin of the street's name.

The first few blocks were the oldest, with small, neat adobe houses, and he could tell by the preponderance of fresh-faced young blond women walking Irish setters or yellow Labradors, and the many fair-skinned men in Miatas and new Jeep Cherokees, that the area had already been heavily "gentrified." He continued farther west, toward the distant Rio Grande. As soon as he crossed St. Francis Drive, the character of the neighborhood changed abruptly. Here, the adobe houses were crumbling and the newer structures were of aluminum prefab, or were trailers set back from the road. The cars were low-riders or wide-back pickups. Dark eyes, filled with deep suspicion, fixed on him as he passed by. Two police cars ripped past, sirens screaming. Welcome to the barrio.

Near the intersection of Agua Fria and Hickock Street, Lowell pulled into the parking lot of a small store that boasted a drive-up liquor window, one of New Mexico's most oft-debated and popular institutions. He got out of the Buick, locked it—feeling conspicuous doing so—and went inside.

"Buenas dias," he offered the proprietor with a smile.

"Hola," came the guarded response. The man—short, with a silvery brush of hair—eyed him with greater mistrust than he did the three teenage boys in the back wearing black gang T-shirts, who looked as though they were hoping to buy, or steal, some beer and cigarettes. The boys, the proprietor probably knew. Or he knew their mothers. Lowell was an Anglo, and a stranger. "Can I help you with something?" the man inquired in good English, with the local singsong accent that lilted and flowed like a mountain stream.

Maybe language was not going to be such a problem after

all, thought Lowell. Maybe the cultural differences had been overstated by his daughter and the white locals he'd met. Besides, this wasn't really a foreign country, was it?

"I'm looking for someone," Lowell told the grocer. *"Voy a mirar por alga persona."* The proprietor's eyes slanted away. Great, thought Lowell. Now he thinks I'm a cop. Nice going.

"¿Quien quiere?" the man asked, his tone harsher.

"Una mujer," Lowell pressed on. *"Se llama Alicia Sandoval."* He presented the photograph.

The proprietor's reaction told Lowell the man knew something. But he wasn't about to share that knowledge with a stranger. *"Yo no conosco,"* the man said, shrugging. He looked away. "Don't know her."

"I'm a friend of hers," persisted Lowell. *"No soy policia.* It's just that I'm from out of town, and I've lost her number."

The three teenage boys in the back had made their selection: a case of Budweiser and a carton of Marlboros. They brought their purchases over to the counter and presented absurdly fake I.D.'s. Two of the boys flanked Lowell, and the third stood behind him.

"Hurry up, José," demanded the leader. "We ain't got all day."

Uh-oh, thought Lowell. Trouble.

"Tito," the proprietor said to the leader, a sprouting sixteen-year-old with a shaved head. "You know I can't sell you this stuff. Where's your mother, by the way?"

Tito backed off right away. "I dunno," muttered the kid. "She's busy." He gave Lowell a sidelong glare, grabbed his fake I.D. and beat a hasty retreat, buddies in tow.

The proprietor grinned and winked. "The young Cholos. The best way to handle boys like that is to mention their mothers. They all live in great fear of the wrath of their mamas, who are very important in the community and are in constant despair about the behavior of their sons."

Lowell glanced out the window and saw one of the boys kick the fender of his rented car. It didn't fall off, which was encouraging. He decided on discretion in favor of valor.

The proprietor, whose name was José Gaspar, let out a sigh of relief. Lowell sensed that the man may have dodged a bullet—perhaps literally. He bought a can of a local root beer, called Blue Sky, and a package of peanuts. He could tell that the man was holding something back, just by the way he avoided eye contact. Perhaps he'd said more than he'd intended. Lowell thanked the shopkeeper and headed for the door.

Just then the proprietor looked out the window and shouted. *"¡Ladrones!"* he yelled.

Lowell followed his gaze. The same boys were clustered around the far side of the rental car, trying to force open the window. It was as though they were deliberately challenging the Anglo *estranjero*. Lowell took the challenge and was out the door as fast as his middle-aged legs could carry him, unmindful of the likelihood that if he caught them, they would probably beat the hell out of him with tire irons, if not shoot him on the spot. They scattered, dashing away down an alley, hurling insults and laughter back in Lowell's—and José's—direction.

"Punks," gasped José, breathlessly joining Lowell in the parking lot. *"¡Cabrones chiquitos!"* Lowell nodded and watched them go. He'd known a few punks in his time. He thanked the storekeeper, climbed into the rental and started the engine. It was time to regroup.

5

For the rest of the afternoon, Lowell prowled the city in growing frustration over his lack of success, combined with the increasingly heavy traffic and accompanying levels of public
distemper. He checked the hotel for messages. There were
none. Finally, he took refuge in the hotel lobby watching the
trendy jet-setters, dark-skinned locals, and pale yuppie new-
lyweds come and go.

A tall man had been sitting there for some time, his face
buried in a newspaper, long, lanky legs extended, wearing a
leather blazer, ostrich-skin boots, and tan cords. Lowell
hadn't paid him much attention. The man's back was toward
him, but he had noted, in the abstract way that detectives
note the seemingly inconsequential, that whoever it was, he
was putting away one hell of a lot of liquor; the waiter had just

brought another refill as Lowell started across the lobby in search of dinner.

As he crossed the path of the newspaper reader, a booted foot stuck out and nearly tripped him. Lowell's reactions were quick enough to avoid a fall, but as he turned to face his would-be harasser, a long-ago familiar voice rang out: "Got to watch your step in this town."

Lowell broke into a grin. "Croft. Son of a bitch! I've been looking all the hell over town for you."

That was when he noticed that his old acquaintance's eyes weren't quite focused. He glanced at the drink, then at Joshua's face, questioning.

Smiling faintly, Croft shrugged. "I'm semiretired," he informed Lowell. "A man of leisure. Care to join me?"

"Maybe later," said Lowell. "But I made a promise to my daughter."

"Daughter?" said Croft. "Big mistake. One should never have daughters. Or sons. Or puppy dogs. No attachments, no broken promises."

"It just happened. Things happen," said Lowell, sitting down in the vacant lounge chair opposite Croft, who pulled his feet back to make room.

"Shit, you mean," said Croft. "Shit happens. No offense to your daughter."

"I don't know about that," Lowell responded mildly. He wondered what kind of shit had happened to render someone he knew to be one of the toughest, sharpest P.I.s anywhere into such a state. It was disquieting. "In any case, I happen to have a daughter. Ergo, I have promises to keep."

Croft smiled. "And miles to go before you sleep." He tossed back his libation and waved to the waiter. "Another

41

Jack Daniels," he called, then turned back to Lowell. "You never struck me as the family type, Lowell. How'd this daughter thing happen?"

"By accident. A long time ago. I found out only a few years ago, so I have a lot of back promises to catch up on."

Croft contemplated that for a while, awaiting a resupply of sour mash. When it arrived, he looked up at Lowell, and his eyes were like dark pools. "Sorry," he said. "I'm being a jerk. That happens, too. More than it used to."

Lowell glanced at the waiter, who was still standing there. "Do you have any Kirin beer?" he asked. The waiter frowned. "Never mind," Lowell sighed. "Bring me that local brew I read about somewhere."

"Santa Fe Ale," said Croft. His voice sounded like it was coming from somewhere far away. "It's not bad."

Lowell nodded at the waiter, then turned back to Croft. "All right, Joshua. So what the hell is up with you? I heard that you'd quit working."

"Slowed down some, maybe." Eventually, after several more drinks, Lowell got it out of him. Croft's longtime love affair with his partner, Rita Mondragon. How she'd been nearly killed by an old foe out to get Joshua. It had been the final spike driven into their relationship. How Croft had felt responsible, and how she'd left him at the end.

Lowell was sympathetic. "Maybe she'll come back," he offered optimistically.

"Right," said Croft. He ordered another drink. By mutual consent, they changed the subject. Lowell told Croft about Ariel and her mother, and finally, about his mission.

"So," said Joshua after a while. "You want to find this

42

local woman, an Hispanic, who may be embroiled in some kind of domestic peril, is that the gist of it?"

Lowell nodded. "That's about it."

Croft looked at him and his eyes slowly focused. Suddenly he smiled. "An outsider Anglo dude poking into local family business. Chasing after a local woman. Messing with a macho husband. And why?"

"She may be in danger," Lowell reminded him.

Croft smiled again. "Sure she's in danger. Shit, she may even be dead. But she's got nothing to do with you. You've got no *business,* don't you get that?"

"Yes. And no. Poking around in other people's business *is* my business. And used to be yours."

Croft looked down at his drink. After a moment, he looked up. "Okay, so your daughter is worried about her friend. Probably rightfully. Great. It shows she's a sensitive, caring human being. We need more of those. But the way the Santa Fe locals are going to see it, it's none of her damn business either."

"What about you?" inquired Lowell. "Is that your position?"

Croft looked at him, focused again, smiled again. "I came here seventeen years ago and I'm still an outsider. You got your Indians. They were here first. You got your Hispanics. You got your rich Anglos from L.A. and Scarsdale and Detroit. Everyone thinks they know what's best for the town. Which means for themselves. Ask them, any of them, what this town is all about, what it needs, what it wants, and they'll be happy to tell you." He sipped at his drink. "One thing they all have in common, though. They came here because they liked the idea of cowboy privacy." He smiled. "You know cowboy privacy? Somebody asks you a question you don't care to answer, you tell them you don't know. They ask you again, you shoot them."

"Great," said Lowell. "I'm lost enough out here as it is."

"The bottom line is, you're up shit creek. Without a speedboat." He glanced down at Lowell's makeshift hiking boots, found in the back of his closet back home, from who knows when and where. "You'll need better boots than those. This isn't the Everglades."

"I'm going to be here for only a few days," protested Lowell.

Croft shrugged again. "When in Rome." He reached into his back pocket, slipped out his wallet, opened it, and found a business card. Reaching up, he deftly swiped a pen from the tray of a passing waiter and wrote a name and number on the card while the waiter stood by, sheepishly hoping for the return of his pen. "Here," said Croft. "Tell this guy you're a friend of mine, and what you're after. If he doesn't shoot you, he can maybe tell you something."

Lowell picked up the card. "Sergeant Hector Ramirez, Santa Fe P.D. Thanks, I'll give him a call."

Croft shook his head. "No, you go see him. He won't talk to you except face-to-face. That's the way it works with the locals here. It has to be *mano a mano.* You look him in the eye, he looks you in the eye. You do your little dance." Once more he smiled. "Santa Fe style." He handed the pen back to the waiter.

"I'll remember that," said Lowell, putting the card away. He'd already figured as much. He thought about what Croft had said, and about what he'd already observed about the state of local race relations—bad, and not mentioned in *Condé Nast.*

Croft was in no mood to eat, but agreed to meet the next day, maybe for coffee, and maybe he'd have some information, or an idea or two of where to get some. "But start with Ramirez," he reiterated.

Lowell thanked him and got to his feet. Joshua recommended a restaurant not far from the plaza on Marcy Street that had good authentic local cuisine and reasonable prices.

"Oh, one more thing," called Lowell, turning back. "Which way is Canyon Road?"

Croft smiled. "You want to observe the tourists in action?"

Lowell laughed. "No, I've already seen plenty. It's just a lead I want to check out."

"I doubt you'll find her up there," said Croft. "But whatever. You go out the front door, cut across the parking lot to the trail, and go left at the corner. Two blocks up, you come to the Paseo de Peralta. Make a right, and Canyon Road will be the first left you come to. It's a narrow road, easy to miss. Good luck." He smiled. "And bring money."

Lowell thanked him and went out into the city. The air was cold and crisp. Even though it was only five-thirty, darkness had fallen and the skies were gray. No expert on southwestern weather, Lowell wondered if snow was coming. He decided to walk.

The restaurant was a small, nondescript cafe that catered primarily to locals, and he was grudgingly shown to a small table near the back. He ordered what turned out to be the best *chile relleno* he'd ever tasted, and washed it down with another Santa Fe Ale. He'd have to watch his drinking, he thought. He didn't want to follow Croft's example. And he wouldn't be able to spend much time in the bars on Canyon Road without ordering yet another drink or two. He declined a second ale, ordered a coffee and a glass of water, and paid his bill.

Crossing the parking lot, he turned left on Marcy and located the Paseo de Peralta with no trouble. Turning right, he followed Croft's directions and found Canyon Road. It was a narrow, winding, cobbled street with low walls and old adobe houses on either side, many of which had been converted to art galleries featuring trendy Southwestern landscapes and Native American art. A few had become restaurants. There was even an old Quaker Meeting House—an odd location for such, he thought—and all in all, the place reeked with charm. And money.

Incongruously dressed foreigners in chic Indian jackets and intricately engraved Texas cowboy boots strolled past, often in the middle of the road, to the vast annoyance of rival tourists who insisted on driving everywhere they went—even window-shopping on Canyon Road. The adobe walls of the shops were adorned and lit with gas or candle lanterns, enhancing the charm effect all the more. Lowell liked that part.

About halfway up the hill, he found the bar he was looking for: El Farol. It proclaimed itself an authentic Western saloon and certainly looked like one—Spanish-style. The floors were wide-pine plank, the bar of wizened, whiskey-soaked oak, the plaster walls adorned with remarkable paintings depicting Southwestern lore, mostly from the Hispanic perspective. Lowell entered and surveyed the room, half expecting a Clint Eastwood reception. No one paid him any attention other than a couple of Texans, who spotted his swamp boots and snickered into their beer. He noted that the patrons were evenly divided between white and Hispanic, the latter the more affluent-looking, dressed for the most part in well-tailored business suits.

It was early, but the place was already jumping to the beat of a passing-fair, all-white blues band that wailed an old Willy Dixon song into the night: "Killing Floor." An appropriate ending for a frustrating day. Lowell ordered a Santa Fe Ale and asked the bartender if he'd ever heard of an artist named Thomas Royster. The bartender shrugged noncommittally and moved on to another customer. Lowell tried the photograph of Alicia out on a few grizzled local Anglos on either side of him without success. The picture elicited a couple of wolf whistles and a salacious comment or two, but no one had seen her.

The band took a break. Lowell was about to move on when the bartender placed a small rectangle of poster board on the bar in front of him. It was an ink-and-blotter abstract impression of a local mesa. "For you," the bartender told him.

Lowell looked down the bar. At the far end, a gaunt, white-haired, follicularly-challenged man with a lined, tanned face waved an empty beer mug at him and grinned widely. Lowell moved over to join him, nodding to the bartender to replenish the man's drink.

"Thomas Royster?" Lowell slid into the vacant stool next to the man. Royster nodded happily. "Thanks for the picture."

"Thanks for the drink."

Lowell waited expectantly. The bartender refilled the mug.

Royster drank, and seemed relaxed. "You new in Santa Fe?" he finally inquired, turning halfway toward Lowell, who

47

had been scrutinizing the picture the artist had given him, trying to decide the best approach.

"That's right. I'm not staying long, though."

"That's what they all say," interjected the bartender, pour-
ing a glass of generic red wine for a bright-faced young blond
woman two stools over. "You won't get away that easily."

"What can I do you for?" Royster inquired, sipping the
beer Lowell had bought him. "You an art collector?"

"Not exactly."

A long-haired man dressed in grungy cowboy attire, sitting to Lowell's right, reached under the bar as though on cue
and hoisted up a black-leather case onto the bartop. He
snapped it open, revealing an assortment of cheap silver jewelry. "Check this out," he offered Lowell, presenting a particularly garish array of ersatz-Indian belt buckles. Lowell
politely declined and turned back to Royster.

"I hear you know most everybody in town," he began.

Royster yawned and took another sip of beer, slapping
his hand on the bar in time with the music. "Most everybody
worth knowin'. There's plenty who ain't. Like Billy Butler
there." He indicated the neighboring jewelry peddler.

The bartender had long hair and deep laugh lines. He
seemed content with his lot in life. He cheerfully included
himself in any conversation that interested him, a self-
appointed master of ceremonies. "This is where it's at," he assured Lowell. "Everybody who's anybody shows up here.
Steven Spielberg sat at that table right over there just last
week." Lowell glanced indifferently to where he pointed. He
wasn't that interested in show business. "Jack Palance comes
in here all the time. So does James Taylor," continued the
bartender. "Santa Fe is the place, man." He leaned closer.

48

"Even Redford shows up once in a while. He digs blues, man. Comes in with his latest babe. Of course he usually stays home in Tusuque, doesn't come out much. Also, now that Ted Turner's bought half of Lincoln County, we're startin' to see a lot of him and Jane. But Bob Redford's the one, you know what I mean? And every once in a while . . . 'Nother beer?"

"No thanks," Lowell replied. "Got any coffee?"

Thomas Royster didn't recognize the photograph and hadn't heard of anyone named Alicia Sandoval. "Although the name Sandoval rings a bell," he muttered, frowning in thought.

A couple of more affluent-looking Anglos edged up to the bar, dressed to the nines, or higher. The woman had on leather pants, a taunt to the animal rightists in town. And a leather hat to match, and a Pendleton wool shirt and scarf. Her male companion wore a suede jacket, a Guatemalan hat, snakeskin boots, and snug-fitting jeans. Both would be considered good-looking without all the trimmings. Lowell thought they must be the epitome of Santa Fe Style, out slumming. Slumming on Canyon Road. They introduced themselves. He was Hoyt, she Tanya, both from Texas. *Urban* Texas, they added. Planter's Park, Dallas. Hoyt was an architect, Tanya a decorator. They lived in Santa Fe six months a year, to do their "creative work." The rest of the time, it seemed, they spent in Texas, making money. Lots of money, they wanted Lowell to understand. They took the only two remaining seats at the bar, just to the left of Royster. Both of them smoked. So did Royster. Lowell didn't. Lowell left.

It was after eleven when he walked back down Canyon Road past gallery after gallery, all of them locked and gated for the night to protect the valuable assets of what he'd read was Santa Fe's number-three industry, behind tourism and state government, just ahead of food service and Santa Fe Style.

Cutting across a school parking lot and through the now-quiet, picture-book back streets of the old city, Lowell crossed over Old Santa Fe Trail, leaning into the cold wind. As he passed a dark, narrow alley, someone stepped in front of him. "Stay away from *la chica*," a harsh voice hissed, barely audible. He hardly had a chance to look up—his thoughts were elsewhere and his eyes on the sidewalk, trying to avoid the icy patches—when the blow fell. It caught him on the side of the head just above the temple, and he went down as much in surprise as shock. As he rose into an automatic defensive crouch, his attacker fled. A police car was rounding a corner two blocks ahead, on routine patrol.

The assailant, or assailants—Lowell thought he had heard other voices in the alley, but wasn't sure—vanished into the darkness as he climbed back onto his feet. His scalp was bleeding. He stanched the flow with a tissue he kept in his pocket, then smiled and waved as the police car drove on past. The cops seemed unaware of what had just occurred, which was fine with him. He didn't want any police involvement. At least not until he'd had a chance to meet Sergeant Ramirez. Besides, he hadn't seen who'd hit him, it had happened so fast. Nor did he expect that the police would give much of a damn. Especially since he hadn't been robbed. They'd chalk it up as another barroom dispute and tell him to see a doctor.

He made it back to his hotel room without further incident. Helped by the cold wind, the bleeding had stopped. He washed his hands, tore off his clothes, and got into the shower. He had just worked up a good cloud of steam when the phone rang. Grabbing for the terry robe the hotel had so thoughtfully provided, he scrambled out of the tiled stall and hurried across the room to the phone by the nightstand.

"Hello?" he barked, breathless, dripping, fighting off a spell of dizziness.

"Would this be Mr. Lowell?" The voice was female, deep and husky, with a West Texas twang.

"It would." He shook off the dizzy spell.

"I do hope it's not too late to call," she went on. "This is Christina Taylor. Y'all left a message on my answering machine?"

He remembered. "Oh, right."

"Listen," she said, "I talked to your daughter and I know who you are. If y'all aren't busy, we have a gatherin' going on out here at the ranch. You might find it interestin'."

"What sort of gathering?"

She laughed: a deep, earthy laugh. He liked her laugh. "Well, I guess you'd call it New Age. Some of my fellow travelers are comin' over to do some drummin'. You'd be more than welcome."

"Drumming?"

"If you haven't experienced it, I can't explain," she said. "You have to be there. But it might be worth your while. There are some folks coming who know Alicia Sandoval."

So, he thought, Ariel has been a busy girl. Good for her. "All right, I'll be there," he said. "Just give me directions. I'll be coming from the Inn at Loretto, near the plaza."

"Darlin'," she said, laughing, "I know where y'all are.

You just get on Old Pecos Trail and go south to the Interstate. You take that north, even though it actually turns south down there to get around the mountains."

"North, going south," he repeated, fumbling for a paper and pen.

"You take the first exit, says Lamy." She spelled it out. "That's where the original Santa Fe Railroad station is. There's some route number or other, I never remember that stuff, but you get off there, go right, exactly two point six miles, no more, no less. You'll see the gate on the left, says Rancho de Cielo. There's an intercom, you just say who you are and come on in."

"Got it. Rancho Cielo, two point six."

"Get here as soon as you can, darlin'. We'll be drummin'."

Lowell hung up the phone, shaking his head. Drumming. What had Ariel gotten herself into on her adventures out here in the Wild West?

Lowell's head was reeling from both alcohol and physical abuse, and he would much rather have curled up in a warm bed than climb into a frigid car in the middle of the night. But he managed to get his head bandaged Willie Nelson-style—which actually looked fairly trendy—to get dressed in clean jeans and pullover, to squeeze two pairs of socks into his boots, and to pull on his parka and head outside once again.

The night was bitter cold now, and the wind was blowing, which helped to clear his head. The car started without trouble and he found his way onto the Old Pecos Trail. He was wide awake by the time he got to the Interstate. He took the Lamy turnoff, drove past a new subdivision called Eldorado on the right, and after doubling back once, managed to locate the Rancho de Cielo gate.

He first heard it when he opened his window to press the intercom button. It came rumbling down from the desert foothills as though from the mountains themselves—a deep, ancient, rhythmic pounding. The beat, the tone, was nothing like the sounds these hills might have known in centuries past—the drums of Apaches gathering for war, the tom-tom rhythms of raiding Commanches from the Great Plains to the east. While the tempo was erratic, he recognized the rhythms to be closer to those he'd heard in New York's Central Park years ago while still a working photographer. He'd even done a prize-winning photo of those drummers: Afro-Americans, as they'd called themselves then. Seeking their roots in the rhythms of the Serengeti. Well, he supposed, either the Africans are preparing to invade Santa Fe, or the New Agers are reaching pretty far out for some roots. Just now he didn't feel much like drumming, but a contact was a contact.

He pressed the button and announced himself. The gate swung open as though a mystical hand had reached out from the sagebrush. He was in.

The dirt road was deeply rutted like a washboard; it made his teeth rattle. Deep pools of slush bore testament of ice to come—probably within the hour. He wished he had a four-wheel drive and hoped he'd make it back out of here some-time before spring.

The house appeared out of the darkness like Avalon in the mist—in fact, it resembled an Arthurian castle, very much not in keeping with its Rocky Mountain high-desert setting, not to mention Santa Fe Style, he thought. For which reason alone, he sort of liked the place, and its owner—presumably Christina Taylor. Facilitating New Age seminars must be a lu-crative business, he decided. As he drew closer, he recog-

53

nized the architecture to be more along the lines of upscale Dallas than Camelot. But it did give him a turn for a moment.

The house was lit for Christmas, even though it was barely November, burning enough kilowatts to heat Anchorage. So much for eco-awareness, he thought. His Sixties hippy pals would've probably burned the castle for heat and stayed in a van.

Lowell parked in front, got out, climbed three steps to the broad portico, wended his way through a forest of wind chimes, made it to the door, and rang the bell. It played about four choruses of Dvorak's symphony *From the New World,* and the drumming stopped. After a brief interlude, a tall, broad-shouldered woman with a ruddy, freckled complexion and a shock of wild red hair answered the door. She wore a comfortable sweatshirt and jeans. She greeted him with a smile the size of West Texas.

"You must be Tony Lowell," she declared. "I'm Christina. Do come in."

Lowell braced himself against the resumption of noise and the accompanying headache sure to follow, and entered. The house was a veritable museum of crystals and candelabra, mystical paintings, and images of Celtic goddesses in sylph-like poses, presumably casting magical spells upon the world. The air was saturated with incense.

Someone thrust a mug of wonderful-smelling, hot mulled cider in his hand. It tasted as good as it smelled. Someone else took his parka and ordered him to leave his boots in the hall.

The drumming resumed, somewhere down a mile or two of hallway toward the back of the house, but the vibrations seemed more soothing than abrasive to his throbbing skull. Christina led the way and Lowell followed obediently, awed

54

by his surroundings despite decades of semi-impoverished, jaded cynicism and bad memories of the mansions of Palm Coast Harbor, where he'd grown up on the servants' side of town. She led the way to a vast chamber—that was the word, he thought to himself whimsically—with tiled floors, paneled walls, a huge fireplace with a beckoningly roaring fire, and tall windows that almost reached the high frescoed plaster ceiling boasting paintings of Greek and Arthurian lore, an odd but somehow logical mix, that took his breath away like a cold, sharp wind. As in the rest of the house, the room was lit by hundreds of scented candles.

A dozen New Age revelers, some wearing elaborate gowns and robes, many of tie-dyed fabric or various kinds of velour, and all of them hung with several yards of beads, greeted him with disconcerting warmth. "Welcome," they told him, one by one, as Christina introduced them. One attractive-if-wispy young woman named Emily was introduced as a psychic. She had long, blond little-girl pigtails and wore a long East Indian dress. She studied him critically, her head tilted slightly. "You have an interesting aura," she informed him. "But it's clouded with pain and uncertainty. Have you adjusted your heart chakra lately? Because I know a wonderful past-life therapist who—"

"Maybe later," said Lowell, thanking her and moving swiftly on. Miraculously, the beverage seemed to have cleared up the fog in his brain. Even his throbbing scalp felt better. There were eight women and three men, all of them drumming their hearts out, and only two of them had even a suggestion of a sense of rhythm. But it didn't matter. They were having the time of their lives. Before long, Tony Lowell, sufficiently recovered from his earlier bout of drinking and blow on the head, was furiously pounding away on a set of congas that had been relinquished in his honor by an anorexic young woman who seemed to vanish into the smoky shadows that dwelt in the corners of the huge room, where large clusters of Eastern incense burned. The fire crackled and smoked, the drums boomed and thrummed, the room shook and its occupants along with it, until the midnight hour was announced with a chiming of bells that rang throughout the house.

"All right, everyone," announced Christina. "Time to give blessings to our nocturnal Spirit Guides and welcome our new friend over tea and sustenance, *a la media noche.*"

The revelers moved almost in unison from the drumming chamber to another, warmer room, which Lowell recognized as the kitchen, except that it was the size of an auditorium. Two Native American servers were preparing a midnight repast of dishes, some of which Lowell vaguely recognized from years long gone by: macrobiotic rice and beans, breads and fish in vaguely Asiatic marinades, hummus and tahini, and various manifestations of tofu. A regular gastronomic New World Order.

Lowell considered himself for the most part a "marine vegan," which is to say that he preferred seafood to meat, and on those unfortunate occasions when vitamin pills were unavailable, he allowed himself such vegetables as were necessary to survive. But as Croft had warned him: when in Rome . . .

The food was surprisingly good. The New Agers, at least in that regard, had come a long way since the Sixties, when the same kinds of food and spiritualism were equally in vogue but with a definite lack of taste. This too, he realized, was Santa Fe Style, since with the coming of Shirley Maclaine and her following, it had become *the* New Age mecca. But something bothered him about the whole scene, and he couldn't put his finger on it. It just seemed . . . *inappropriate* somehow.

As he mingled with the group and warmed his bones with tea and nourishment, he fended off the more biased inquiries regarding Florida, and how could he stand all those bugs and tourists, all those molds and allergens, all that heat and humidity, all that crime and conflict? He even grudgingly admitted to his hostess, when she asked, that he was enjoying himself. Sort of. "I liked the drumming," he said. And at that moment, he realized what was bothering him.

"You helped a lot," he heard her saying. "Most of us couldn't keep a beat if we had pistons."

While that was eminently true, his mind was elsewhere. "I have to ask you something," he said. Christina turned toward him expectantly. "I know this is going to sound ungracious, but this is all so . . . I don't know . . . otherworldly. Do you people ever get *involved*?"

"Whatever do you mean?" she asked, her voice suddenly wary.

"I mean, do you ever get involved? With anything other than your own personal, I don't know what . . . betterment?"

He saw a change in her, but it passed quickly. "Oh, yes, I haven't forgotten, Mr. Lowell. You are a man with a mission."

Lowell decided that before he put his foot in any farther and was shown the door, it was time to ask her about Alicia. "Speaking of which, what did Ariel say when you talked to her?" he asked.

"Oh, she told me about her concerns and how nice you were to come out here," she said airily, "and I am sorry if you got the impression I know Alicia personally, but we *do* travel in different circles, after all. I mean, she was very nice and all, but she really was somewhat of a fish out of water up there in Denver."

Lowell masked his irritation. "You said on the phone that there would be people here who knew her."

"Oh, there are, just be patient," she told him and hurried off to change the audio CD from George Winston to Enya. Annoyed, Lowell circulated through the group, and despite Christina's promise, he could not find anyone who admitted to knowing Alicia Sandoval. One young Native American guest, however, a woman, reminded him of what he'd already observed from checking the phone book: that Sandoval was one of the most common names in the Rio Grande Valley, not just in Santa Fe. "It's also one of the oldest," she added. Lowell thanked her for sharing that wisdom and was about to call it a night when Christina suddenly appeared before him, accompanied by a handsome, dark-eyed, affable young man of probable Hispanic origins.

"*There* you are, Mr. Lowell!" she exclaimed, over the noise as though he'd been hiding in the woodwork all evening. "I want you to meet Michael Baca." The young man with her smiled vaguely and gazed at the wall. "Michael is one of our leading artists in Santa Fe. He's studied in New York, sold paintings in San Francisco for big money, and now we're all thrilled that he's decided to return to his roots."

"A pleasure," said Lowell, wondering what roots she meant.

"Likewise," said Baca, vaguely.

"Darlin', I told you there'd be someone here who knew her," she whispered as she swept past him to relight an incense burner. "And here he is. But don't press him. He'll come around."

58

Lowell and Baca talked for a while about art, and music, and Indian artifacts, and the Santa Fe scene. Baca seemed bemused by the New Agers and intrigued by the Floridian, and they sat in lounge chairs near the fire sipping mulled wine while the drumming resumed, this time accompanied by random chanting and singing. Finally, Baca got to the point during a break between chants.

"You're looking for someone?" he asked.

"That's right. It doesn't seem to be a very productive pastime around here."

"This is a highly private community," said Baca. "But I heard about your daughter."

That got Lowell's attention. "What did you hear?"

"Don't worry, man, I heard she's a cool *chica*, is all."

"And who did you hear this from?"

"A friend of mine. Alicia Sandoval."

Lowell sat up abruptly and leaned toward him. "Then you know where she is?"

Baca put up his hands. "Hey, easy. I haven't seen her since summer. She always kept pretty much to herself."

"But you know that Ariel asked me to come out here and find her?"

Baca nodded. "I heard."

"Ariel thinks Alicia may be in trouble."

Baca frowned for a brief moment. "I think she's been in trouble for a long time," he said cryptically.

"Then help me find her."

The artist shrugged uncomfortably. "I'll check around. "But like I said, I haven't seen her in months. If I were you, I'd stay away from her, though. It's more than you want to deal with."

"Why?"

"I heard she's married, or was. To nobody you'd want to meet."

"I wouldn't want to meet a lot of people. But it comes with the job. Who was he?"

"I never met him, but I think his name was Lopez. What I hear, he's got a history of violence. Especially toward women. I've worried about her too, more than once."

"Where can I find this Lopez guy?"

Baca looked incredulous. "Listen, man, one thing you should never do is approach somebody like that. Not in Santa Fe. Especially not some macho hombre about his wife. Even if your Spanish is perfect, they'll still know you as an outsider and you won't get anywhere, except maybe have your head caved in."

"They already tried."

Baca looked at Lowell's bandaged head and raised his eyebrows. "Oh?"

"I'm fine. No big deal."

"You might try one place," Baca suggested after a pause. "But I'd be very careful. There's a bar on St. Michael's called the Green Pepper, where some people who call themselves the 'DeVargas Compadres' hang out. If they'll talk to you, and I'm not saying they will, you might learn something. She's got a brother who hangs there sometimes. But you have to be very cool, and very careful. *Comprende?*"

"*Comprendo,*" said Lowell. "Los Compadres. At the Green Pepper."

It was better than nothing. Lowell thanked Baca and said good night to his hostess.

"Y'all sure you wouldn't care to stay?" Christina proposed with a wistful smile. "They say it might snow."

"Isn't that unusual this early in the season?"

"It wouldn't be the first time. El Niño is doing some pretty strange things to our planet."

"The human race is doing some pretty strange things to our planet too. But thanks for the invite. I better get going."

"You sure? We party all night long, darlin'." He sensed she had more than one kind of party in mind.

"Maybe next time," he said, pulling on his boots.

"Oh, right. The man with the mission." She put her hand on his arm and looked serious for a moment. "Y'all be careful out there, it can get mighty slippery."

"I will," Lowell promised, wondering if her words portended anything deeper than falling snow. As he left the castle, snow indeed began to fall, thick, soft dry flakes that made a gentle hissing sound as they drifted down. Although he skidded a few times in the frozen slush, he managed to maneuver the Buick back down the drive, surprised at how quickly the snow was accumulating. Plows were already out on the roads, their blades making a harsh scraping noise on the roadbed, yellow lights flashing like angry warnings in the darkness.

Lowell inexpertly spun and slid and skidded his way back to Santa Fe, doubting more than once that he'd make it, and finally fell exhausted into bed at 3:00 A.M., with a splitting headache and little closer than before to his goal.

6

Lowell arose late, opened his hotel-room shutters and was nearly blinded by the brilliance of the day. The weather had cleared completely. He turned on the radio, found a news station and checked the time: nearly noon. The early season snow was already dissipating in the midday sun and would be gone by mid-afternoon, according to the radio. Lowell noted, with some appreciation for Christina's prediction, that the on-air talk focused on El Niño. Against Croft's advice, he placed a call to Sergeant Ramirez at the Santa Fe P.D., with a vague notion of dropping Lieutenant Bedrosian's name in there somewhere to grease the skids. It didn't work. The desk sergeant asked his business, and when told it was personal, dusted him off as a flake and told him Ramirez was off duty. Use of Joshua Croft's name didn't help, either.

Once again, Lowell was on his own. He called Ariel at her grandfather's house and was told she had gone shopping with her mother. He remembered Michael Baca's suggestion—a local bar on St. Michael's. But he wasn't ready to face another bar just yet. And it was too early in any case.

Outside, two police cars tore past, sirens screaming and lights flashing. Maybe it was the effect of spending most of the night doing New Age drumming. Or hanging around all those crystals. Or crystal gazers. But he was getting one of those feelings again. It felt as though the sirens were for him, warning him that he had no business here in Santa Fe. That was when he felt an urge that came out of nowhere: to go back to the barrio and find the storekeeper named José Gaspar, who knew more than he'd said. Something, a sixth sense, told him there was an urgent need for him to speak to the man again.

He drove west on Alameda, crossed the river to Alto, and came around the back way, toward St. Francis, trying to retrace his steps from the day before. He had almost driven past the small bodega when something caught his eye, and he recognized both the store and the situation at the same moment.

The teen gang was back, and with just a quick glimpse through the plate-glass front window as he drove by, he saw that José was in trouble. They had surrounded him at the little checkout stand and the leader—Tito, was it?—had him by the shirt collar. Lowell had a bad feeling that the confrontation taking place had something to do with him. He didn't hesitate. He skidded quickly over to the curb, jumped out and ran back to the store. Barging in as if he didn't have a care in the world, he yelled out in a booming voice: "*¡Hola! ¡Que pasa, amigos!*"

The teenagers spun around and gaped at him in surprise. José stared at him, both hopeful and bewildered. Tito let go of the storekeeper's shirt. *"¡No esta finito!"* he warned him and shot Lowell a venomous glance. The other boys turned toward Lowell and moved in his direction almost in unison. He calculated his chances of taking them on *mano a mano,* as Croft had put it. The boys gathered around him, Tito hissing in venomous tones.

"Hey," he said. "It's the *cabron.* Hey, fuck you, man. What're you doin' back around here?"

"Just visiting," said Lowell pleasantly. "I like it here. It's a nice place."

Tito snorted, reached into his pocket and pulled out a very large, very nasty-looking bowie knife. Lowell looked at the knife, then at the boy, trying to decide how serious the kid was. He decided the kid was serious.

With a quick feint right and another left, Lowell used a move he'd allowed Perry Garwood to teach him one time after they'd smoked a couple of joints and were messing around, combined with a few moves he still remembered from his military days, and suddenly the boy was facing the other way, his arm bent behind his back and Lowell holding the knife.

"Leggo, you bastard!" shrieked the kid as his buddies backed away. By this time, José had recovered his wits and reached behind the counter, where he kept a very old, somewhat rusty Colt pistol that looked like it was left over from Billy the Kid.

"You, Tito! Get out. *¡Ve te!"* he shouted.

"I can't! *¡No puedo!"* whined Tito, who had a point, because at that moment, Lowell had him pinned against the beer cooler.

"It's okay," José told Lowell. "He just lost his head for a while. He won't be bothering me anymore."

"You sure of that?" Lowell asked.

"I'm sure," said José. "I know his mother."

"That's what you said yesterday."

"Yes," conceded José. "But this time, I intend to *talk* to her!"

That seemed to do it. Tito's shoulders slumped and Lowell let him go. The boys were out the door and running in about three seconds flat. José came over and joined Lowell at the window as they watched the gang's rapid departure.

"Sort of like little roadrunners, aren't they?" said José.

Lowell decided he liked José. "Maybe," he said. "But who's the Wile E. Coyote?"

José looked at him in recognition. "You're the one looking for Alicia Sandoval," he exclaimed, putting the gun back under the counter.

"I have to tell you, I haven't made much progress," said Lowell. "It's amazing, a town this size and nobody ever heard of her. It makes me wonder if she even exists."

José hesitated, then leaned conspiratorially across the counter. "Yes, she exists. I know her parents," he said, now speaking in perfect English. "The Sandovals are like family to me. We have shared communions, taken part in Fiesta together. Little Alicia used to baby-sit my two girls, who now have children of their own. Yes, I know her. What is it you want of her?"

"She's a friend of my daughter's. I'm trying to deliver a message."

José considered that, frowned, and nodded gravely. "How does your daughter know her? You are not from around here."

"They took a seminar together in Colorado."

"Colorado?" The storekeeper studied Lowell with his dark eyes, as if wondering what kind of trouble Alicia had gotten herself into this time. He shook his head slowly. "It would be better if you stayed away from her."

"People keep saying that. Why? Because of her ex-husband?"

"Maybe. Also because of her brother."

A distant alarm went off in the back of Lowell's head. Hispanic brothers were notorious for their protection of family members. Especially their women. He wondered how they might regard violence against a sister or a daughter—say, from a spouse. It might depend, he thought, on the relationship between the brothers and the spouse. He had learned the hard way that male bonding could be stronger than sibling loyalty in some cases. He wondered if this was such a case. He hoped not. He also hoped it wasn't a problem within the Sandoval family. Such things, of course, were possible in any culture, which didn't improve the outlook for Alicia.

"Her younger brother," José was saying, "is the one who's been the big troublemaker around here lately. You would do well to steer clear of him and those Compadres of his."

"Compadres?" Lowell recognized the old Spanish word for companions, or "comrades." He'd heard the same word just last night.

"The DeVargas Compadres. Little more than a street gang, a bunch of Cholos, basically. Like those little punks who just left. But they are grown-up hombres who talk like they're the saviors of our Spanish heritage. Last thing this town needs," he reflected sadly. "More gangs. More violence. More threats

66

of violence. It's bad, but it won't keep the newcomers away. It will probably just bring in the National Guard if the Cholos do what they're talking about."

"What sort of things are they talking about?" Lowell's internal observer, the photographer-journalist part of him, became alert and took notice.

"Burn houses, shoot tourists. Locos, all of them. She's not like them, but I bet you they won't let you near her."

"Why is that?"

Gaspar sighed. "That," he said, "stays in the family."

Lowell tried another tack. "I heard a rumor," he said, "that she is, or was, married to somebody who might be a danger to her. Any truth to that?"

The storekeeper frowned in consternation and glanced sideways fearfully. Lowell knew he had struck a nerve.

"She married that *bastardo*," José muttered, his tone hushed. "We were all afraid for her, but she wouldn't listen."

"Maybe nobody would listen to her."

Gaspar thought about that and pursed his lips. "Her father is a Sandoval, and even so, she married badly."

Lowell pressed him gently, finally getting somewhere. "And this man she married so badly. Where can I find him?"

José looked terrified and shook his head. "Please, Señor, I have a family."

"Yes. Daughters, you said. Is his name Lopez?"

José nodded. He barely breathed the name. "*Sí, Lopez,*" he whispered. "Danny Lopez. He hangs out sometimes with the Compadres."

"I think it's time I met these Compadres of yours," said Lowell.

Gaspar sighed once again, as though expelling the last breath he would ever breathe. "There's a place down on St. Michael's Drive," he said. *"Una taverna."*

"The Green Pepper?"

Gaspar looked surprised. "You know it?"

"I've heard of it," said Lowell grimly. He was halfway out the door when José Gaspar came after him.

"Please, Señor," he urged, wringing his hands. "It is very dangerous for you there. Maybe you should go home. There is nothing you can do for Alicia Sandoval."

"We'll see," said Lowell.

He got back into the Buick, checked his map of the city and located St. Michael's—a main east-west thoroughfare. He drove east to St. Francis, headed south for about a mile, and turned right onto St. Michael's Drive.

He slowed down as he crossed the old Santa Fe Railroad track. The bar was just ahead. He pulled into the parking lot and squeezed between a low-rider and a blue pickup truck. He knew that from this point on, the rules of engagement would very likely change.

Lowell pulled back the heavy door and entered the bar. By the way the place fell silent and from the high percentage of dark heads that turned his way, it was immediately clear that he had just gone where no sensible Anglo had gone before. At least not recently.

The Cholos had gathered, about a dozen of them. The same teenagers from the bodega were here, sort of like apprentices, Lowell decided. Hail, hail, the gang's all here. The boys gaped at him from around the pool table, which they had just taken over. Their look was mostly one of astonishment.

The older *patrones* lounged around a table at the opposite

end of the room, listening to a solemn-faced young man in good ranch clothes; he looked oddly familiar to Lowell. He was tall, slender, and handsome. Lowell guessed him to be in his mid to late twenties.

Lowell bestowed smiles and nods around the room—some of which were sullenly returned—and strode over to the bar.

"*Una cerveza, por favor,*" he requested. "*Dos Equis.*"

The bartender glanced at the Cholos, then complied. Lowell, too, glanced at the Cholos. The leader, whose name was Peso, looked him over, scowled, shook his head as though to say "crazy gringo," and resumed talking, speaking in low, intense tones.

"You new on the force?" the bartender asked conversationally.

"What force would that be?"

"Police force. Haven't seen you around before." He spoke with the same lilting, singsong accent Lowell recognized as unique to the region.

"What makes you think I'm a cop?" inquired Lowell, feeling slightly resentful. The answer was immediately apparent. The bartender and patrons naturally assumed that no Anglo but a cop would dare to venture in here. Lowell quickly realized this had probably saved him from getting his head caved in at first sight.

The bartender shrugged and turned away to greet one of the Cholos who had come over for another beer.

"I'm not a cop," Lowell heard himself informing the many.

"So what are you, then?"

"Photographer. That, plus odd jobs."

The bartender raised his eyebrows, then shrugged again. The Cholo, overhearing, looked over and reappraised Lowell

69

with some interest, combined with skepticism. He was about the same height and weight, with a similar pony tail to Lowell's.

"That true? You one of those celebrity chasers? Or maybe you work for *National Geographic,* man?" The Cholo asked this with a smirk. It was a local joke, obviously.

"Not anymore," Lowell said, grinning. "Too many farmers' wives."

Wives were a touchy subject in these parts. The smirk vanished. "So where's your camera, man?"

"My hotel room. I'm off duty." He saw snickers form on the faces of the group at the table. He kept on smiling. He guessed the Cholo to be around thirty.

"So, Photographer Man. Whereabouts you from?" the Cholo inquired.

"Florida. Near Tampa Bay."

Lowell might as well have mentioned Londonderry, or Pago Pago. "You're in the wrong place, man," the Cholo advised him. "You want La Posada, someplace like that. That's where the film celebrities and all you other paparazzi types hang out."

"Thanks. But I'm not into chasing celebrities. I'm looking for a friend of mine, actually."

The Cholo had walked away. Lowell heard him explain to his friends in skeptical tones: "The dude says he's a photographer. From Florida."

"Fuck that shit," he heard the teenage boy Tito say. Lowell looked at them, wondered if one of them might be named Danny Lopez. He decided he didn't want a direct confrontation just yet. Not in this setting, on these terms. He needed to know more first.

"Yo," exclaimed one of the group at the table. "Peso, maybe he should take a picture of us."

There were several hoots and barks of laughter. Peso shook his head.

"Why not?" insisted the one who'd made the suggestion. "It's free publicity, man!"

"Like I said, I'm off duty," Lowell told them.

"He's a jerkwad!" complained Tito loudly. "He was hasslin' us, man."

Peso spoke to Tito in rapid Spanish, something about his lack of cranial matter, and the boys reluctantly trooped out of the bar, looking resentful. The biggest member of Peso's group came over to Lowell and sat next to him. He was stocky, had an army crew cut and a gold earring. "Yo, dude," he said. "You got any I.D. proves you are who you say you are?"

Lowell shrugged and fished out his Florida driver's license and a business card he'd saved from his teaching days at the junior college. The Cholo looked them over, then back at his friends. "Name's Tony Lowell. A fucking photography teacher, man. From fucking Florida," he confirmed, surprise mixed with incredulity. Lowell reached out and retrieved his I.D.

"Flor-ee-da!" someone exclaimed in mocking tones.

"I'm out of here," announced Peso, who was already on his feet. "I got better things to do than this."

"Hey, c'mon, man, he ain't no cop," protested the one who'd come over to Lowell.

"He's Anglo, Luis," retorted Peso, and stalked out. The others looked at each other in consternation. The stocky one shrugged insolently.

"He's uptight," he told Lowell with a grin. "Doesn't like Anglos."

"I noticed."

"He thinks maybe we should get rid of them all."

"That's a tall order," observed Lowell.

The stocky Cholo, Jaime, laughed. "It's worth a shot! They take over our land, take over our town, bring in all these damn *turistas*, drive up all the prices—"

"Jaime, you're talking to a *turista* right now, you dumb shit," snapped the only woman in the bar. She was dressed like one of the Compadres, and Lowell hadn't noticed her earlier. She blended in, a regular, one of the boys.

"Hey, fuck off, Marta," Jaime told her.

"How do you know he's not undercover?" she objected.

" 'Cause he ain't local. And who else is gonna give a shit? The fucking Feds?" He laughed harshly.

That seemed to settle it. After that, they pretty much ignored Lowell and resumed their discussions in low, inaudible tones, switching freely between English and Spanish. Lowell heard bits and pieces of conversation, but nothing significant.

Luis, the Cholo who'd spoken with Lowell earlier, came back after a while, as though he had just noticed Lowell was still there. "So what was it you said you were doing here, man?"

"I said I was looking for a friend," Lowell reminded him.

"Oh, yeah. I forgot. What friend?"

"A woman friend. Her name is Alicia Sandoval."

It was as though Lowell had thrown a bucket of ice on everyone. The whole room fell silent, for the second time since his arrival.

"Peso's gonna be sorry he missed this," said Marta with a sharp, quick laugh. Lowell wondered what that meant.

"Him and Danny," remarked Carlos. No one laughed.

The stocky one, Jaime, looked Lowell up and down with renewed assessment. "Hey, man, you're new in town, right?"

"That's right."

"And you ain't a tourist or nothing, right?"

"That's right."

"Then you won't miss much if you were to just turn around and leave, know what I mean?"

Lowell felt the tension rising. But he held his ground. "Yeah, I would. I'd miss seeing my friend. Not to mention all this great photographic scenery of yours."

They seemed to assess that, what it meant, as though they were sampling some strange, alien fruit. The woman looked at him with something new in her eyes, perhaps curiosity. Perhaps something more. She moved over toward him, her hips swaying unconsciously, as though resuming a feminine pose she'd set aside before, perhaps for the benefit of the Compadres. Despite her fatigues and mannish attitude earlier, he noted that she was in fact a very attractive young woman, barely into her twenties.

"So tell me, mister. How well you know Alicia?" she asked.

"Actually, she's a friend of my daughter's."

She let out another sharp, harsh laugh. "You dating her?"

"Nothing like that."

The other Cholos laughed at that. Their laughter had an ugly sound to it.

"Even so, you better leave town, man," Jaime repeated. "She's married, don't you know that?"

"You mean divorced. But like I said, I'm not here to date her."

"She's Catholic," Marta spat, as though talking to an ignorant child. "You don't just get divorced."

"I've never even met her, actually. She knows my daughter."

"Anyway," Lowell heard someone else mutter, "Danny didn't go along with it."

"Danny?" Lowell decided it was time to test the name.

"Her husband, Danny Lopez. A friend of ours," said Luis.

"Yeah, I heard," said Lowell ironically.

That didn't go over well at all. Jaime moved over to his right, reached out and tapped him on the arm. "You do what you want, but I wouldn't stay around here, if I were you."

"I'll keep that in mind," said Lowell, getting to his feet. "Thanks for the tip." Putting three dollars on the bar, he headed for the door. They watched him leave, the atmosphere charged with hostility.

Lowell left the Green Pepper Bar without looking back, half expecting to be overtaken by footsteps, or even a bullet, at any moment. He heard the tavern door open behind him as he got into the rental car.

"Yo, hold on," shouted a voice Lowell recognized as belonging to Carlos, the tall, older youth with the beard. Lowell stopped and waited for him to catch up. Carlos glanced around furtively and spoke in a hushed voice. "Alicia Sandoval is one of my people. She also happens to be one of my favorite people." He sounded agitated. "She's had a bad time in this town, and she deserves a chance to live her own life. I don't think you'd be stupid enough to come here to do her any harm. I think maybe she's been done enough harm already."

Lowell turned and faced him. "How much harm has she been done?"

"Enough." Lowell could see veiled anger in the young man's eyes. "I can't even tell you some of the shit she's had to take. But I'll tell you one thing—I don't think he's finished with her."

"He?"

"That's all I can say, man."

"Then help me find her. Help me get her out of whatever hell she's in."

Carlos shook his head. "I think you're crazy, man," he said. "But I believe you mean well by her. And the Sandovals can take care of their own if you're lying." He let that sink in. Lowell did the same. "Okay," Carlos went on. "Her father's name is Manny. They live over on Alto Street, it's the biggest house, north side facing the river. You can't miss it. They probably won't let you talk to her. But if you want to give it a try, I got no problem with that. Just don't tell them I sent you."

Lowell didn't press Carlos for directions. He could find it on the map. Two blocks away, he pulled into a 7-Eleven and went over to a phone booth. Sure enough, there was a Manuel Sandoval in the book, on Alto Street. He got the map of Santa Fe out of the glove compartment and studied it. Alto Street was only two blocks away from Agua Fria, where he'd been earlier.

He found the address within five minutes, pulled up at the curb a few doors farther down, and studied the house. It was large and ancient, of genuine adobe, two stories and rambling, with a huge yard, by local standards. There was even an orchard in back. The Sandovals, he realized, were people of some substance in the Santa Fe community. That could be good. It could also be bad.

As Lowell contemplated his next move, a car came down

75

the street toward him, moving slowly: a shiny, black '67 Pontiac Bonneville. It glided up behind him and stopped. The windows were dark-tinted, and he couldn't make out anyone inside. Moments later, from the other direction, a white Datsun pickup truck came around a corner and also pulled over at the curb, facing the wrong way, directly in front of him. Its occupants were two young Chicano males in black T-shirts. They grinned at him. It wasn't a friendly grin. Lowell managed to grin back and waited to see what would happen next.

A young Hispanic man in his twenties got out of the Pontiac, taking his time. He came over to Lowell's window. Lowell obliged him by rolling it down. Only then did he recognize the tall young man from the gathering he'd just left. Peso. The gang leader who'd walked out.

"*Hola,*" said Lowell.

"Hello," said Peso. "You looking for something?" By his demeanor, Peso seemed distracted and not in the best of moods. He hadn't yet recognized Lowell in the bright daylight.

"Yeah, I'm looking for the Sandoval residence."

The eyes narrowed. "Fuck for?"

"I'm looking for Alicia Sandoval. I have a message for her." Lowell remembered only then the woman Marta's cryptic remark: "Peso's gonna love this." At which instant he remembered what José Gaspar had told him. Peso had to be the brother.

Peso did a classic double take in recognition. "Hey! It's the dude from the bar," he shouted. "You crazy? What the fuck you want with Alicia? Who the hell are you, anyway? And don't give me that photographer crap or I'm gonna hurt you, man!"

76

The other two Cholos were out of the pickup in an instant, drawn by Peso's visible agitation.

Lowell knew he'd better talk fast. "What I told your people in the bar is the truth. My name is Lowell. Tony Lowell. I didn't know you were her brother until just now."

"Fuck that!" screamed Peso. "You gotta be some kind of cop or something!"

"Not exactly. More like private investigator."

Peso studied him for a long moment, then shook his head. "Investigating what?"

"A missing person."

"Say what? Fuck you, man. Nobody's missing!"

"Then you won't mind if I talk to her?"

Peso shook his head again. Then, with sudden brutal swiftness, he drew his fist back to slug Lowell, and to his surprise, Lowell moved even more quickly than he and the blow missed. What was worse, Lowell now had hold of his arm and was levering it against the edge of the window. Peso let out a yell, at which moment Lowell then seized his hand, shook it, and let it go.

"Nice to meet you, too," he said.

By this time, all three Cholos stood in a row, staring at Lowell like he was an escapee from a colony of demented lepers.

"All right, man," Peso said, rubbing his arm and flexing his fingers ruefully. "Let's cut the crap. What do you *really* want?"

Lowell sighed. "Once more from the top. My daughter is a friend of Alicia's. She is worried about her. Your sister tried to call, she was afraid about something. Then when Ariel called her back, the phone had been disconnected. Alicia left no forwarding address, and my daughter is convinced something is wrong. She asked me to find out what and see if I could help."

"You? Help my sister? Like *how*? She don't need no help from you, man."

Lowell raised his hands. "If not, that's good. But I'd like to hear that from her."

"You come all the way out here because your daughter got some notion my sister was in trouble?"

"Is she?"

Lowell could see the hesitation for just a brief moment.

"That's none of your business, Anglo. You don't even know her. So how do you—"

"You care about your sister?" Lowell cut in.

The question caught Peso off guard. He whirled angrily, ready to strike out once more. Lowell didn't flinch, which made the Cholo pull his punch. "Yeah, I care about her, she's my sister, man."

"That's important. People *should* care about their sisters. They should also care about their friends. And my daughter considers your sister her friend."

"Maybe my sister doesn't feel the same way. Anyway, I never heard of your daughter."

"I haven't told you her name yet. It's Ariel. Besides, how many of your sister's friends do you actually know?"

"Most. Fuck's that got to do with it?"

"Just give her the benefit of the doubt for one second. Then tell me one thing and I'll go."

"Tell you what?"

78

"Can you absolutely guarantee to me—and I'll take it back to my daughter on your word—that your sister Alicia is *safe*?"

Peso hesitated once more at that, and Lowell had his answer. "Nobody is safe no more, it's too late for that," he said cryptically. It wasn't the answer Lowell had been hoping for. What he'd been hoping for was that it was all a mistake, she was fine, come on in and ask her, she'll tell you so herself. Now he knew Ariel's instincts, or whatever they were, had been right. He could see it in Peso's eyes. Doubt. Doubt and rage. A dangerous combination.

Peso was silent for a long moment, studying the Anglo *estranjero*. "You're in front of the wrong house," he finally informed him, pointing at the big one half a block away. Then, with a nonchalant shrug, he said, "So do something about it. Not that anybody is gonna want to talk to you."

Lowell glanced at the two Cholos and back at his inquisitor. "Do they have a reason not to?"

"Yeah, man," said Peso, his temper suddenly flaring. "You come from out of town, out of state, we don't know you. Now you say my sister don't know you, you got some crazy idea that's none of your business. Why should anybody want to talk to you?"

"Well," said Lowell, "You do have a point." But what you're telling me, he thought, is that she really is *not* safe. Not safe at all. "Anyway, as Virgil said, 'Fortune sides with him who dares.' "

Peso shook his head and grinned slightly. "I don't know this Virgil dude, but I admit you got *cojones*, bro'." He studied Lowell some more for a moment. "Wait here," he said finally and walked over to the pickup. He spoke with the two occupants in rapid Spanish. They started their engine, backed up, and drove away. He came back to Lowell.

"Here's what I don't want to know about. I don't want to know about you going to the house and asking for Mrs. Sandoval, my mother. I don't want to know about whether or not she knows where my sister is, or whether you should see her or not. I don't want to know about you talking to my other sister, Micaella, or my big brother Roberto, the big shot lawyer. And most of all, I don't want to know about you or your daughter anymore," said Peso. "We clear on that?"

"Clear as a dust storm," said Lowell.

Peso grinned. "So long, Anglo." He turned, walked back to his Bonneville, got in and sped off, mufflers rumbling like a desert dragon.

Lowell watched him go, took a deep breath, got out of the car and walked up to the Sandoval residence. He rang the bell and waited. After a moment, a small viewing window slid open in the main door and someone peered out at him.

"Quien es?" called a female voice of indeterminate age.

"Excuse me. *Por favor, estoy buscando por Alicia Sandoval."*

There was a long pause. The little door slid shut, and after a pause, Lowell heard the bolt slide open. The door opened a crack, and a small, gray-haired woman looked out.

"What do you want?" she demanded.

"Sorry to bother you," he told her. "I'm here with a message from a friend of hers from back east. I'm in town, and thought I'd stop by and see how she's doing."

The woman frowned. "What do you know about her?"

80

"Only that my daughter lost contact with her a few weeks ago and is worried about her."

"*¿Cómo se llama?* What is your name?"

"Tony Lowell."

Her eyes narrowed, as though sorting through some long-forgotten data bank. She opened the door wider and called behind her into the house: "Micaella! *Venga!*"

Another, younger woman appeared in the hallway, behind the woman at the door. She looked to be around thirty. Lowell could see a resemblance to the photo of Alicia at once.

"I'm Mrs. Sandoval," the first woman told him. "This is my daughter, Micaella."

Micaella looked older than she probably was. She looked tired. She stared at him blankly.

"This is Señor Lowell," Mrs. Sandoval told her. "He says his daughter is a friend of Alicia's." Micaella's eyes were inscrutable. "You better come in," Mrs. Sandoval told Lowell, and opened the door.

He stepped into a wide entry hall. It had reddish brown tile floors, yellowed adobe walls, and wooden ceiling beams blackened by untold years of wood and cigar smoke.

Mrs. Sandoval gave her daughter a look. Micaella blushed, then turned and hurried away. Lowell thought he heard children somewhere in the house. Probably hers.

"Please sit, Señor," said Alicia's mother, gesturing at a boxlike, straw-woven wooden chair against the wall. "You must have come a long way."

"Is Alicia here?" he asked, looking around.

Mrs. Sandoval shrugged noncommittally. "I can't tell you. How do you like Santa Fe? You been here before?"

"This is my first visit," he replied, perching on the edge of the chair, studying his surroundings. "This is a beautiful house."

"This house has been in my husband's family for ten generations," Mrs. Sandoval told him, observing his reaction with some satisfaction. "It was once a hacienda, part of an original Spanish land grant."

"It's very nice."

"All my children were born here, in the front room upstairs," Mrs. Sandoval said, a note of pride in her voice. "Micaella's husband is in the army, so she still lives here with her children. We are a very close family, Señor."

"Speaking of which, I was asking about Alicia."

She wasn't ready to talk about Alicia. Instead, she told him about Roberto, her son the lawyer. She was very proud of Roberto, who had an office near the plaza. Then she began naming the ancestors whose portraits lined the walls. A few minutes later, Micaella reentered, carrying a silver tray bearing an elegant china tea service.

"You like some tea?" she asked nervously. Lowell nodded and accepted an ornate Mexican cup and saucer, watching the women intently as Micaella poured the tea. They looked at each other while Lowell took a sip.

"My youngest daughter Alicia is not well," the mother told him at last.

That set off an alarm in his head. "I'm sorry to hear that. What's wrong with her?"

There was another pause, another look. "Nothing. Just that her constitution isn't so good," Micaella interjected.

He felt the danger again, the presence of something unspoken and ominous. "Where is she?"

"She went away," Micaella told him.

He had already figured as much. "I see. Can you tell me where? And why?"

"You some kind of bill collector or something?"

Lowell laughed despite his anxiety. "No, Señora. Nothing like that. I'm a friend, nothing more."

"That sounds like something a bill collector or a gangster would say. Are you a gangster?"

She cocked her head when she said it, and he liked her right away. "No ma'am," he said and grinned.

The women looked at each other again, but they had no answers for him.

"She was all right when I saw her last," said Micaella finally.

"How long ago was that?"

"A while. Look, Señor, I don't think—" Mrs. Sandoval began.

"So she lives here, except she's not here right now. Can you tell me if she's back with her husband? With Danny?"

Micaella looked alarmed. "Danny Lopez? *Madre de dios!*" she gasped. "No, Señor! We just can't tell you where she is, is all."

"And you can't tell me how she is?"

It seemed to them like a strange question. Mother and daughter looked at each other quizzically.

"Maybe," said Lowell finally as though speaking to himself, "she'll come back here because she has nowhere else to go."

That startled them. "Of course she will," said the mother.

"Please, Mama. Just tell him," Micaella pleaded. "He's not going to hurt her."

83

Alicia's mother shook her head. "We can't tell you," she told Lowell, fear—and was that sorrow—in her eyes. "We can't tell anyone. She's gone away, where it's safe."

Lowell put his cup down slowly, carefully, so as not to spill the tea. "Safe? You mean safe from Danny Lopez?"

The Sandoval women weren't about to say any more.

"You better go," Micaella said as she went to open the door. "I'm sorry."

7

Tony Lowell knew one thing about insular cultures and small towns, even Santa Fe. Whatever quaint and distinctive characteristics any particular locale might offer, the one thing that everybody had in every town in America was a phone book. What was tricky, however, was to find copies of back issues.

As he left the barrio and headed back across St. Francis toward the plaza, Lowell pulled into the next of the ubiquitous strip malls with a pay phone, got out of the car and in the book there looked up the location of the nearest Southwestern Bell Telephone Company office in the white pages. Checking his map, he saw that it was only a few blocks away.

Five minutes later, he strolled into the phone company office and sauntered up to the reception counter. There was no one around, so he waited, studying the prints on the wall of famous Native Americans and New Mexican landscapes. After a while, an attractive young Hispanic receptionist returned to her desk and stifled a cough, apparently startled to see someone standing there.

"Can I help you, sir?" she asked. From her flushed appearance, the fact that she smelled of tobacco smoke and had a cough, Lowell concluded she'd been in the ladies' room, sneaking a cigarette.

He proffered his best smile, remembering that his friend Joshua Croft smiled a lot. Maybe that was the thing to do in Santa Fe. She smiled back tentatively. "Yes," he said. "As a matter of fact, I was hoping you could."

Her smile faded slightly. He could tell from her look that this wasn't part of her job description—helping people. "I'll do my best," she said. "Is it an address change? Or did you want to open a new account, maybe? For that, you have to go upstairs to the business office."

"No, nothing like that," said Lowell.

She regarded him doubtfully. "What was it you needed, then?"

"Something pretty big." She looked alarmed. "Phone books," he explained.

Her expression relaxed into a smile of relief. "Oh! Is that all. For those, you just call your—"

"Old ones," he added.

"Oh. You wanted to see some of the past editions?"

He nodded. "That's right."

"They're in the back. You want the last three years?" Her voice had assumed a note of boredom.

"That would be nice."

"Wait here," she said. "I'll be right back." She left the

86

room and returned shortly with a stack of books, white and yellow pages together. "Here you go. You can sit at that table over there," she said, handing the books over. "Just leave them on the counter when you're through, sir."

Lowell thanked her, sat down and opened the most recent phone book first—the one prior to the current edition, which he had already thoroughly perused. He checked under Lopez—two pages of entries, and then Sandoval, two more pages. No Danny, and no Alicia. He moved on to the year-old, with the same results. Finally, he found what he was looking for, two years back: Daniel Lopez, with an address on West Alameda Street. He wrote it down and returned the books.

"You find what you were looking for?" asked the receptionist.

"Maybe," he said.

Lowell drove out on Alameda, once again west, toward the river from St. Francis, and found the place, a dreary, gray-block apartment off Columbus. He parked the Buick and walked up to the entrance. The air stank of urine. Several small brown children played on the barren lawn, fighting for possession of a few broken toys, their faces already reflections of broken dreams. Lowell found the manager's apartment on the row of buzzers and rang.

A gaunt, white-haired Hispanic man came to the door.

"The buzzer doesn't work," he said, "but I saw you coming. Who you looking for?"

Lowell told him. The man frowned and shook his head. "I remember the guy Danny, all right. And his wife, too. She was a good-looking girl when they first moved in. Didn't look

87

so good later on. Always fighting, them two," sighed the old-timer. "Too bad. These kids. No respect for their elders, or traditions, or nothing."

The apartment manager confirmed that Alicia had finally left one day and never returned. "Mr. Lopez moved out a year ago," the man said, not looking too heartbroken about it.

"You know where to?"

"Don't know where, don't want to know where." He shook his head again and turned away. "Anything comes for him, I put 'return to sender.' Nothing but trouble, that one. As for the *chica*." He just shook his head once more and shut the door.

Lowell returned to the plaza and stopped by the Blue Corn Cafe for coffee—a popular hangout and pastime in Santa Fe—and ran into Mike Baca, who brought his latte over to the table and asked how Lowell was doing.

Baca seemed amused to hear of his lack of progress on the Lopez/Alicia front and offered an additional word of cryptic warning. "Danny Lopez is a dangerous one," he said. "But watch out. So is Alicia." He didn't elaborate.

"Do you know if her divorce is final yet?" Lowell asked.

"Haven't you heard? Far as I know. But it's not that easy, you know. Around here."

"Family values," said Lowell, nodding sagely.

Baca gave him a shrewd look. "Did you make it over to the Green Pepper? Speaking of family values."

Lowell nodded. "Yep. Had a fine ol' time."

"I'll bet. Did you meet Peso?"

"Yes. A regular family man. Very helpful."

Baca cocked his head and grinned. "Glad to hear it."

They sipped coffee in amiable silence. Lowell decided to

change the subject. "Listen, do you know where I can get hold of a computer?"

"What for?"

"To access a database. Criminal records, last known addresses, that sort of thing."

"Cool!" exclaimed Baca. "I've been meaning to get a computer so I can access museums and galleries, not to mention some other interesting things. That detective—what's-his-name, Josh Croft?—used one of those to find the guy who shot Rita. He tell you about that?"

"No, but he wasn't in a very talkative mood when I saw him."

"Never is, from what I hear. But maybe Croft would lend you his, or you could try the library, or Kinko's copy place. They also rent computers." Baca snapped his fingers. "Hey, I think Alicia used to be into computers. I was going to sign up for one of those classes, you know? At the community college. She was there at the same time. I asked her what she was up to, hadn't seen her in a while, and she said she wanted to try to get into computers because there's good money in them. 'Course, that was a while back, before she left Danny and showed up in Denver for those seminars. Things change, I guess."

Lowell nodded, wondering if that piece of information could prove useful.

He paid for the coffee and headed north across the plaza, remembering that Santa Fe had a good-sized library just up the street, plus a couple of colleges somewhere on the south side. If he could get onto a computer, he could access one of the special databases available only to registered legal investigators. Lena Bedrosian had convinced him to sign up

89

several years ago. Sometimes, he admitted to himself, she came in handy.

The main Santa Fe Library was surprisingly large for a city of only seventy thousand. There was a whole roomful of computers, but they could only access publishing data. Lowell needed more than that, but while he was there, he logged onto the periodicals search base and ran a search on Danny Lopez. An article jumped out at him from the screen, and he immediately clicked on "Print Now." It was a wedding announcement, from 1990. It included a nice photo of the happy couple. Lopez was a handsome, beaming, post-adolescent groom. There was mention of his football and basketball heroics at Santa Fe High School.

The bride was not Alicia Sandoval. Recovering from his shock at that revelation, he read on. The girl's name was Amanda Cortez, her age, eighteen. The article said nothing about her, except that her family was from nearby Española and that "the bride wore a traditional white satin gown with a lovely tulle veil and train." He searched further and came up with several more articles on Lopez, including one about charges being dismissed for an armed robbery. And a year later, another about charges being dismissed for aggravated assault. The writer of the second article took pains to point out that Lopez was a "good local boy who'd never been in trouble before." The same, evidently memory-impaired judge apparently agreed, and the records had been expunged. Another article, a few years later, mentioned the marriage of Daniel Lopez to Alicia Sandoval. But nothing more about Amanda. It was as if Amanda Cortez had suddenly ceased to exist.

On a whim Lowell checked the phone books for an Amanda Cortez. There was none. He called Croft at the agency, left a message on the ubiquitous machine, and went to Kinko's, down on St. Michael's Drive, not far from the infamous Green Pepper Bar. The employees were all bright, young, peppy, and eager to rent him a Macintosh with Internet access. But then he ran into another problem: his database was in Florida and he was unable to log on. Croft found him there still trying an hour later.

"You called Hector," he stated, sitting on the stool next to Lowell's rented workstation. "I told you that was a bad idea."

"When you're right, you're right," said Lowell, not looking up. "Sorry about that."

"It's your case, not mine. He said to tell you that if you'd stopped by, maybe he'd have found some time."

"You win some, you lose some," said Lowell.

"He said to tell you that he wants better references than me."

Lowell thought of Bedrosian. "Okay. I'll see what I can do." He looked up. "Thanks for the tip."

"Was there something else you wanted?"

"Yes. Have you ever heard of a guy by the name of Danny, or Daniel Lopez?"

Croft frowned. "Not offhand. It's a common name."

"He was Alicia Sandoval's husband. Does that ring a bell?"

"Should it?"

"Maybe you crossed paths once or twice. But here's the thing. He was married before. And his first wife may also have disappeared."

"I'll ask around," said Croft after a pause. "But I have to go. People to do, things to see. Plus a very important case. Two ex-spouses think they own the space the other one is in. Both want the other one out. Preferably dead. Life marches on." He got up to leave.

"One more thing," Lowell said quickly. "Do you have access to the state criminal data bank?"

Like Lowell, as a legal investigator, Croft had access to certain databases intended for law enforcement, but each state had its own, and there was no central source except for the National Crime Information Center in Washington, D.C., to which only state law-enforcement agencies and the FBI had access. Available information included credit reports, most-recent addresses, in some cases fingerprint files, police blotter, aliases, and criminal records. Lowell had gotten access in Florida through Lena Bedrosian from time to time, but only when he was assisting her in her own investigations. This was another matter. She wouldn't lift a finger for this one, he was quite sure.

Croft shook his head. "I don't do computers," he said. "Not if I can help it. That was Rita's department. But I know who does." He picked up the customer courtesy phone on the counter and made a call. He spoke quickly, listened a moment, scribbled some notes on the provided notepad, then hung up. "Okay. If you're a *Data Tech* subscriber, you call your local server and dial this code, use this password and name, and you're in." He wished Lowell good luck. "By the way, you still need boots," he said, and left.

Lowell accessed the Web, typed in the Internet address of his server, followed Croft's mysterious contact's instructions, and feeling like a burglar on a caper, hacked his way into the New Mexico data bank. Using the "Find" command, he entered "Alicia Sandoval" and came up with nothing. Ditto "Amanda Cortez." Next he went for the big enchilada, "Danny Lopez." Unfortunately, it was a very common name.

Even in crime circles. He came up with one hundred and fifty-six entries. Methodically, he narrowed the field: first to Santa Fe County, then to the city proper.

Adjusting the brightness on his computer screen, he continued to plow through the menu options, ever narrowing the fields. Finally, an entry flashed boldly on the screen: "Daniel Lopez, b. 5/16/1966," followed by the address he'd already checked out, and a list of charges confirming the ones mentioned in the newspaper articles, and adding a few more besides—check kiting, armed robbery, felonious assault, and attempted rape. All dismissed. There was also an expired driver's license and a list of unpaid fines of various kinds. Then the following: "m. Amanda Cortez, 6/12/90. m. Alicia Sandoval, 11/5/95."

"Bingo," he muttered to himself and printed out the data sheet. He was about to exit the server when a thought struck him like a bolt of desert lightning. Ariel, when she'd first spoken to him about her friend Alicia, had mentioned that she'd gotten an e-mail from her. Which meant that at least as recently as last summer, Alicia'd had an account, or access to one. Somewhere. Maybe she still had one. Lowell went to the customer service desk and arranged for a local e-mail box, charged to his Visa. Then he reclaimed the Macintosh and this time accessed the Web through the Kinko account on one of the major Web servers. The screen went through its customary series of graphic images, welcoming bulletin boards and twirling icons, logged onto the Net and offered him the usual dazzling array of amazing and incredible ways to waste time. He clicked on the Internet icon, accessed the gopher and followed the prompts. He typed in the names: "Alicia Sandoval Lopez," and "Santa Fe, New Mexico." The machine hummed, clicked, beeped, and went to work searching for a screen name that might finally lead him to Ariel's mythical friend.

Knowing this might take time, perhaps even days, Lowell was about to sign off when the screen went blank, and then a list of prospects began to appear. He scrolled and scanned it, his pulse quickening. There were a hundred-odd names, many of them combinations of Alicia Sandoval and/or Lopez. As was the case with Internet addresses, there were no locations indicated. The Internet was the ultimate form of anonymity. You could send and receive messages, from anywhere to anywhere, with neither party having the slightest clue as to the whereabouts of the other. With a laptop computer and modem, or just with access to a public one, the e-mail was entirely mobile. Have modem, will travel. At least until some newer, better technology came along, cheerfully rendering several hundreds of billions in global time and capital investment obsolete.

But it was a start.

He decided to delete all the Lopez versions, because an abused wife, even one of Hispanic origins, would be unlikely to retain the name of her ex-husband once she'd finally managed to extricate herself from his domination. So he focused on the Sandovals, and there were plenty of them. He decided to create a de facto newsgroup and send a message to each Sandoval name at once. Not only was it simpler and more efficient, it could be done in seconds. Then he had but to wait.

He made several attempts before settling on the content of the outgoing message. Then he typed:

To Alicia Sandoval. Formerly Lopez. If you are in or from Santa Fe, New Mexico, and remember Ariel Schoenkopf-Lowell, she sends her love. Help is on the way. Please contact her in Florida for a number. Her father Tony Lowell is in Santa Fe, c/o the Inn at Loretto. Or e-mail LowellPI @ Kinko.com.

He added the return address and pressed "Send."

He waited a while, got no responses, then finally shut down and called it a day. Lowell was no big Net surfer, but he knew enough to realize that most people didn't get or respond to e-mail instantly, even though theoretically it was available and waiting. Most people, other than avid surfers, and unless on line at the time a message came through, were likely to check their mail every few days at most—or even just once a week. Ironically, people still tended to check snail mail with much greater frequency, even though it usually brought nothing but bills and junk—not that the Internet wasn't catching up in that regard in a big way.

It was late afternoon when Lowell left Kinko's and headed back to the plaza, when he remembered seeing the local newspaper office on Marcy, not far from there. He managed to find a rare parking space in the lot adjacent to the newspaper office and went into the building. The paper was called the *Santa Fe New Mexican.* He wanted to talk to somebody about Amanda Cortez. He kept seeing her in his mind, a shadowy, insubstantial form, no longer that high-school ingenue, something more ephemeral and elusive. Once again he faced an indifferent, if not hostile, reception at the desk. This time, he presented one of his old photographer press credentials. It seemed to work.

"Just a minute, Mr. Lowell," said the woman, pronouncing it as though it rhymed with "foul." He didn't bother correcting her; she might change her mind and tell him to go away. He was getting tired of being told to go away. Especially in a city that allegedly prided itself on being an international must-see destination with world-class hospitality. He watched her try a number, give up and ease herself heavily out of her swivel chair. "Be right back," she told him, and went through a door that led into the editorial offices, taking his card with her.

Lowell sat for a while on a stiffly ornate Mexican-style chair and thumbed through today's paper—mostly local political sniping about this and that, with a tad of national and international news thrown in with all the depth of a CNN sound byte.

A tall woman with long, sandy hair tied in a ponytail that—Lowell suddenly realized—wasn't all that different from his, came through the door and smiled coolly.

"Mr. Lowell? I'm Carla Martin, senior editor. What can I help you with?"

Surprised to be afforded such rank, Lowell stood up and accepted her extended hand. It was a working person's hand—rough, reddened, and calloused. She was broad-shouldered and looked strong, as though she'd been range-fed on some big spread in West Texas, or maybe had migrated from Lake Woebegone. Nearly his height, she demonstrated a good grip. Her smile, however, was as fresh and genuine as a Rocky Mountain breeze.

Lowell decided directness was in order and got right to the point. "Thanks for your time, Ms. Martin. I'm a private investigator from Florida, working on a case involving a missing woman. Possibly two women."

She raised her eyebrows. "Interesting. Follow me," she

said and led the way through a doorway and down a narrow hall, past a row of cubicles occupied by frowning, earnest young reporters laboring over word processors, to a small office with an actual window. "Have a seat. Now then," she said, "tell me about it."

Lowell left out the parts about Ariel's New Age manifestos, dreams, and premonitions and stuck to the facts: that one Daniel Lopez had married twice—to an Amanda Cortez, and then to an Alicia Sandoval, and he found it troubling that now neither woman could be located.

"And what's your interest in these people?" Carla Martin asked, her expression polite and guarded.

"My daughter befriended Alicia Sandoval," he said. "She took it hard when Alicia seemed to just disappear. I told her I'd look into it."

The bushy red eyebrows shot up again. "You came all the way out here just to do that?" He nodded, slightly embarrassed. "Dang," she laughed wryly. "My father wouldn't cross the street if I asked him to unless there was a bar on the other side." She gave him a sideways look that he suspected was more than just inquisitive. It was as though she wanted to say something more, then thought better of it. He didn't encourage her. The moment passed. She let out a sigh and stood up.

"Wait here a minute," she said, her tone of one accustomed to giving orders. "I've got a reporter here you might want to talk to." She left the room and returned a few minutes later, accompanied by a thirty-something Hispanic male dressed in casual-conservative style, wearing wire-rim glasses, tan Dockers, a striped Arrow shirt open at the collar, and a beige cashmere sweater.

"Mr. Tony Lowell, meet Peter Herrera. Peter works in the

97

news department. Mr. Lowell is here from Florida on a private investigation." Herrera shot him a speculative look as Lowell nodded and considered getting up. They were too far apart to shake hands, as the editor's desk was between them. Herrera didn't look as if he minded. "Mr. Lowell, tell Peter what you've got."

Lowell pulled a vertically folded manila envelope from the inner pocket of his parka, unfolded it and took out the copies he'd made of the articles in the newspaper of nearly a decade earlier. "I'm looking for a missing person," he explained. "A former wife of a man named Daniel Lopez." Lowell saw Herrera frown at the mention of Lopez's name. "I gather you may know the man. And maybe you know something about this woman? Amanda Cortez?"

Herrera accepted the sheaf of clippings and looked them over. He focused on the first item, the one about the wedding to Amanda Cortez. "I remember this," he said. "And I remember her. From high school. She was an honors student. We took debating together, and she worked on the school paper for a while. Nice girl."

"When was the last time you saw or heard from her?"

Herrera looked pained. "Can you wait a few minutes? There's something I'd like to check in the files." Lowell nodded again as Herrera stood and left the room, taking the clipping with him.

Carla picked up the remaining clippings, glanced through them, then looked at Lowell. He wondered if she found him a refreshing change from all the cowboy wanna-bes and New Agers hereabouts. He also suspected she smelled a story.

"Of course Peter has a much better awareness than I do

of what goes on in the Hispanic community," she said matter-of-factly. "But the name Daniel Lopez rings a bell. It seems to me he's been in trouble fairly recently. I remember that he was a sports star a decade or so back."

Lowell told her what he knew. And what he'd found on the rap sheet. He'd also printed a copy of that from the Internet, and he showed it to her. "What's interesting about that," she commented, "is more what *isn't* there than what *is*."

"You mean the fact that he has no convictions?"

"Exactly." She smiled at him. They were on the same wave length.

Herrera came back looking somewhat flushed. He was studying the contents of a manila file folder with a dark frown. "Shit," he said and looked over at them.

"What?" demanded Carla.

"I should have wondered about this a long time ago. We all should have wondered."

"What?"

He glanced at Lowell and showed Carla the file. "It's from five years ago. I kept it only because I was working on the Community Section back then. Obituaries, weddings, graduations, that sort of thing."

"It's where we start them out," Carla explained.

Lowell knew only too well. He'd had almost the same job himself once, at Palm Coast Harbor.

"Man, I blew it," muttered Herrera, shaking his head. He sat down and looked at Lowell. "It didn't look back then like it looks now. I think we just assumed she'd run out on him. I think that's what he told the judge. Said the marriage was never consummated."

Lowell felt something heavy flip over in his stomach. "What are you getting at?" he asked.

"He got a divorce," explained Herrera. "On grounds of desertion. Nobody'd seen her in a long time, and nobody questioned it. Her parents had moved away by then. And Lopez still had this reputation as a good guy."

"A regular hombre," muttered Carla, which made Lowell wonder if she'd met the man.

"So nobody challenged it, and in cases of desertion, why would they? So . . ." He shrugged.

"And no one ever saw her again?"

"People come and go all the time in Santa Fe," Carla pointed out.

"Even locals—from the community?" asked Lowell.

Herrera shook his head. "Technically, she was from Española. But even so, you're right. I should have wondered." He dug into the folder once more. "I did a story on her—it was one of my first pieces after graduation, when I came to work here." He pulled out an old yellowed article and gingerly handed it to Carla.

She glanced at it, frowned and shook her head. "Oh, Lord," she said and passed it over to Lowell.

He read it quickly. It was from about ten years before, an announcement of that year's National Merit Scholarships. The one and only local winner was a promising young honors student named Amanda Cortez, from Española. There was a nice photograph, showing a young and pretty Hispanic girl.

"It's a damn shame, really, what happened," said Herrera sadly. "Some people around here just can't let go of the old ways."

"How so?" asked Lowell.

Herrera sighed. "Amanda had created quite a stir in the community with all those scholarships she won," he said. "It wasn't . . . common. Especially back then. I think it's changed some, but not too much. The kicker was when she accepted a scholarship to some hotshot Ivy League school. Maybe even Harvard. The pity of it was, everyone was so proud when she got the scholarship. That was one thing. Real good for local pride, that kind of thing. But the minute she actually accepted it, the shit hit the fan."

Carla leaned forward, her lips pursed tightly. Lowell sensed she knew what was coming.

"It was as if she was a traitor to her culture," Herrera said with a sigh. "Girls weren't supposed to go to college, unless maybe locally for a teacher's certificate or something. But to go away, especially back east, it just wasn't done." Instead, he explained, she'd been chastised into submission, then forced into a marriage with sports star Danny Lopez, whom the locals considered quite a catch due to his fire-captain father, athletic prowess, and good looks.

"Let me get this straight," said Lowell. "Amanda Cortez, the pride of Santa Fe High, is forced to turn down a top college scholarship and marry a local jock, presumably so as to get her barefoot and pregnant and tie her down to where her folks or whoever could keep an eye on her. Then, shortly thereafter, she vanishes, and is never reported missing."

Herrera and Martin exchanged uncomfortable glances. "Something like that," said Herrera softly. He shook his head. "Even today, parents are afraid to let their daughters leave home, for fear of losing them to—God knows what—cultural contamination, I suppose."

"Sex, drugs, and rock and roll," suggested Lowell.

Herrera looked embarrassed. "Maybe. In any case, traditionally the girls stay at home until they are married. And even then, the groom moves in with the in-laws, rather than the girl moving out." He didn't look very happy about it, which made Lowell like him and wonder if he had in-laws, too.

"And so after a year or two—I can't believe this—nobody misses this woman?"

"I wouldn't say that," said Herrera defensively. "I think it's more like she fell through the cracks. From what I gather, she didn't get out much, didn't have many friends here in town—remember, she was from up north of here—so I don't think too many people were aware of her."

"So you're saying Lopez kept her at home, possibly against her will?"

Herrera looked pained. "It isn't that simple. Nothing is that simple. You're talking about a particular culture, the oldest culture in the Americas of European origin, which has a very strong moral code and its own ways of doing things, Mr. Lowell. I myself would like nothing better than to change some of them. I get in trouble quite often with my own people, even with my own family, when I report the way things are. Or suggest, in my own way, that maybe some things should be different than they are."

Lowell could relate to that. "I was a newspaperman myself once," he said.

"Staff photographer, *New York Times*, Washington Bureau," cut in Carla Martin. "I made a call to an old editor friend of mine I went to school with at U.C.L.A. You quit right after Watergate." She turned to Herrera. "He took some very famous photographs in his time, and I'm not talking paparazzi celebrity chases, either. Although he did take a pretty

102

good picture of Lennon and Yoko mugging at the Dakota, and some people questioned the one of Senator Muskie when he—"

"Please," said Lowell. "That's ancient history now."

"In any case," said Carla, "you understand the ambivalence we feel and the fine lines we have to tread in regard to some issues here. Particularly issues pertaining to cultural values and differences."

"And as I said," said Herrera, still defensive, "sometimes people fall through the cracks." There was silence for a moment. Herrera looked at Carla. "With your permission," he said, "I'd like to reopen that file. I know someone down at Missing Persons who might know something, or at least might still be wondering about her. There has to be some information on her whereabouts. She had to have had a Social Security number, tax returns, a driver's license . . ." He trailed off, lost in thought.

"You do that," said Carla. Herrera got up as though to leave.

"One more thing," said Lowell. "Amanda was Lopez's first wife. I'm concerned about what's happened to the second one."

Herrera stopped in his tracks. "Second one?"

"That's right. Her name is Alicia Sandoval."

Herrera sat down again. "Oh, God," he said.

Carla got that tight-lipped look again. "Peter, I want you to provide Mr. Lowell with whatever assistance you can in the location of these two women. And that includes assisting in the reopening of a police investigation. Maybe one that should have been conducted a long time ago."

"Maybe it's nothing," said Lowell. "But thanks."

Herrera looked at Lowell thoughtfully. "This is gonna take me a while. Is there a number where I can reach you?"

Lowell gave him the hotel number and left, feeling a little better about the good people of Santa Fe. And a lot worse about the health, welfare, and personal prospects of one Alicia Sandoval.

He stepped out into the low, slanting light sloping in from the west. Zipping his borrowed parka against the rising cold wind, he climbed into the Buick and went back to his hotel in search of a warm fire and a cold drink.

As he crossed through the lobby, the concierge hailed him from the desk: "Mr. Lowell? I have a phone message for you. She said it was urgent."

Lowell detoured over to the desk and picked up the slip of paper. He recognized the number at once: Ariel's. Hurrying to his room, he dialed out.

"Dad?" She sounded breathless. "I've heard from Alicia! She's alive!"

Inexplicably, he felt his heart pounding. "Where is she?"

"I don't know!" she exclaimed, sounding slightly mystified.

"You don't know?"

"That's just it. She sent me an e-mail!"

Lowell tempered his enthusiasm. He was not much closer to his quarry than before. On the other hand, it was a good indicator that at least she was alive. "So," he said. "What did she say?"

Ariel's tone of mystification increased. "She wanted to know about you, and why you tried to contact her. Dad, what do I do?"

Lowell remembered that Ariel was not up to speed on computers—something he would have to see about correcting as soon as possible. "All right, honey, what server are you on?"

She hesitated, scrutinized the on-screen logo and told him. It was one of the big three.

"Fine. You see a little box on your screen that says 'Reply'?"

There was a moment of muttered consternation. "Yeah, found it."

"All right. Just move the arrow there and click on it twice with your left mouse button."

He heard some fumbling noises, and a clicking sound. "Okay," she said. "There's like a big blank form letter."

"Good. Her return address is already in the top address box. Copy it down for safe keeping. Then put something in the 'Subject' box, like 'Hi' or whatever. Then move your pointer down to the main letter box, click on the upper left-hand corner and type in whatever greeting you want to. Just explain who I am and so forth, that I'm here in Santa Fe, don't alarm her, just have her call me here at the hotel. Got that?"

She sounded uncertain. " 'Kay, I think so." He heard some typing sounds. "It's hard, with you on long-distance like that. Why don't I do it and call you back?"

"Fine," he said, privately relieved. Hotel long-distance charges were murder. "Just click on 'Send' if you're already on-line, or 'Send Later' if not. If you're off-line, pull down the mail menu to 'Activate Flash Session' and do what it says. Got that?"

He heard her scribbling breathlessly. "I think so. I'll call you back if I mess up."

"You won't mess up, honey. But let me know it went through. I'll be right here."

"Okay. 'Bye, Dad. Love you!"

She hung up. He lay down on the bed, his stomach churning, contemplating calling room service for dinner—another outrageous expense. He decided he'd wait it out. He switched on the television and watched the news, not absorbing anything.

The phone rang. He snatched it up. "Yes?"

"It's me," said Ariel. "It went through. This means I can communicate with her! This is so cool!"

"If she's all right, it's cool," he said. "I still want to talk to her."

"Sure, Dad, I told her in my e-mail. Let me know if she calls," she said, and hung up.

Lowell had trouble getting to sleep, but finally he managed to drift off as the wind established a rhythm against the shutters on his window and fatigue overtook him at last.

8

SANTA FE
NOVEMBER 19, 7:15 A.M.

Lowell was awakened by the telephone. He opened his eyes
slowly, at first unable to remember where he was. He blinked
at the unfamiliar surroundings, shook his head at the irritating, intrusive, high-pitched noise piercing his skull, and finally recognized the source. He reached over and seized the
receiver from the nightstand, as much to silence it as to answer it.

"Yeahwhut?"

"Lowell? This is Peter Herrera from the *New Mexican*.
Sorry to bother you so early, but I just found something I think
you should know about."

"What time is it?"

"Seven-fifteen. Can you meet me here at the office in
twenty minutes? It's important."

"I'll be right there."

He hung up mystified. Dragging himself out of bed, he went into the bathroom, carefully avoided looking in the mirror and splashed cold water on his face. That woke him up enough to contemplate himself. Displeased with what he saw, he took time to shave, threw on some clean beige cords and his one and only sweater, and raced over to the newspaper office.

Herrera met him in the lobby and took him to a small conference room down the narrow hallway.

"Any chance you have some coffee around here?" Lowell asked.

Herrera winced. "Of course, but you're not going to like it. It isn't exactly what they serve at the plaza."

"I'll take my chances, as long as it's roughly the color of molasses, reasonably hot, isn't chicory, and has caffeine in it."

"That it does. How do you like it?"

"Two-percent milk and some honey. If you don't have that, I'll take it black."

"Don't blame you. I can't stand those fake substitutes either. Be right back."

Herrera went out. Lowell glanced at the coffee table, where Herrera had left a manila folder along with a copy of the morning paper. He was tempted by the folder but decided on good manners, figuring he'd learn its contents soon enough, and opted for the newspaper. The headline story was about a tourist who'd been assaulted at an ATM one block from the plaza. Someone had walked up behind him and shot him. He was in fair condition in the local hospital, and the Chamber of Commerce was "concerned." The mayor and police chief had expressed outrage. An investigation was underway, and according to a police spokesman, several local

108

gangs were under suspicion including, he noted, the "DeVargas Compadres." The gangs had been getting increasingly bold in their activities lately, according to the spokesman, but the Santa Fe Police Department would not stand for crimes of this kind against visitors to the city, and arrests were expected at any time. Lowell wondered whether the police regarded Peso Sandoval's little group as a "gang." Something about the incident, though, just didn't sit right.

Herrera came back in, carrying two steaming mugs. "Don't say I didn't warn you," he said with a grin, handing Lowell his coffee. "Starbucks it isn't."

Lowell took a grateful gulp anyway and let those miraculous toxic chemicals do their work. He tapped the headline. "What can you tell me about this DeVargas group?"

Herrera frowned and looked at him. "I talked to some people this morning. I don't know if there's any connection, but I hear that your friend Danny Lopez was involved with this crowd for a while. From what I gather, he wanted to turn them into one of those Aryan Nations-type groups, except pro-Hispanic and anti-Anglo. Word is they didn't like that idea too much, to their credit. The cops are just blaming the group because they're too incompetent or lazy to get the real perps, who are probably one of the teen gangs. The DeVargas thing is something else. They have a political agenda, which doesn't go over too well at City Hall."

"I bet," said Lowell. "I met some of them."

Herrera looked at him in surprise. "No kidding? Where?"

"At a bar called the Green Pepper."

"You went *there*? You gotta be either pretty brave or pretty loco, hombre."

"Just too ignorant to know better. Anyway, their leader

just so happens to be the brother of the woman I'm looking for. Alicia Sandoval. Which also makes him ex-brother-in-law of Danny Lopez."

"Peso is one of *those* Sandovals? No shit!" Herrera seemed embarrassed at having such knowledge revealed to him by an outsider.

Lowell smiled and shrugged. "I found out purely by accident. A local storekeeper from over in the barrio sent me down there."

"Probably so you could get your head caved in, Anglo."

"I don't think so. It didn't happen, in any case."

"So you met Peso Sandoval." Herrera whistled. "What's he like?"

Lowell raised his hands. "Slow down. Is that what you called me up about? To pump me for all my inside knowledge of the ways of Santa Fe?"

Herrera laughed. Then scowled. "Okay, Okay. As a matter of fact, I called you because I found something else in the archives that's bothering the hell out of me."

He picked up the manila folder from the table, opened it and took out a clipping. He slid it across the table to Lowell. "This was from three years ago. I did some checking this morning, and there was never any follow-up at all, which I think is pretty bad."

Lowell read the article. It was about the skeletal remains of a woman's body that had been discovered in one of the many caves in the Sangre de Cristos, above Chimayo. Two local boys had found it, and according to a relative, they had also found some jewelry, which the boys later denied and were not further questioned about.

"She was never identified?"

110

Herrera shook his head. "That's just it. That's the sheriff's domain, and I'm afraid he dropped the ball on that one. Nobody was reported missing, and no one came forward." He showed Lowell a subsequent article from a few weeks later, which recapped the grim discovery and went on to say that the unclaimed remains had been buried in an unmarked grave in the church cemetery in Chimayo.

"Did anyone ever contact the Cortez family about this?"

Herrera pursed his lips. "That's what I'm saying. They moved away after the wedding, I think to Albuquerque. I've heard rumors that they'd received threats of some kind. Between you and me, I think the threats had something to do with the dowry."

"Dowry?"

"An old tradition with lots of cultures, including ours. Hadn't you heard?"

Lowell shook his head. "Only in books. Never had one myself."

"The Cortez family were, basically, obligated to give the groom a dowry for marrying their daughter. In the case of Amanda Lopez, I think she also had some jewelry. She may have suspected something and held back on some of it."

"Do you know how much, or what any of it was worth?"

Herrera shook his head emphatically. "Are you kidding? This is very private, personal business between the bride's family and the groom. It's something you just don't ask. Especially not in this community."

"Maybe it's time somebody did." Lowell was thinking about the Sandovals and wondered what kind of dowry Danny Lopez had demanded from them. He looked at Herrera. "I appreciate your telling me this," he said.

"I hope I don't regret it. So, have you made any progress in finding his second wife, Alicia? The one you say is Peso's sister?"

Lowell wondered whether to mention the call from Ariel and decided there was no harm in it. "Yes, as a matter of fact. She contacted my daughter by e-mail, and I'm expecting to hear from her directly."

"Well, that's good news, I suppose."

"Sure," said Lowell. "It means she's still alive. Presumably. Anyhow, thanks for the information."

"That's okay. I hope it helps." Herrera hesitated. "*Now* will you tell me what you know about Los Compadres?"

Lowell grinned. "They remind me of the young people who used to populate the cafes in Gainesville back in the Sixties. Talking about the war, maybe smoking a little dope, listening to revolutionary rock songs, shouting rhetoric, that sort of thing. Using the name of some obscure historical person for its ring of authenticity. I didn't sense they wanted to blow anybody up. So I agree with you, I don't think they are dangerous per se."

They shook hands and Herrera got up to return to the newsroom. "Oh, Peter," Lowell called after him. "You know where I could find this Cortez family?"

Herrera stopped and looked thoughtful. "All I know is I heard they moved to Albuquerque, like I said. Cortez is a pretty common name, but I have some cousins who were neighbors of theirs in Española. I'll give them a call and see what I can find out."

"Thanks," said Lowell. Herrera turned again to leave. "One more thing," called Lowell. Herrera waited expectantly. "Can you tell me how to get to Chimayo?"

Lowell decided to call Lena Bedrosian again, back home in Manatee City. She hadn't helped much before, other than to confirm that neither the Santa Fe Police Department nor the Santa Fe County Sheriff were likely to be very useful about Alicia. But she still owed him. Plus, an unclaimed body and some missing jewelry were a lot more tangible than an allegedly missing person.

He checked the time—it was just before noon in Florida—and placed the call. Luckily, she was in. Unluckily, she was in a meeting. After some huffing and haranguing between himself and the desk sergeant, he got through to her.

"Hello, Lieutenant."

"Who . . . Lowell? What is it *now*? I'm in the middle of a—"

"This is important, Lena. I'm still waiting for reimbursement for the Pappas reports, not to mention the—"

"Is that what you're calling about? I thought you were in Mexico or somewhere."

"*New* Mexico. Santa Fe, to be exact, and I need some help with a little problem out here."

"You better not be in jail again," she cut in, "because if you are, you need a bail bondsman, not a—"

"I'm not in jail," he said quickly. Not yet anyway, he thought to himself. "I need a favor."

"What a surprise. Such as?"

He told her what he wanted. Predictably, she blew a cloud of steam probably visible in Taos. He calmed her down, reminded her once again about friends in need and so forth, and finally got her attention when he explained to her that he

113

was trying to prevent a possible domestic homicide. Lena Bedrosian, being a mother, had a certain soft spot for the victims—almost always women—of domestic violence. Lowell had once overheard her tell a female patrol officer that if her husband ever, ever, laid a hand on her, she'd bust him so hard he'd need a doctor, not a lawyer.

"You realize you're asking me to compromise my position as an officer of the law," she snapped.

"Not at all," he protested. "I'm just asking you to assist in preventing a possible crime, in addition to help in solving one that might otherwise go unsolved."

Grudgingly, she relented. "All right," she said. "I'll see what I can do. But you're going to owe me for this, Lowell."

"Sure," he said. Anything to appease her. "Remember, the name is Ramirez. Hector Ramirez. He's a sergeant. You outrank the man."

"Yeah, right. I'll get back to you. Just stay out of trouble in the meantime."

"I'll do my best," he said and hung up.

Two hours later, Lowell was armed with a search warrant, thanks to Croft's friend, Sergeant Hector Ramirez. Bedrosian had won the sergeant over by telling him the one thing Lowell himself would never mention to anyone: that he was the son of a police chief. Ramirez had then requested his presence at the police station and demanded to know his business. Lowell had again mentioned Croft's name, gotten the expected displeased reaction, then stepped gingerly around the issue of Alicia Sandoval's whereabouts. He'd mentioned Amanda Cortez instead, and asked if he could see the investigation files on her disappearance.

"Why?" Ramirez wanted to know.

"Because when an attractive, intelligent, gifted young woman seems to disappear from the face of the earth, I think someone should care. At least enough to ask what happened to her. Is that 'why' enough for you?"

Ramirez glowered and made a quick call. A young, over-weight female clerk brought in a file after a while, gave Lowell a quizzical glance and left. Ramirez looked through the file, his scowl increasing by the page. Finally, he tossed it on the table, in Lowell's general direction.

"There's nothing," he announced in disgust. "Her husband reported her as missing. She didn't turn up. Case closed."

"How convenient. So that gave Lopez clear sailing to get a divorce and marry the next victim. That sound about right?"

"That," Ramirez practically snarled, "sounds pretty damn presumptuous."

"Sorry," said Lowell. "Presumptuous is my middle name. But it would be nice if at least one of these wives of your Danny Lopez could be found, if only to reconfirm what all of you around here seem to think, namely, what a great guy he is."

Now Ramirez looked like he wanted to shoot him. "I shoulda known," he muttered, shaking his head. "You and Croft. Two of a kind. Christ!"

But he agreed to ask the sheriff's department to send a deputy up to the ancient village to meet Lowell and show him where the remains had been found. "They don't know anything about any jewelry," Ramirez warned him.

Lowell went to pack his gear, including his Nikon. There was a message for him at the hotel from Christina Taylor, Resident Queen of the New Age. "I hear you are looking for Amanda Cortez," she told him when he called her back. "I have someone who can help you."

"Whoa," he said. "You knew Amanda Cortez?"

"Knew *of* her."

"How did you know I was looking for her?"

"I picked up on your energy," she told him. "And checked with my channeler."

"I should have known," he said.

She laughed her bawdy Texas laugh. "Apparently she still has a strong Spirit Force around here. There is much about her that is unresolved. I think she senses you might help resolve her."

"Resolve her?" He thought about that and felt a chill that wasn't leaking in through any cracks in the window frame.

"You know," she said, "it kind of bothered me, what you said the other night about being involved."

"Sorry about that."

"Don't be. The upshot of it is, I think you were right. A lot of us have gotten very self-absorbed with our various quests for personal fulfillment. But we do live in this world."

"So who is it you've found to help me? Your channeler?" He regretted the sarcasm at once—her contrition seemed genuine—but she took it in stride.

"No. For this, you need a psychic."

"Oh," he said, then laughed. "I knew that."

"Of course you did!" she teased. "You obviously have some latent abilities of your own."

"Sure," said Lowell. "I predicted that the end of the Sixties would be followed by the beginning of the Seventies."

She chuckled. "There, you see? Her name is Emily. Emily Tartikoff. You met her at my party, actually. The little blond gal with the pigtails. She's very good. She's helped the police more than once with something like this."

Lowell thought about refusing, but decided what the hell. He'd already offended enough people in Santa Fe just by showing up here. No point in offending those who actually wanted to help.

"You'll have to pick her up," Christina told him. "She doesn't have a car."

Now that's eccentric, thought Lowell, and took down the address. It was on Galisteo, near San Mateo, a nice neighborhood of mostly large, ranch-style homes just south of the historic government district. He found it on the map and was there in fifteen minutes.

He recognized Emily Tartikoff right off. She was the one who'd kept talking about chakras and past lives. A petite, skittish, potentially attractive thirty-something woman with dirty-blond hair plaited into two long braids like Pippy Longstocking, and nervous green eyes that flashed right and left, ever alert. She was wearing another long dress, and over it she had a bulky cloth coat. She also wore hiking boots, suggesting a practical side.

"Hello again," she said, extending her gloved hand, with which she gripped his hand quickly and firmly. She frowned, glancing around the car and looking him up and down. "You don't have any animal hair on you, I hope."

Lowell glanced down at himself doubtfully. "I sleep with animals only when I'm back home in my barn," he said. "Why do you ask?"

"Allergies. Why else?"

He opened the rental-car door. She sniffed the air and balked immediately. "Deodorizers," she announced in disgust.

"What?"

"You didn't get a chemical-free car," she accused him.

"Now why didn't I think of that? A chemical-free car. Gee, I would have if I were psychic like you and knew you were coming," he said. "Even better, I would have reserved a biodegradable, nontoxic, solar-powered self-levitator. Made of wood."

"No need to be sarcastic. All I meant was that you should get one without those damned cardboard pine trees that smell like toilet cleaner." She pointed at the offending object he hadn't even noticed, hanging from the mirror. He quickly removed it and deposited it in a neighbor's curbside trash can.

"There," he said. "Feel better?"

She took a deep breath and let it out ever so slowly, as though to demonstrate a limitless capacity for patience. "Never mind, I'll take some B-Twelve later," she said and got in the car. "Christina told you about my fee?"

Now it was Lowell's turn to balk. "Whoa. No, she didn't. What is it, a finder's fee?"

She wasn't amused. "I happen to be sensitive to cosmic tremors and spiritual anomalies," she informed him with a pert sniff. "I get fifty an hour."

"Oh, is that all? Do you guarantee your work?"

She looked at him as if he was the world's rudest person. Or biggest fool. Or both. "Never mind, let's just go," she snapped. "I'll take it up with Christina later. I owe her a couple of favors, anyway."

"Consider it a public service," suggested Lowell. "The woman we're looking for is, or was, a local resident. And I'm sure she'll be grateful for you helping her get *resolved*."

The road to Chimayo wound its way high into the mountains above the exclusive Indian pueblo-turned-trendy en-

118

clave of Tusuque, toward the bald dome of Tusuque Peak, now blanketed with early snow. As Lowell drove north out of the city and onto the old Tusuque Road, he told her what he knew and didn't know about Amanda Cortez. Her eyes opened wide at the mention of Danny Lopez.

"I've heard about him," she said. He thought he saw her shudder slightly. "He's the one who raped that girl with a tire iron."

Lowell hadn't known about that. There was a lot he still didn't know about, didn't want to know about, but needed to know. His fear for Alicia intensified. "If I'm right about this, he may have killed Amanda Cortez up here where we're going. What I'm afraid of is that he is going to kill his second wife, Alicia Sandoval, if I can't get to her in time."

"Yes," she said, frowning darkly. "I know." She surprised him by informing him she'd known about the discovery of the body three years ago. So he told her about the confession of the two boys and the identifying ring and pendant. "They denied there was any other jewelry," he said.

"That's interesting," commented Amanda. "She owned a fair amount of jewelry, according to my Spirit Guides."

"What do you, or your Spirit Guides, claim to know about Amanda's jewelry?"

Emily closed her eyes as the Buick labored up the steep mountain road below Tusuque. "Sapphire," she said finally. "Pendant, I think. And a set of diamonds . . . wait . . . a ring, and . . . earrings. Not too big, maybe a carat at most. Some gold heirlooms, I can't quite make them out. Pearls . . . a pearl necklace. Some of them are still out there, I can feel the beacon."

"Beacon?"

"They put out an energy field, almost like a lighthouse signal."

"Does it mean keep away?" he asked. "Or come hither?"

Emily visibly shuddered and didn't reply. They passed a sign shaped like an arrow, inscribed, simply, "Chimayo." "Why are you going up here?" she asked. "Do you hope to find confirmation that she's dead?"

"Something like that."

"Well, you needn't bother," she said, staring out the window. "She's dead, all right. Her Spirit Force is all around here."

"Like swamp gas?" His efforts to be glib were falling flat.

"It's diffused, like ions. If she were alive, it would be concentrated in a single place."

He didn't argue. If there were spirits about, he'd just as soon they do their talking to Emily rather than to him. He wasn't all that enthusiastic about spirits. But if there were any, this small, remote, ancient adobe village he was approaching was a good place for them. He could feel the weight of centuries of superstition on the very markers and monuments, walls and edifices, even on the rock walls above. Many ancient and not so ancient cultures had clashed and converged here, and a lot of what had resulted had been bloody and desperate. If there were spirits out there, there must be a lot of them. He had a bad feeling that things had turned out very poorly for Amanda Cortez not far from here—the sudden awareness of which startled him. If her spirit still lingered, along with others far more ancient, was she any better off in their nether world than the real one she'd presumably, and violently, left?

Lowell found the turnoff to Chimayo and began to climb,

high above the Rio Grande Valley. Changing the subject, Emily told him about the Hispanic faithful who had followed this trail for centuries to commemorate the ordeal of Jesus, carrying the cross. They still did so every Easter. But this was autumn and there weren't any pilgrims.

At one of the wide turns, Emily pointed out the huge towers and wisps of smoke high on a plateau far across the river valley on the rim of the Jemez Mountains. She told him it was Los Alamos, where the Nuclear Age had been spawned. He wondered what horrors might still lurk over there in some forgotten laboratory . . . what else might have been forgotten here in this godforsaken place, which some thought to be paradise itself?

They were high in the mountains now, the Rio Grande Valley spread out below, tinted with the same brown haze spread across all landscapes these days. He turned onto a small lane leading toward the church tower, visible through the piñons and chaparral.

"I really don't know what we're looking for," he explained. "I'd just like to see where they found her. I don't think there was much of an investigation. No forensics were done. They just kind of spirited her off to the graveyard. No pun intended."

"I want to visit the grave," she said.

He looked at her. "Do you know where it is?"

"No, but I can find it." He was starting to believe her.

They reached the old church at last, and the graveyard filled with elaborate white crosses and stones, all heavily embellished with floral displays. The sheriff's patrol car was parked near the gate. A tall, dark-skinned deputy stood by the front of the car, smoking a cigarette. He stubbed it out when he saw Lowell's rental Buick approaching. Lowell pulled up behind the deputy and got out of the car, camera bag over his shoulder.

"Hello," he said, approaching. The deputy was Native American and wore a ponytail not unlike his own, except for being coal-black. "I'm Lowell. Thanks for coming."

The deputy gave Emily a speculative look and shrugged. "It's my job," he said. Belatedly, Lowell introduced Emily.

Lowell wished his friend Perry were here. Perry knew about Indians. And mystics. Although Perry would probably point out that he himself was part Creek, whereas this person was totally Pueblo and therefore no more closely related to him than a Serbian was to a Scotsman, Lowell nevertheless believed there was a brotherhood between all Native Americans.

Two young Hispanic boys appeared, seemingly out of nowhere. They'd been playing in the graveyard, and watched with veiled eyes from behind the wall. The deputy spotted them at once. "Yo," he called over at them. "Come here. *Venga.*"

The boys obeyed, as much out of curiosity as fealty to the law. Emily regarded them expectantly. They seemed wary of her, almost afraid. Lowell could relate.

"Sí, Señor," said the taller one. "We live over there, in the pueblo." He pointed vaguely toward a small cluster of adobe houses on the hillside.

"You kids ever go exploring around here?" asked the deputy.

Both boys nodded hesitantly. "Si, Señor."

"They're the ones who found her," said Emily matter-of-factly. The tall one, Florio, stared at her as though he'd seen a ghost. Lowell looked at her, then at the boys. He hated to admit it, but knew she was right.

The boys seemed mesmerized by the sight of Emily. She took full advantage. "What did you do with the wedding ring?" she demanded bluntly.

They looked terrified. No one had ever bothered them about the ring for the simple reason they'd never mentioned it. They'd been congratulated for their dutiful reporting of their grisly discovery to the padres, who'd lovingly patted their behinds and sent them home. The padres had called the sheriff in good time and the holy fathers had the body interred with a minimum of fuss. Now, ignoring Emily's question, and against Florio's wishes, Ernesto told them about the amulet with the photograph, how the padres had insisted it should be buried with the body, as being sacred to the memory of the unknown woman.

"What amulet?" Lowell demanded to know.

"A little gold one, Señor, the kind with *una fotita*."

"It opens and shuts," explained Emily.

The sheriff's department had not been informed of the pendant, which might have confirmed the identity of the woman. And no one in the village had said a word of it. There had been no mention of jewelry outside of the village. Whoever she was, she'd been returned to the saints and that was good enough for the deeply superstitious villagers. Until now.

Florio and Ernesto exchanged terrified glances as Emily bore down on them like an avenging angel, which they may well have thought her to be.

"You also found her wedding ring," she declared. "You will show it to me at once." Lowell stared at her in astonishment.

"Wait a minute lady. What's this about a ring?" the deputy wanted to know. He could see for himself the fear in the eyes of the boys. Ernesto was trembling. Florio gave him a warning look, but it was too late. Ernesto cracked.

"*¡Fue en la tierra!*" he burbled, bursting into tears. He pointed an accusing finger at Florio. "*El dice que sera nuestros. ¡El dice que nadie puede saber como aquello!*"

"You stole a ring from a dead body?" The detective was appalled. He placed his hands on his hips sternly. "You kids know what kind of crime that is?"

Now Florio cracked too, as though the magnitude of their little secret had suddenly dawned on him. Maybe it had. If anything, his tears exceeded those of Ernesto.

"Show us the cave first," requested Lowell.

The boys led Lowell, Emily, and the Indian deputy to the cave. It was empty now, once more abandoned. It had a dirt floor that had been dug up, musty rock walls stained with ancient smoke. Ernesto showed them where he'd found the body. "The ring was just laying there on the ground!" he sobbed.

Lowell snapped in his 50mm lens and took a few pictures to establish the site location. The boys then led them to a small thatched hut behind one of the oldest houses in the village. It looked abandoned. They'd kept the ring, along with some Indian pottery shards—also illegal to pick up, the deputy told them—in a painted mason jar that reminded Lowell of Dennis the Menace's cookie jar.

The deputy picked up the ring and studied it, then held it while Lowell changed to his macro lens and took some close-ups. Emily concentrated on the shards, spreading her hands over them, much to the annoyance of the deputy, who had been elbowed aside by the woman. The boys stood sniffling by the doorway, awaiting further punishment. It was not forthcoming.

"Is this it?" demanded the deputy.

Lowell looked at Emily expectantly. "You said she had a lot of jewelry."

She looked at the boys, then held the jar in her hands and closed her eyes. "She did. Some of it was taken from her before she died." She set the jar down, put her hands to her head for a moment, and then cried out as though in pain. "He was looking for the blue stone," she said. "He never found it." She picked up the ring. "Omigod!" she screamed suddenly.

Everyone froze. Especially the boys.

"What?" Lowell demanded.

"He's strangling her!" cried Emily. "For the blue stone! He knows she has it somewhere. He wants it and she won't give it up!"

"Shit," said the deputy, squinting at her. "You some kind of shaman?"

Emily let out a long sigh and opened her eyes. The boys edged toward the door fearfully.

"He already had most of it, most of the rest," she told them, her voice suddenly flat. "The ring. She hid it in her—" She stopped, embarrassed.

"Who got the rest?" asked Lowell after a moment. "Was it Danny?"

She looked at him blankly. "I think it was him, I could only see him vaguely. There's something frightening about him. Something almost . . . prehistoric, predatory." She looked at the boys again. They quailed before her. The deputy appeared pretty nervous himself.

Lowell took the ring from Emily and examined it closely.

"It has an inscription on it," he announced, focusing his camera for an extreme close-up. The inscription read: "DL loves AC." Along with something else, he couldn't quite make out. "Cute," he muttered, mostly to himself. "A regular lover boy."

That was when Ernesto volunteered to show them the grave site. "Maybe you can dig up that other thing, the one with the picture in it," he boldly proposed. "It's buried in there with her."

Emily looked at him sharply. "Where?" she demanded.

It wasn't far. The body had been interred in a simple grave at the far edge of the graveyard. The burial stone was unmarked, but the boys knew which one it was.

The deputy got on his police-band radiophone and called the dispatcher. "This is Corona. I'm up at Chimayo. Better get me the sheriff, and call Judge Gonsalves. I think we're gonna need to exhume a body up here."

"It really isn't necessary," Emily tried to tell him. "Other than to recover her property. I know who she is."

Lowell and the deputy glared at her. She met their gazes calmly. "Her name was Amanda Cortez. She was murdered." She pointed toward the mountain towering above them. "Up there."

"And how do you know all this?" the deputy demanded before Lowell could say "Don't ask."

"Because," Emily calmly replied, "she told me so." The boys turned and fled, taking their chances with the demons and padres.

The deputy looked at Lowell. *Now* Lowell said: "Don't ask."

9

Lowell pulled up in front of Emily's house, fully intent on dropping her off as though she had the plague.

"We'll be in touch," she promised him, but her blue eyes were livid pools of an almost biological loathing.

Lowell responded in kind. "I don't doubt you mean it, but it doesn't make me feel warm and fuzzy," he said. She gave him a quick look of cool appraisal, and turned away.

She didn't bother to say good-bye. Turning left at the corner, he headed back downtown to drop the Chimayo film off at a custom black-and-white photo lab he'd seen in the phone book, not far from the plaza, leaving instructions to print high-contrast five-by-sevens of all exposed frames.

"How soon can I get them back?" he asked.

"Maybe in an hour," the young woman at the counter told

him. "You're in luck, it's a slow day." He thanked her, got back in the car and returned to the hotel. There were no messages. But before he even had a chance to kick off his boots and relax for a minute, the phone rang.

"Mr. Lowell? It's Peter Herrera again." He sounded anxious. "I located Amanda Cortez's mother down in Albuquerque. The father passed away a couple of years back, and I don't think she'll talk to you, but maybe you could—"

"What's her address?"

Herrera hesitated, then gave it to him, along with the directions. "Two-seven-seven-five Calle del Rio. It's on the east side, not far from the river. You should be able to make it in less than two hours, but I wouldn't go until—"

"Thanks, I'm on my way," said Lowell, hanging up.

Herrera called back immediately.

"I was trying to warn you about rush hour, but I guess you're going against it anyway. It shouldn't be too bad. But listen," he added quickly, "what did you find out up in Chimayo?"

Word sure gets around, thought Lowell wryly. He considered putting Herrera off, then relented and told the reporter about the hidden ring, the possible identification—without saying how—and that the sheriff's office was going to reopen the Amanda Cortez case.

"That's excellent news!" exclaimed Herrera. "Can you give me the name of the deputy?" Lowell told him it was Corona something and hung up.

His mind cluttered with confused and contradictory images of three women—one dead, another in jeopardy, and the third somewhere in mental Machu Picchu—Lowell took a quick shower and was out the door in twenty minutes. He stopped by the plaza for the film, glanced through the shots quickly, tucked them in his pocket, grabbed a Whopper from the Burger King on St. Michael's and headed for Albuquerque, some ninety minutes in the opposite direction from Chimayo.

The afternoon sun was low as he sped south through the barren desert on Interstate 25, following the descending tiers of mesas past Pueblo Indian reservation after reservation: Cochiti and Santo Domingo, San Felipe and Santa Ana, through Bernadillo, following the Rio Grande Valley and watching as towering Sandia Peak loomed closer and closer in the southeast. Lowell tried and failed to fathom how and why a family would raise a young woman to be an honor student, full of promise, gifted with talent and beauty, then turn her over to someone like Danny Lopez and walk away. There was something missing here. Something he was trying desperately to understand.

The sun set as he wove his way through the sometimes quaint, sometimes ordinary, middle-class suburban neighborhoods to the north and east of Albuquerque. It was clear that the Cortez's didn't live in a barrio. Not that it was Beverly Hills. The gray-stucco ranch house at 2775 Calle del Rio was drearily ordinary, distinguishable from its neighbors only by its elaborate array of unlit Christmas decorations on the otherwise drab, flat roof. It was still early for Christmas, and something about the ornaments, perhaps an evident shabbiness, made him wonder if they hadn't been there since the Christmas before. Or even longer. There was the prerequisite triptych of Jesus, Mary, and Joseph, along with a sun-bleached Santa Claus and his reindeer, all in a tableau of tangled wires and bulbs reminiscent of an old *Home Improvement* episode gone awry.

The house had a chain-link fence that completely enclosed the perimeter of the darkened yard. Tony Lowell hated chain-link fences. They always meant one thing, and one thing only: dogs. Invariably, big ones, with bristly coats and big teeth and red gums slavering with drool at the very sight of his apparently succulent form. There were two of them: a Rhodesian Ridgeback and a big rottweiler. His first thought was that it was a wonder they didn't kill each other. Out of sheer ill-natured boredom. After all, they could devour only so many trespassers and mailmen before they'd need spicier fare.

There was a cowbell hanging on the gate, but it was superfluous. No way could anyone inside hear it ringing, with all the racket the dogs were making in their frantic desire to terminate Tony Lowell on the spot, combined with their inordinate rage at being prevented from doing so by something so flimsy and insubstantial as a chain-link fence.

After a while, a floodlight came on and the front door opened six inches. A large woman peered out apprehensively. Lowell wondered what the hell she had to be so wary about. They were, presumably, her dogs.

Her look of apprehension changed to truculence. *"¡Callaté!"* she shouted at the dogs in a voice even louder than the rottweiler's. The dogs fell silent instantly and slunk away as though they'd been whipped.

"May I help you?" she asked, stepping out onto the front stoop and regarding him in the growing darkness with acute suspicion.

"Are you Mrs. Cortez?" he asked, one eye on the retreating dogs.

"They won't bite," she told him. "Unless I tell them to."

"Thanks, that's reassuring."

"What is it? If jou're here about the gas bill, I already told them—"

"I'm not a bill collector, Señora."

She frowned, as though bill collectors were the only species besides rottweilers and Ridgebacks with which she was familiar.

"Jour're not a bill collector? Jou a cop?"

"No, I'm not a cop," he said.

"Then what jou want?" A look of sudden recollection crossed her face, followed by renewed truculence. "Jou're the one that reporter called about."

"I want to talk to you about your daughter, Amanda. I have reason to believe—"

Her face had turned dark red by then. "I told him I never wanted to see you!" she exclaimed. "Jou tell that sonuvabitch he can go to hell. And jou can tell her, too. We give her all we got and she don't even call. She don't come home for Christmas, she don't even take calls no more, nothing. Five years we don't hear nothing. My husband nearly broke his heart, and then he say we don't even have no daughter no more."

"That's what I'm trying to tell you," said Lowell. "I'm very sorry, but I'm afraid it's very probable you don't."

She stopped, her rage vented, an expression of doubt replacing it. "What jou mean? Jou talk to her?"

"Can I come in?" he asked mildly. "I won't take much of your time. I have some information I think you should know about."

She chained the dogs in back and grudgingly admitted him to the house—a veritable museum of brightly painted icons, mostly of a suffering Jesus in many poses and forms.

She told him to sit and he asked her what she could tell him about Amanda's marriage. She just shook her head. Then he asked her about the forsaken scholarship, without saying what he thought about it.

The tears flowed at that, and the regrets. She tearfully explained to him how difficult it was for a mother to let her daughters go, how, for her people, the family was everything, how children should always live at home until married, which is why their daughter couldn't go away to college.

He felt at a loss, all the rage and righteousness gone, leaving him with a sense of futility and exhaustion. She and her husband had only done what they knew to do, what centuries of tradition older than America itself had taught them, dreading so much that they might lose their daughter that they'd driven her straight into the arms of someone who would make absolutely certain that was exactly what would happen.

Her name was Donna. She confessed to him how afraid they had been, how torn they had been, she and her husband, over the scholarship. "He was not healthy even then. Two bypasses, and the doctor said he'd have to stop working in construction, but he wouldn't listen," she sobbed. Her husband, she told him, had died two years ago. "Of a broken heart, jou ask me," she said. "His only daughter not calling, not nothing after two years, and that—" She groped for a suitable adjective for such a person as Daniel Lopez. "We didn't know what he was like," she said, her eyes pleading, "or we never would have let her marry him. But everybody said he was so wonderful, he was this big hero and everything, and my husband was impressed with him."

"And you?"

"Me?" she asked, putting her hand to her ample breast. "I just wanted her to be happy!"

"Of course," said Lowell. "Go on."

"He was all with the smiles, and the flowers, and the fancy new Chevy, and always talking sweet nothings to our daughter, until her head was turned this way and that, even though she wanted to go to school and he said no way. And everybody, all our friends—some friends!—and the grand-parents, even the padre, they all say oh yes, this is the man for my Amanda—" The tears came again, and this time it was Lowell who found his way around the kitchen and orga-nized a cup of tea.

"I'm very sorry, Mrs. Cortez," he told her at last. "A body was found north of Santa Fe." He didn't tell her it had been found three years before. Or that it had been hastily shoved into the ground in hopes of being quickly forgotten. "I'm afraid your daughter may be dead."

Her eyes widened. He told her about the two boys and their discovery. He showed her the photo close-up of the ring, and related the boys' story about how they had come across it. She listened stoically, beyond surprise or sorrow.

"It says 'DL loves AC.' I can't make out the rest of the in-scription," he said, "but it appears to be in Spanish."

She looked. It didn't take her long. *"Siempre amor,"* she barely murmured. The tears finally came, and she thrust the picture away as though it was haunted. "It's hers," she wept. "It was my mother's. He had those letters put on it." Lowell put the photo away. "So it's true. She's been dead all this time. My husband would have had a heart attack for sure, he knew about this."

He told her the sheriff's office was still investigating, but that positive I.D. of the remains was expected soon. "One other thing, Mrs. Cortez. We have witnesses who said she was wearing some kind of necklace. Does that sound familiar at all to you?"

"The *zafiro*!" she exclaimed suddenly.

"Excuse me?"

"The *zafiro*. The sapphire. A blue stone. It was my great grandmother's, come down from the time of the Conquistadors. The pendant was where my daughter hid it, because nobody would think to look under the picture inside. She bought the pendant at Woolworth's 'cause she thought it was pretty. And maybe to hide the stone, maybe she knew something."

Chalk one up for Amanda, he thought grimly. One small victory against a lot of losses, including her life. Chalk one up for Emily Tartikoff as well, he admitted to himself.

"The sheriff will probably be in touch with you," he told her. "I'd appreciate it if you'll keep our conversation private."

She nodded dumbly. But now, oddly, no more tears came. She just kept on nodding, as though to tell him she already knew, that she'd known for a long time.

He approached the next question delicately. "Señora, if you can remember, was there anything else of value that she had? Diamond earrings? A pearl necklace, anything like that?"

She looked at him wide-eyed. "*Sí, sí.* They found those things?"

"No, I'm sorry to say they did not," he told her. But she'd had them! So Emily—or her celestial informants—had been right. He wondered what else Emily might know. It was not a comforting thought.

Amanda's mother blew her nose, sipped more tea. Then

she told him about the dowry. "I have a list," she said, and shuffled into the next room. He heard her rummaging around, and she finally brought him a yellowed piece of paper. "It was for the insurance," she said. "But they wouldn't cover it no more when she left home."

Lowell looked at the list. It almost exactly matched what Emily had described. He wondered for a fleeting moment if Emily could be some kind of accomplice, a partner in some bizarre scam. He decided not.

"It was that boy," sniffled Mrs. Cortez. "That Danny Lopez, and all his friends with the *policia*, they wouldn't do nothing for her. Even after he threatened my husband and had him beat up. My daughter didn't have nobody to turn to. She told me he was selling her jewels, but what was I to do?"

More tears came. He sat down next to her and put his arm around her shoulders while she swayed back and forth. Tony Lowell had long ago forsworn violence, after the horror and mayhem of 'Nam. But the more he heard about Danny Lopez, the more he wondered if he could keep such a vow.

"One thing," she asked, after a while. "Could jou tell me where she is? I'd like to visit the grave."

"Sure," he said, and told her.

"But it's possible this is the wrong person they found, that she's still alive," he added, unconvincingly. She didn't believe it, and he didn't either. "Remember, they haven't made positive identification yet." She just shook her head.

He thanked her for the tea. "Oh, one more thing, Mrs. Cortez."

"Yes, what is it?"

"I wonder if you'd do me the favor of letting me make a copy of your list of Amanda's valuables. It could be useful."

She shrugged, then shuffled into another room and returned with a pen and pad. "About the insurance," she said while he copied down the list. "Do you think we could make a claim, if she's really dead?"

"I don't think so, unless it can be proven the jewels were stolen. But if they came with the dowry, then he may have had every right to sell them."

She shook her head, just more bad news in a long saga of bad news regarding her long-lost daughter. Lowell thanked her for her help and for talking to him, bade her good-bye and took his leave. The dogs watched him from the side yard, strangely subdued, as though they too understood the gravity of his mission.

The sky was pitch-black as Lowell headed north back to Santa Fe, preoccupied by the jewels. He wondered where Danny had sold them. He'd noticed a lot of jewelry stores around Santa Fe. There were probably a lot more in Albuquerque. But the trail was very cold, and he doubted they'd ever be found.

He wondered what sort of heirlooms, what sort of "dowry," Danny Lopez had managed to weasel out of the Sandoval family. He decided to find out.

10

Ariel Schoenkopf-Lowell sat at her mother's computer desk, boldly surfing where no Schoenkopf had surfed before—the infamous, mysterious depths of the World Wide Web. It was after sunset, the sky a deep rose and violet hue. The breeze had turned chill, and another late-autumn storm was blowing in from the Atlantic, tearing at the palm fronds in the yard, slapping the stays and rigging on the two sailboats her grandfather still kept on the pier, neither of which he'd used in years.

Someone had sent her an anonymous e-mail, inviting her to visit a Website called "Lizard King." On a whim, she'd clicked on the hypertext icon and had been instantly transported into another nightmare, featuring an animated man with reptilian scales on his body, glowing red eyes, and di-

nosaur teeth. Choking back a cry, she groped for the telephone . . .

SANTA FE, 8:50 P.M . M.S.T.

Lowell made it back to Santa Fe in seventy minutes, grabbed
a quick bite at one of the old Mexican restaurants on Cerillos,
and headed up Canyon Road. He found an illicit parking
space in the alley behind the Chinese restaurant across from
El Farol, parked the rental near a big Mercedes, and emerged
onto the sidewalk. An art opening was still going full swing at
one of the small, chic galleries he had noticed the day before.
A somewhat wine-besotted cluster of patrons hovered by the
portal, collectively deciding where to adjourn for dinner.

"Yo!" Lowell heard a voice hailing him from the midst of
the gallery group. It was the artist Thomas Royster he'd met
at El Farol's earlier. He waved back.

Royster gestured emphatically for Lowell to join him.
Lowell politely obliged and walked over to the gallery. One of
the charming aspects of the art scene—not just in Santa Fe,
but also in Florida—was the gala opening reception. It involved an elegantly mounted display of the latest works of
the Artiste-of-the-Month, lots of knowing-looking yuppie patrons also on display, usually in sartorial splendor, a few actual buyers disguised as ordinary people, plus wine and hors
d'oeuvres. The more expensive the art, the more upscale the
gallery, the better the wine and hors d'oeuvres.

Unfortunately, opening receptions being open to the public, there was always a certain number of "patrons" who were
regulars at these events. These "regulars" never bought art,

usually being devoid of funds. What they did do was to eat a lot of hors d'oeuvres and drink a lot of wine. They'd wink and nod and look knowingly at the works on display, make clever comments, hobnob with the yuppies, and stuff themselves. Some of them were artists themselves, and considered these events to be sort of an entitlement. One such was Thomas Royster, who looked like he'd stuffed himself pretty success-fully. Especially with wine.

"You're the photographer dude from back east!" He ex-claimed, wobbling slightly.

"Yes. You gave me a painting. Not bad, actually."

"Not bad?" Royster stared, his bloodshot eyes widening. "Not *bad*? Man, I got shit in the Corcoran, the Chicago Insti-tute, MOMA. I got mentioned in *Fine Arts* magazine six times. What do you *mean,* not bad? My shit is *good!*"

"Of course! *Good.* That's the word I was trying to think of," said Lowell. "What's up?"

Royster leaned toward him into the wind, his breath as volatile as lighter fluid. He cast a nervous glance up and down Canyon Road. "A Spanish dude was in El Farol looking for a babe named Alicia. Somethin' like that. Alicia in Wonder-land, man. Isn't that who you been looking for?"

Lowell felt his skin crawling. "What about her? What did he want?"

"Didn't say, man. But he looked bad. One of the waiters knew him, said his name was Danny something."

Lowell caught his breath. "He looked *bad*? As in sick?"

"No. As in 'not good.' "

Lowell nodded, his heart racing. "He still there?"

"No, man, I don't think so. Not his scene."

"Thanks for the tip. He talk to anyone else?"

"I don't know. Ask Leon. The bartender."

Lowell headed for El Farol. Loud electric blues music was booming out through the doorway, and a competent-looking bouncer was busy collecting a cover charge.

"Five bucks," he told Lowell.

"Which one is Leon?" Lowell asked, grudgingly shelling out tomorrow's lunch money. The bouncer gestured toward the same bartender who'd been on duty at Lowell's prior visit.

"Hey!" complained Royster, appearing at his elbow, apparently having followed him from the gallery. "What about me, man?"

Lowell looked at him in annoyance. "Depends. You know anything about jewels?" Several people edging past him to get into the bar gave him a funny look at that.

"What kind of jewels?" Royster seemed taken aback, like one who has himself been caught with his hand in somebody's jewel box. Lowell didn't consider that such an unlikely scenario. "Not stolen ones," he said. "Just, say, do you know somebody who buys family heirlooms."

"Spanish?" Royster inquired with a knowing grin.

Lowell shrugged. "Maybe."

"Hey, can I get in here?" Royster demanded. Two people behind him agreed.

Lowell sighed and paid another five bucks. Royster elbowed his way in and headed straight for the bar. Lowell spotted another familiar face: Mike Baca. Santa Fe was a small town after all. Baca, sitting on a stool at the near end of the bar, had already seen him and grinned. Lowell signaled to him to wait a minute and went after Royster. He had to get past two very good-looking blond women with Texas written all over them—concha belts, big earrings, white cowboy hats,

fringed vests, frilly skirts, and inlaid Acme boots—to get to
him. Royster eyed the Texas women, threw Lowell what was
intended to be a meaningful look, and barked his order to
Leon. "Red wine!" Leon, no fool, looked to Lowell for the
green light. Lowell shrugged and nodded grudgingly.

Royster drank half the glass in a single gulp. Four-fifty,
Lowell was informed as another fiver vanished for good. "All
right," he said. "Now talk."

Royster wiped his mouth, looked longingly at the two
Texas blondes, who had just crowded in behind Lowell. "How
y'all doin'?" said the first one to Lowell.

"We're doin' great," Royster answered for him, with a las-
civious grin. The blondes left quickly. Lowell glared at him.
"All right, all right, yeah, sure. Jewels. Why, you wanna fence
something?"

"As I said, I want to know where somebody would go to
sell some heirlooms. Grandmother's rings, that sort of thing."

"No questions asked?" Royster had that irritating grin
again. He finished his drink and waved his glass at Leon
meaningfully. "Yo, Leon," he called. "This is the other guy
that was looking for what'sername."

Leon gave Lowell a look of recognition and appraisal, and
poured Royster a refill from the Gallo jug he kept next to the
Napa cabernets. Lowell saw that and pointedly lay down the
three dollars listed on the menu for house wines. Then added
five more, for whatever Leon had to say. He was going to have
to get a real job if this kept up. He wondered if Ariel had any
clue whatsoever about economics, having been raised in a
millionaire's household. True, she had been out on her own for
two years, even though she had—just temporarily, she insisted—returned to the Admiral's fold. On the other hand,

traveling with a major college sports star might not have provided the most practical demonstration of reality economics.
Somehow, major college sports stars always seemed to have
plenty of money.

"You the guy from Florida?" Leon was asking him.

Lowell looked around. "Am I the only one?"

"A dude named Danny Lopez was looking for that chick
you asked about," said Leon, scooping up the money. "Said
something about her being his wife."

Lowell could almost sense people moving away from him,
like in the old Westerns. He couldn't help glancing around.
"He here?"

"He never comes this side of town," interjected Royster.
" 'Less he's got a major reason. She must be the major
reason."

"I'm looking for his *former* wife," Lowell said. "Nobody
around here seems to know her whereabouts. Unless you do?"
he asked Leon pointedly.

Leon didn't. Then Lowell remembered that Mike Baca
was waiting for him. "Excuse me," he told Royster and Leon
and moved down the bar. The two Texas blondes had moved
in on Baca, whose impressive Latino good looks seemed to be
just fine with them.

Lowell joined them. "Excuse me," he said to the women
with a smile. They smiled back, misconstruing his intentions.

"Meet Tiffany and—?" said Baca, gesturing at the two.

"Stephanie," said the second blonde.

"This is my friend," said Baca.

"Tony Lowell," said Lowell, introducing himself.

The blondes smiled some more. "Hi," they said.

"Hi," said Lowell, and turned back to Baca. The young

women reminded him a little too much of Ariel for his comfort. "So," he said. "What's up?"

"You're getting popular," said Baca.

"Word gets around."

"Where y'all from?" asked the first blonde.

"Florida," replied Lowell without looking at her. He didn't want to see her. She looked too good. Even with the hat.

"I ran into Emily Tartikoff," Baca told him. "She said to say hi."

Lowell nodded noncommittally.

"Everything is so *quaint* around here!" bubbled the second blonde.

Lowell ignored her. "Maybe you should level with me," he told Baca. "I wish somebody around here would." He looked at the women. "Excuse me, ladies?" Then at Baca. "Can I speak to you a minute?"

"What about?" Baca brushed his long black locks from his eyes and smiled for the Texas ladies.

"Danny Lopez," said Lowell.

Baca's expression changed to wary, then to wistful. "He was something else, that Danny Lopez. A regular local hero. A bunch of his high-school teammates are on the police force. Did you know that?" Lowell had heard. "Maybe that's why you can't find him. People don't want you to. People around here, at least, have this tendency to protect their icons—even if they get tarnished over time. Danny was quarterback. How many guys with Spanish names you know of play quarterback? And he was good. If he hadn't been such a fuck-up, he would've had a full scholarship to U.N.M. He led the Blue Devils to their only football and basketball state championships in three decades. He had these great moves like you

143

wouldn't think he had, the way he was built, kind of low to the ground, always moving his head from side to side, looking for an opening. I think he was a big fan of O.J. Simpson. Him and Jim Morrison."

"O.J. I can see. But Jim Morrison? Of The Doors?" Lowell didn't like the idea of having a common interest with his quarry.

"Yeah. Jim Morrison used to call himself the 'Lizard King.' I think he even lived in New Mexico once. So Danny kind of related, even took the name for himself. Seeing as how," he chuckled, "Jim Morrison wasn't needing it anymore."

"So this wife beater I'm looking for is a popular sports hero. What else is new?"

Baca's smile vanished. "I advised you to stay away from him," he said. "I'd take that very seriously now."

"That might not be so easy. It would help to know where he's at, and which way he's coming from."

"And headed."

Baca turned away and stared out into the night. The two blondes gave up and headed for greener rangeland. "You've got a point," he said. "One thing you have going for you is that he doesn't know much about you yet. He may not even know that you exist."

"It's nice to exist. Despite the sordid perils."

"I have heard that he's into kids these days."

That chilled Lowell to the core. "Into kids? What do you mean?"

"Not what you think. I don't think so, anyway. I mean he has a job, working with kids."

"Great," said Lowell with a shiver. "Don't tell me. He's a social worker."

"Sorta. I hear he works at the City Rec Center, down on Agua Fria."

"I've seen it." Lowell remembered passing it several times. It was barely two blocks from the Sandoval residence. That really chilled him.

"If you plan on going down there, which I personally would not do, be careful," Baca warned him, his eyes serious. "I told you. He's a bad dude."

Lowell wondered why nobody had warned the City Rec Center. But then, there were a lot of things he wondered just now.

"Thanks," he told Baca. Royster was gesturing emphatically at him from the other end of the bar. Apparently his glass was empty again.

"Emily has a message for you," Baca was saying. "She's seen Alicia."

"What?" Lowell stopped cold and stared at him.

"She's seen Alicia."

"Where?"

"In a dream."

Lowell threw up his hands, not caring to mention he'd seen her himself in dreams. They seemed to be the only place she really existed, he thought as he worked his way back down the bar. Dreams and cyberspace.

"I thought of a place," Royster shouted to him over a bold rendition of Willy Dixon's "Ain't Superstitious," the way Howlin' Wolf used to do it. Lowell wanted to hear the song. But he also wanted to hear what Royster had to say.

Royster waved his glass at Leon. Lowell nodded to the bartender and put another fiver on the bartop. It was his last one. "This better be good," he said.

"There's a place out on Cordova Road," Royster told him. "Buys antique jewelry, rare coins, old gold, that kinda shit. Santa Fe Jewelry Exchange. Some shit like that."

"Where'd you get this, the Yellow Pages?"

Royster looked insulted. Or tried to. "No, man! I been there. I sold them my old wedding ring down there, last year."

"I hope you got a great price."

"Not bad," said Royster. "Kept me in art supplies for a couple months."

"Art supplies," said Lowell. "Good for you."

"Hey, don't get critical!" Royster protested. "I get drinks for free, remember?"

He had a point.

Lowell turned and left, before Royster had any more information he couldn't afford. When he made his way past the other end of the bar, he saw that Mike Baca was gone. The band was rocking. Nobody paid any attention as he slipped out the side door.

He thought about the little surprise attack his first night in Santa Fe, three nights earlier. The side alley was empty. He moved quickly down it toward Canyon Road. Suddenly a door burst open right behind him and he whirled, hands raised defensively, as a short Hispanic man in white kitchen togs came out, carrying a garbage can. The kitchen worker stared at Lowell in surprise, set the can in the alley and went back inside, throwing Lowell a look of dark suspicion.

Lowell reached the sidewalk, where a crowd stood waiting to get into the bar. He edged around it and scanned the area for anyone questionable. It was a problem. He was going to have to be wary of anyone who looked Hispanic. Just like a lost tourist might act on Calle Ocho in Miami. Or East Man-

146

atee. His survival in Santa Fe might require a considerable degree of political incorrectness for the foreseeable future.

His next problem was the alley behind the Chinese restaurant, across the road from the bar. He'd picked it instead of the public parking lot not so much for a free parking space—a rarity in Santa Fe—as to arrive unobserved. But now his choice could well work against him. The vacant alley behind the restaurant was the perfect place to jump someone. Or to get jumped.

Lowell didn't want to get jumped. His head was still sore from the last time. He joined a group of yuppie revelers gathered on the sidewalk and moved with them to the end of the block, then dropped out and ducked behind a white BMW with California plates that was moving up the road, and reached the other side of the street unobserved. Taking shelter behind a huge oak tree on the next corner, he had a view of the rear of the restaurant and the alley.

At first, the alley appeared vacant. He could see the Buick, and the Mercedes next to it. Then he spotted the two dark figures, standing almost motionless behind the Dumpster. He would have walked right past them if he hadn't been alert. He watched the watchers, noting with grim amusement when one of them lit a cigarette, illuminating his face. Lowell thought he might have seen him before but wasn't sure, and the light flickered out too quickly to tell. The man had been a perfect target for a sniper. Good thing for him I'm not a sniper, he thought. Bad for me that *he* might be.

Lowell considered his options. Not being armed, the likelihood of his surprising and overcoming the two of them seemed doubtful. That worked great in bullshit movies, but not so well in real alleys. A ruse might work. Or might not.

There was no reason to assume his watchers were gullible. Or stupid. He wondered if one of them could be Danny Lopez. He didn't like that thought at all.

Lowell slipped back around to the front of the Chinese restaurant and walked inside behind several well-dressed tourists hankering, presumably, for some good old Mushu Gai Pan. He had nothing against Chinese food, but couldn't see spending a fortune visiting a quaint former Indian and Spanish settlement in the Rocky Mountains in order to eat egg rolls. He asked the smiling host for the nearest pay phone.

"By men's room," he was told. "Men's room for dinner guests only." Lowell apparently didn't resemble a dinner guest.

He faced the scowling man, who was wearing a tuxedo. He thought of the Mercedes parked near his rental Buick. "Then maybe you can save me the trouble and make the call yourself," he said.

The man blinked. "What call?"

"The one to the police, to report the two men breaking into the Mercedes Benz sedan in your back alley."

Bingo. The man turned pale. The Mercedes obviously belonged to either the man himself—presumably the manager— or to one of his bosses. He grabbed a phone from under the counter. "Give me police!" he shouted into the receiver. "Right away!"

Lowell beamed, and waited for the action to begin. He timed them. It took seven minutes for three prowl cars to block off both ends of the alleys and Canyon Road in front, and sweep the parking lot. The two young men in black sweat suits were flushed out right away. Lowell watched them as they were handcuffed and placed in the back of a cruiser.

"Hey, we didn't do nothin'!" protested one of them. Lowell recognized him. He was one of Peso Sandoval's Cholos. Interesting, thought Lowell. He wondered why Peso would have sent them. Or if not Peso, who had.

Unfortunately, the Cholos also spotted him. "You're dead meat, man. You're road kill!" The nearest one continued to shout at him angrily as they were driven away.

"That sounded like a threat to me. Isn't that a violation?" Lowell asked the nearest cop.

The cop smiled. "Not in Santa Fe. But if they do turn you into road kill, then *that's* a violation."

Lowell returned to the hotel, bone weary. Stopping in the lobby bar, he ordered a double Barbados rum, hoping to dampen the high desert blues that continued to dog him. Tomorrow, he decided, it was time to confront Danny Lopez. If he could find him. Tonight, he played everything he could find on the jukebox to soothe his mood, from Dylan to Peggy Lee. Nothing worked except, inexplicably, an a cappella version of "Little Red Riding Hood" by a group called The Bobs. It was the vocal bass, he decided. The guy's voice, whoever he was, was so good it rendered all electronics dispensable.

It was close to midnight when the waiter brought him a phone. "Call for you, Mr. Lowell."

Startled, he took the call, having no reason to expect anything but more bad news. He had already come to realize one thing about himself: he hated failure.

The voice was soft, hesitant, and impossibly alluring. "Is this Mr. Tony Lowell?"

149

He knew who it was at once, without knowing how. "Alicia Sandoval?"

She affirmed that it was.

"How are you? Are you all right?"

"About as well as can be expected. I guess you know I heard from your daughter."

"Yes, yes. Can you tell me where you are?" He asked cautiously, fearful she would become skittish and hang up.

She hesitated, then seemed to reach a decision. "In Colorado. A place called Pagosa Springs. The Best Western."

"Stay there. I'll come up," he told her.

"Are you crazy? There's snow everywhere. I was lucky to get here myself."

"Snow?" He looked out the window. "How far is it?"

"I don't know. Three, four hours. In good weather."

"I'll be there for breakfast. Please, don't go anywhere. Don't talk to anyone. Just wait for me. I'll be the guy with the swamp boots."

"Excuse me?"

"Just a joke."

"Oh." She paused, as though to think it over. "Is Ariel with you?"

"No. But I'll bring I.D."

She sounded like someone who was too tired to run anymore. "Fine," she said, her voice barely audible.

"Wait! Give me your number!" he said quickly, but she'd already rung off.

Lowell hung up, feeling a strange sense of dread mixed with euphoria, the latter beyond all reason, considering what had happened that day. But she had called him, which was better than he could have hoped for.

Danny Lopez would have to wait. The fact that Alicia was safe from his grasp was good enough news for now. Lowell got dressed, grabbed his carry-on and was on his way down the elevator in less than thirty minutes. The desk clerk waved to him as he crossed the lobby, and handed him a slip of paper. "Call for you, Mr. Lowell. Said she was your daughter."

He'd have to call her tomorrow, this was urgent. He headed for the door.

"Are you checking out, Mr. Lowell?" the clerk called after him, noting the bag.

"No. I thought I'd just take a little side trip and have a look at Taos while I'm here."

"That's over sixty miles, sir, and this is the middle of the night!"

"I'm aware of that. I like to drive at night."

"It's snowing up there, sir!" A note of incredulity crept into the clerk's voice. "They say it's El Niño."

"Yeah," said Lowell. "I love El Niño."

The rental car had chains. The roads, specifically Route 84 north out of Española to Chama, were still open. Stoking up on coffee at an all-night 7-Eleven in Pojoaqui Pueblo, Lowell drove through the night, blind to the pristine beauty of the virgin, snow-covered desert and snow-clad, moonlit mountain landscapes. He had one single vision in his mind: rescuing Alicia Sandoval. He didn't feel tired at all. He felt enervated, like a soldier before a battle. Maybe he was feeling what a paramedic might feel, trying desperately to maneuver an ambulance through an icebound maze. There was no sense of panic. In any case, it didn't matter. What did matter was that Alicia Sandoval had surfaced, was still alive, and he was on his way.

As he drove north, and the frequently replenished cups of caffeine kicked in, he began to question his own motives. Why was he doing this? Was it just because of Ariel's request? Or something deeper, more—mysterious. Wasn't it enough to know she was somewhere safe, away from Santa Fe? But something else nagged at him as well. Shouldn't he have called Ariel back before leaving?

No, he told himself. What he was now convinced had happened to Amanda changed the whole complexion of the case. Ariel's fearful premonitions might bear more weight than he'd been willing to admit.

He sped up, watching his rear view carefully, just in case. It was very bad news, finding out that Lopez was also actively searching for her. He could already be one step ahead, which meant that Alicia Sandoval was in more imminent peril than ever, at this very moment. He had to warn her, and move her to a safer place.

Something else worried him as well. If Danny Lopez was actively stalking Alicia, he had a huge advantage over Tony Lowell: he knew the woman and her patterns, her secrets, her favorite places, perhaps even her childhood haunts. And he knew the territory.

11

It was the purple-violet hour before dawn when Lowell finally reached Pagosa Springs, slipping and sliding into town like a drunken miner down out of the mountains while the sober world slept. His wheels made virgin tracks in the new-fallen snow after a night he would never forget. He spotted the Best Western sign shortly after entering the city limits from the south. Pulling into the office breezeway, he climbed out, stretching in the crisp mountain air. It smelled of firewood smoke and the odor of sulfur from the nearby hot springs that had given the town its name. He shuffled through the blowing drifts in his old swamp boots and went into the office.

"I'm looking for a friend of mine who's staying here," he informed the bleary-eyed clerk.

"What's the name?"

"Sandoval. Alicia Sandoval."

The clerk checked the computer. "Sorry," he said with finality. "No such person."

Lowell felt a sinking sensation.

"Was she here before? Last night, or yesterday?" It made sense she might use another name. But what name? He felt the adrenaline that had driven him all this distance ebbing away.

The man, a wizened, retired cowboy by the look of him, inexpertly thumbed the keyboard once again.

"Sorry."

Lowell turned away. He was halfway out the door when the cowboy clerk called after him. "You might try the other one," he suggested, as though an afterthought.

Lowell stopped. "Other what?"

"The other Best Western. East end of town, out toward Wolf Creek Pass."

Lowell was already out the door, sprinting for the car.

Alicia was registered as Mrs. Sandoval—a common name. Her room was on the ground floor, facing the parking lot. Lowell pulled in front, got out, checked the area, and knocked.

There was a fumbling, shuffling sound from within, and he recognized the sultry, sleepy voice that responded: "Who is it?"

"Tony Lowell."

"Just a minute."

After what seemed an interminable delay, the door

opened a crack, only as far as the chain lock would allow, and he could just make out a dark, sleep-reddened eye peering out at him, fear mixed with suspicion.

"You have I.D.?"

"Sure." He fumbled for his wallet, his fingers freezing, and flipped it open to show both his P.I. and driver's licenses.

She looked at them for a long time, then at him. "What's your daughter's name?" she asked suddenly.

He grinned, admiring her cautious savvy. "Ariel," he said. "Blond, about your size, a couple years younger."

She closed the door and released the safety chain. "All right, you can come in," she said.

She was fully dressed, and he realized she must have been waiting for him all those hours. He'd seen the picture, and seen her in the dreams. But even in this disheveled state, or perhaps because of it, seeing her in person took his breath away. She was stunning. The bed was still made, unslept in. She brushed her jet-black tresses out of her eyes and held the door for him as he stepped cautiously into the room.

"Sit down," she said, and perched herself on the edge of the bed. He hesitated, then pulled up the only chair and sat.

"I'd offer you some coffee," she said, "but there isn't any. Maybe if we went to the coffee shop in the motel."

Lowell checked the window and decided no. "Too public," he said. "Do they have room service here?"

She shook her head.

"I'll go get some and bring it back," he told her. "You stay put. I'll knock twice, then twice again. Got that?"

"Got it," she said, nodding. "I take mine black," she called after him.

The motel coffee shop was open and bustling. He bought two large coffees to go, and two bran muffins that somehow a baker had managed to deliver that morning, snow or no. He took the cardboard tray back to the room and signaled. She let him in and they talked, warily sizing each other up. She seemed shaky. He studied her closely, noting the pain in her eyes despite their inpenetrable depth, like a quarry lake, unmasked by her dark beauty. She blinked and shrank back into the shadows.

After an awkward moment, both agreed they should call Ariel. They did so from her room, and Alicia reassured Ariel that she was all right, was recovering, and that she was happy Lowell had found her. "He seems like a nice guy, Ariel," she said.

Lowell wondered how she would know.

"Dad!" Ariel exclaimed when it was his turn. "Are you okay?" She'd wanted to tell him about the lizard Website, but now it seemed foolish. Probably just a coincidence, anyway.

"Of course I'm okay," he said, laughing somewhat stiffly. "Alicia's safe, and that's the main thing."

"So what now, then?"

"I have to get her out of here," he told her without saying why.

"Well, whatever you do," she warned him, "please don't fall for her. She's not ready—damn it, *you're* not ready. Please tell me she's not falling for you and all your charms."

He forced a laugh. "Ariel, I just got here," he replied, bothered by her perception. "We're getting to know each other."

"Just talk to her. That's all either of you can handle right now. Just talk to her!" Lowell agreed and insisted that everything was fine, everything was under control. And for the moment, everything was. There was an awkward silence as father and daughter finally said their good-byes.

"Are you going to be my bodyguard?" he heard Alicia asking, a slight tone of challenge in her voice.

"For the moment. I promised some people, particularly my daughter, that I'd make sure you were safe." He thought for a moment. "I have a friend, a private investigator in Santa Fe. He knows a number of people on the police force who are trustworthy, as well as some of the D.A.s. I think we can get you some protection, certainly a restraining order, possibly press charges—"

She drew away with a derisive laugh. "You've got to be joking. I used to call the cops all the time, and every time they showed up, they were friends of my husband's. They all got a big laugh out of that, let me tell you."

He suddenly felt fearful for her once again. "Come on, get dressed," he ordered her. "I have to get you out of here."

"Nobody knows I'm here. Except you."

"Even so, it's not safe for you to stay in one place this long." He thought for another moment. "Did you make any calls? To anyone?"

She hesitated. "Just to my sister." Peso had answered, actually, on his fancy new cellular phone, but Lowell didn't need to know that. "Not that it's any of your business. What's with you men, anyway? You're always trying to control everything. Do you have to own us, own every moment of our lives?" She burst into hot, angry tears.

He understood his mistake at once. She simply wasn't ready to trust a man—any man—so soon. It was just too dangerous for her, and her psyche was coming to her defense.

"Sorry," he said gently. "You're right. No man should presume anything about a woman or her feelings, and I need to earn your trust."

She watched him while the television flickered in the background, illuminating her profile. "I've heard it all before, is all. That's how it started with—" She put her hand over her mouth suddenly and ran for the bathroom. He heard her throwing up and left her alone. Then, when the heaves had subsided, he brought her a wet washcloth. She wiped her face, but fresh tears followed.

When he led her back to sit on the bed, she raised her hand as though to fend him off. Then she recoiled in horror and collapsed in his arms, weeping. "Oh, God, I'm sorry," she wept. "I'm so sorry!"

"No, you have every right. It's all right," he assured her, "It's all right."

He sat on the chair beside her, trying to recall how to be tender and ministrative. It was hard to recollect. There hadn't been much tenderness, many ministrations, in his childhood. His mother had died when he was young, and he'd missed his chance with Ariel by a decade.

She looked at him, questioning. Then she seemed to make a decision.

"I want to tell you about my husband," she began. It all came out, hesitantly at first, then in a gush of anguished words: the possessiveness that became ownership, the jealous rages that led to the beatings, then the chokings, the betrayal by her friends, the jokes from the police, the blindness of her family, the many times Danny had nearly killed her.

"I finally got up the courage to take that seminar in Denver. A girlfriend had told me about it. It was Ariel, your daughter—God, are you that old?—who finally made me aware of how I was trapped by what she called my *victimhood*. God, I hate that word! Then Christina, the facilitator, told me it would be years before I'd be really free and able to move on. And I *wanted* to move forward, but I couldn't!" She was crying again. Lowell sat and listened quietly.

"I couldn't cherish it, though," she sobbed.

"Cherish what?" he asked, bewildered.

"The pain. The way the seminar—the way they wanted us to. They kept saying, 'Cherish the pain until it is yours to own.' I just wanted to be rid of it, once and for all."

"I'm with you," he said.

Then she told him about the first rape, when she was only fifteen, by some macho creeps from the west side. It was after she'd finally convinced her parents to let her go to the mall with some friends, and then her mother had said the assault was her own fault for running around loose and not staying home, and it had haunted her every relationship since.

"That probably had something to do with my having so little self-esteem that I wound up choosing a man like Danny Lopez," she said with a sigh. "At least that's what Christina said at the seminar." Then she told him about the pain of the police laughing and teasing her, some of them fathers of the same boys who'd assaulted her. Lowell made a note to pass on some of these revelations to Sergeant Hector Ramirez— who, he sensed, would not have acted that way—and continued to listen as she shared with him the anguish of her own cousins castigating and blaming her, calling her *"puta."*

"Small wonder," he told her, "that this time, you chose to get away." She nodded, wept some more, and blew her nose. Then she told him of how, after the last, final, most savage beating, which had broken four of her ribs, followed by a choking that had nearly crushed her windpipe, she had tried to convince the doctors the injuries were from a bicycle accident, and they hadn't believed her and told her to get help. She had managed to leave him then for a women's shelter and to file for divorce. But her silence afterward, she explained, had mostly come of knowing that like all the other times, ultimately the blame would be put on her—for how she dressed, or for talking back to her husband. She managed an ironic laugh at that.

He shook his head angrily. "How did your family react when they finally learned the truth about your marriage?"

"Deaf, dumb, and blind. I was raised to do what I was told. Well, never again." Then she went on to tell of how Danny wouldn't let her go, kept pleading for her to come back, promising he'd be better, it would be better, how her father and brothers had urged her to "recant" her divorce and forgive her husband. And how she'd stood firm against them all. Only her mother and sister had defended her, but they, of course, had been ignored. She'd been in the women's shelter off and on over the past three years, she informed him. And then, just when she was finally beginning to recover from the ordeal of her disastrous marriage, he had found out where she was, stalked her, and raped her.

His eyes blazed. "When was that?"

"Last April. I went to stay in another shelter after that, but he found me again! That was when I had to get out."

"That's when Ariel got worried that you'd disappeared."

She nodded. "I'm sorry she worried so much. They had a computer at the shelter. I was using it for e-mail and stuff. But look, I really don't know her that well. I know we were friends, but I didn't think she was that concerned." Her eyes showed interest and puzzlement. Lowell decided to change the subject. "Did you ever hear of a woman named Amanda Cortez?" he asked cautiously.

She frowned, as though it rang a bell deep in her past. Then she shook her head. "No, why? Who is she?"

He hesitated. "Never mind, it doesn't matter. Not now."

There was a shuffling noise outside the motel room. Both of them froze. Warning her to remain silent, he crept to the window and carefully drew the venetian blinds apart, just enough to see out. An elderly couple was checking out next door.

"Es nada," he told her and returned to the bedside still worried. "I don't understand one thing, though," he finally said. "Why didn't you just leave, start life over somewhere new? Why in God's name, after getting a taste of freedom and friendship in Colorado, did you go back to Santa Fe?"

"I don't know. Maybe just some crazy hope, some dream of reconciliation with my family, some foolish need to finally get just a little acknowledgment and support from them."

"Do you think it could possibly have been something even deeper, some need to face the demons that continued to haunt you?"

She looked away. "I don't know. Whatever it was, I made a mistake. Nothing was going to change. Anyway, where else was I supposed to go? I don't know anyone anywhere else but there."

"You know Ariel."

She shrugged. "Not really."

"Well, you sure made an impression on her. She told me how concerned she was for you, and how you suddenly broke off contact. That's why she asked me to come out here. She is so worried about you, you have no idea. Frankly, I'm not even sure why myself, unless she's been places I don't even know about."

She gave him a calculating look. "You may not know her as well as you think. She's had a few knocks of her own."

That stopped him. "What do you mean?"

She shook her head. "It wouldn't be appropriate to say, but you ought to know at least that she was crazy about some pretty shitty guys."

"That basketball player!" It dawned on him. He felt like a fool. Then a flush of rage swept him, that some faceless, egotistical jock had abused his flesh and blood. At least Ariel hadn't married the creep.

Alicia laughed suddenly, as though reading his mind. Then her mood darkened once more.

"You really don't understand, do you?" she snapped, pulling away. "This is just business for you. You don't know anything about me, or what I'm going through!"

"Then tell me," he said, checking the window once more.

Hesitantly, she resumed her tale and told him about what had happened last April.

"I was visiting my parents, maybe for one day. It was raining, half rain, half sleet. I was sitting by the upstairs window looking out at the weather. I knew Danny was out there. I guess I'd known all along he'd be waiting for me. But I had to live my life too.

"Anyway, I couldn't hang around the house all day. I had no intention of being a prisoner in my own home. I had to get out just to clear my head. So after I waited until I thought he'd gone, I took my car and drove to the market. I was just going to pick up a few things when there was, like, this shadow that fell on me. I looked up, and there he was."

Lowell glanced involuntarily behind him, feeling her fear as she recounted her tale. How her heart almost stopped for a moment. How she wasn't ready to deal with Danny. And how, at that instant, she'd realized how foolish she'd been in thinking she ever would be.

"He just stood there and grinned at me," she wept.

"What did he say?"

"Nothing. Just something stupid like 'Hello, baby.' So I had no choice," she went on, "but to brave it out. 'Excuse me, Danny,' I said, 'but I have a court order and you have to stay away from me. So if you don't mind, I'm going to do some shopping here.' "

"Of course he ignores that," she continued after a moment. "So he's following me around. I'm pushing my cart past him, looking for someone—anyone—who might help out. Of course there's no one. No one would help anyway, judging from past experience. Anyway, I make it to the end of the aisle, and the nearest person is the cashier, this teenage girl chewing gum."

Alicia tried to laugh at the scene, of herself hurrying to the checkout stand, Danny right behind her. Of how she tried to get the girl's attention, trying to send S.O.S. messages with her eyes. Of how the girl didn't even look at her, said something like "Paper or plastic?" with her mouth full of gum.

She trembled as she recounted the way Danny stood looming over her and her sense of deep despair and helplessness when he seized her arm.

"What did you say to him then?"

"I just told him to let go," she said, shaking with this strange laughter now, as though surprised at her own courage. Danny, apparently, had been surprised too, and let go, mum-

163

bling something about how he only wanted to see how she was doing.

" 'I'm doing great,' I told him. 'Never better. Now will you please just go?' So then the checkout babe finally looks at me, then at him, for the first time. She looks back at me, and asks, 'You want I should call the manager?' I almost had to laugh. So I say, 'No, it's all right, everything's fine.' Can you believe it? So then I turn back to Danny, all defiant, and say, 'Goodbye, Danny. I mean it.' "

"What did he do?"

"He backed away, his hands up like he's not gonna do anything, still grinning like some kind of T-rex or something. So the guard is finally looking in his direction now. Not, mind you, that the old fart would be much use. Anyway, Danny gets this strange look on his face, turns around, and just walks out."

"Then what happened?"

She took a deep breath and shuddered.

"As soon as he was gone, I kind of went blank. Then I guess I ran—desperate, without seeing—for the car, not stopping to look, not stopping to think, with this one goal in mind: to get away."

Lowell stood up and paced up and down in the room, waiting until she was ready to tell him the rest. How she'd driven blindly through the city, thinking only of how to escape, and of what a dreadful, foolish mistake she'd made, returning to Santa Fe. How she'd stopped at this light where Cerillos Road crossed St. Francis Drive. And how he had followed her, how she had so blindly and foolishly led him straight to her hideaway.

She cried again. "The worst part of it was," she wept, "I loved him."

That sickened Lowell more than anything he'd yet heard. "What about now? Do you still love him, after all that?"

She shuddered. "No. God, no."

His relief was palpable.

"Alicia, I'm sorry," he told her. If there's anything I can do to make sure none of that ever happens again to you, I'm here to do it."

"And how the hell do you plan on accomplishing that?"

"I haven't a clue."

She fell asleep at last. Lowell, in the chair beside her struggled to stay awake.

Finally he too slept, restlessly, exhausted, disturbed by incoherent dreams and thoughts, dark, fearful images. One that kept recurring over and over involved a great, terrible, green lizard. With fangs. He thought he heard the phone ring, but he couldn't wake up to answer it despite a gargantuan effort. It was as though he'd been drugged. Through the dream-woven mists of Avalon, he heard a soft, impossibly seductive voice answering, the sounds of whispers quarreling in the night, of stifled murmurs of disagreement, and a shush for silence. He dreamed on, of serpents and sandstorms, and relentless desert winds blowing through the night.

He awoke at dusk with a strange sensation that made his skin crawl. He sat up with a start. In trepidation, he looked at the bed next to his chair, then around the room. It was empty but for the one bag he'd brought with him.

"Alicia?" he shouted. Heart pounding, he leaped to his feet and checked the bathroom. It was empty. Alicia Sandoval was gone.

12

SOUTHERN COLORADO
NOVEMBER 20, DUSK

Lowell feared the worst. Frantically, he searched the motel room one more time, as though somehow she could still be there and he just did not see her. He threw open the door. "Alicia!" he shouted into the biting wind. There was no reply except from a barking dog somewhere up the road. A deep feeling of terror, mixed with dismay and tinged with failure, gripped him unlike anything he'd felt since 'Nam. He could not bear the thought that she had somehow slipped away, through his fingers, while he'd slept on the job. And then the worst thought of all struck him like an Indian arrow: what if he'd led Danny straight to her? No, he'd been careful, he'd watched his tail. It was probable that Danny didn't even know who he was yet. Or did he? He couldn't know, for sure.

He rechecked the parking lot for some sign, some clue,

knowing it was next to useless. Snow had filled any tracks hours before. He got his camera from the car, loaded it with infrared, and snapped a few stills of the room and the area, seeing nothing out of the ordinary but hoping something might turn up on one of the negatives. Then, returning to the room, he noticed an empty pack of Marlboros on the walkway near the door. Several butts were stubbed out in the vicinity. They could have been dropped by anyone, but he carefully gathered them up and sealed them in a plastic trash liner from the motel room.

Back in the echoingly empty room, he picked up the phone and called the motel operator. A sleepy female voice answered. "Best Western. Good evening."

"This is Room Twelve. Did anyone call or come here today?"

"Just a moment, sir." She put the phone on hold, then came back on the line.

"Just the gentleman."

Lowell's heart stopped for a moment. "Gentleman?"

"Mrs. Sandoval's husband." Her voice grew suspicious. "Who is this speaking?"

Lowell slammed the phone down and his head swam with a red haze of fear, rage, and frustration. Cursing himself, he searched the room once more, quickly, for any signs of forced entry. There were none. Nor any sign of a struggle. Evidently, horrifyingly, Alicia had left willingly with a man who'd said he was her husband: a "Mr. Sandoval."

He grabbed his belongings and hurriedly loaded them in the car, one eye on the office door. His name wasn't on the registry, and the motel office didn't know who he was, which was all right with him. Except now the motel management had probably gathered that Mrs. Sandoval had been with a man other than the alleged Mr. Sandoval, which could be trouble. And they would probably be coming to remove him, if not to present him with the bill, very shortly. He pulled out of the parking lot just as the woman who'd answered the phone came out of the office, glaring after him like someone who has just been burned and is not pleased. Luckily, Lowell's license plate, not to mention the car, was covered with mud and ice.

The roads had been plowed, and he was able to drive with minimum slippage to a small strip mall down the road, where he stopped and placed a call to Hector Ramirez from a pay phone. Luckily, he was still on duty.

When a grudging Sergeant Ramirez came on the line, Lowell shouted. "Ramirez? This is Tony Lowell! The son of a bitch got her!"

"Wait a minute, slow down," growled Ramirez. "Who got who?"

"Lopez, dammit! He came up here and got her and took her away!"

"Took who away from where?"

"Alicia Sandoval. From Pagosa Springs, Colorado. Where she was hiding out, and where she called me from!"

Ramirez sounded incredulous. "She called *you*?"

"That's right. She was here, and now she's gone, and you had better find her before he hurts her again and probably for the last time!"

"Wait a minute. Are you sure it was Danny Lopez? What I hear, he's been lookin' for her for months."

"Well, he found her, dammit! Who the hell else would it

168

be? He's been looking for her. He tracked her down, came up here and took her away. I swear, Ramirez, if something has happened to her—"

"Maybe you led him right to her, Lowell. Don't be so quick to blame us. She calls you, you go running up there like some kind of Don Quixote—"

"Okay, okay, I apologize. I watched my butt, I always do and have ever since 'Nam. Nobody followed me."

"So maybe it wasn't Lopez, then. How do you know it was anybody?"

"The office clerk said it was Mr. Sandoval who came."

"Let's back up a second," Ramirez cut into his thoughts. "You say Danny Lopez came *there*? Where were you at the time?"

"With her. Nearby."

"I see."

Lowell resented the tone. "Not *with* her in the proverbial sense, if that's what you're implying. I was sitting in a chair. I fell asleep. When I woke up, she was gone."

"You were sleeping with Danny Lopez's wife."

"Go to hell!" Lowell yelled. "I was bodyguarding her."

"Nice body," said Ramirez, irony dripping like molten metal. "Nice job guarding it, since apparently she's gone. But I have one question."

"Find Lopez and ask him. I'm out of here." Lowell started to hang up.

"Wait! My question is," Ramirez shouted, "if you were with her and Danny Lopez found her, how come," he wanted to know, "you're still alive?"

Lowell heard him. Ramirez had a point. Everything Low-

169

ell knew about Danny Lopez indicated he'd have woken up with a knife in his ribs, or his head bashed in. Which is to say, not woken up for long, if at all.

"Dammit!" Lowell swore. "Somebody came to the motel desk some time today. A guy. Said he was Mr. Sandoval. They assumed or he told them he was her husband. I assumed he used the name Sandoval because that was the name she's been going by."

"Maybe," said Ramirez. "Or maybe he really *was* Mr. Sandoval."

Lowell had been so blinded by dreadful images of Danny Lopez dragging Alicia away by her hair that he hadn't thought of that. "The father?" He suddenly felt both foolish and hopeful at the same time. Manny might slap his daughter around or call her some bad names, but unlike what he feared of Danny Lopez, Manny wouldn't kill her. At least he didn't think so. On the other hand, Manny Sandoval might be just as likely as Danny Lopez to kill *him* for being with Alicia.

"Could've been either the father or one of the sons," Ramirez said.

"One of the sons?" He hadn't thought of that, either.

"Could've been Peso. Or Roberto."

It was an interesting concept. He liked the Roberto idea a lot better. Either way, she was gone. And having searched so hard for her and finally having found her, only to lose her so quickly, he'd feared the worst.

"By the way," said Ramirez. "We just got the report from the M.E. on that body they exhumed."

"Amanda Cortez? Was it her?"

"The mother hasn't arrived yet. But there was an amulet thing around her neck. And something else."

170

"What?"

"Some kind of a blue gemstone. It was hidden inside. Looks like a sapphire, according to the coroner. I'm surprised the sunovabitch didn't steal the damn thing, except that the pendant it was hidden in wasn't worth much. Oh, one other thing. The skull was caved in. In the front."

"Nice," said Lowell.

"There's no proof Lopez did it, you know."

"Maybe he'll confess."

"Sure. When he sees you coming, he's bound to."

"Thanks for the confidence. If you happen to know where Joshua Croft is, tell him I'm on my way back."

"We can all hardly wait," said Ramirez.

As Lowell got back into the car, the sun set behind the fourteen-thousand-foot peaks of the San Juan mountains, their snowy caps sparkling like vast celestial gems beyond the meadows and above the surrounding forests. Lowell didn't notice. He raced back south on Route 85, through stunning mountain scenery he had not seen the night before and couldn't see now. Southern Colorado and northern New Mexico were more densely forested than the high desert where he'd been, the mountain slopes blanketed with tall stands of ponderosa pine and aspen that glistened in the moonlight. He noted all this in the vague sort of way that photographers file away mental images for future capture, his mind imprisoned by thoughts of Alicia.

Lowell had slept only a few troubled hours in the last two days. The fatigue was almost overwhelming. He didn't want to think about what he would say to Ariel. He couldn't get his mind off Danny Lopez and what he might do with Alicia. He could hardly stand the thoughts that crept into his head, and tried to drive them away with tinny cowboy music on the only radio station he could get.

Find Danny Lopez and you'll find Alicia, he told himself. Just as soon as he got . . . some sleep. The endless drive south on the winding, snowy road had begun to lull him into a stupor. He fought to stay awake but kept losing ground, until finally exhaustion swept him under like an avalanche and he fell asleep. He woke up with a start just as his right front wheel struck a snow-clogged shoulder of the highway. Momentarily panicked, he hit the brakes and barely avoided piling sideways into a telephone pole as he skidded to a stop. He shut off the engine and got out of the car. The biting wind helped some, but he knew he had to rest for a while. He also knew he would freeze if he fell asleep for too long. But he had no choice. He could no longer stay awake.

Thirty-five minutes later, he was dragged out of a fitful sleep that had been constantly disturbed by the roar of passing trucks that sent slush splattering against his tightly shut window. He became conscious of two things. First, that he was freezing cold. Second, that someone was rapping on the car window with a nightstick. A Colorado state trooper looked in at him, his expression a mix of concern and suspicion. Lowell quickly rolled down the window.

"You all right, sir?" inquired the trooper, looking at Lowell intently. He peered into the back seat.

"I'm fine, thank you, Officer. I was starting to fall asleep, so I pulled over."

"There's a gas station and restaurant two miles ahead on your left. I'd move on and stop there, sir. It's not safe to park on the highway. You could get hit by another vehicle. Or you could freeze to death."

172

That would be ironic, thought Lowell. He could see the headlines now in the *New Mexican:* "Florida Man Dies of Hypothermia on Wild-Goose Chase." He thanked the trooper for his advice, and took it.

Lowell made it back to Santa Fe by midnight, and was up at nine. He raced straight to Agua Fria Street, and found the City Rec Center with no trouble. It was a big, purely utilitarian, gymnasium-type structure of steel framing and stucco, with no attempt at adobe styling. There was a large mural on one side that he hadn't noticed when driving by before; now it chilled him more than any Rocky Mountain winter wind. It depicted anthropomorphic images of animals as kids, playing at various sports. Dominating the scene was a large desert lizard, displaying much the same attitude as the late, unlamented Joe Camel. Except that this lizard wore a football jersey and had teeth.

The Rec Center was abandoned. Then Lowell realized why. It was Sunday. People went to church, and to brunch, and took picnics on Sundays. Maybe did some yard work. He had lost track of the days. This whole trip, this entire experience, had plunged him into a time warp. For the last thirty-six hours, he had been completely focused on his intended first encounter with Danny Lopez, the usurper Lizard King. He was going to quietly, peacefully, but forcefully, demand to know what Lopez had done with Alicia Sandoval. Despite his unsettling conversation with Sergeant Ramirez, he was still convinced Lopez had taken her somehow. What he couldn't think about, if it was so, was that she had gone without a struggle.

Wearily, Lowell headed down Cerillos Road to police H.Q. Maybe Ramirez worked Sundays also. If he couldn't talk to

Lopez, he needed to talk to Ramirez. About how come a dangerous, violent man like Danny Lopez worked at the City Rec Center, for starters. And also about what Mike Baca had told him: that Danny had friends on the force.

The desk officer informed him that Ramirez was out on a case. Lowell hoped it involved bringing in and questioning Danny Lopez. The desk officer said she wouldn't know.

Ten minutes later, Lowell pulled up in front of the Sandoval residence. He locked the car, walked to the house, and rang the bell.

A wiry, weathered man of around sixty answered it. His nose was red, his eyes bloodshot. "Whaddaya want?" he demanded, his breath thick with alcohol. Apparently, this being Sunday, he'd been into the sacramental wine. Lowell guessed it was Manny, the father.

A handsome, well-dressed Hispanic man in a dark suit and close-cropped dark hair came toward them from the parlor. He appeared to be near forty. Lowell decided this had to be Robert, the older brother. "Who is it, Dad?" He asked, his voice calm and competent.

"Some gringo."

"I'll talk to him." The younger man took the older man's elbow and moved him gently aside. "Sit down, Dad," he ordered.

"I don't want to, Roberto," complained the old man, but he sat down obediently on the ornate wooden chair in the foyer.

Roberto turned to face Lowell. "This better be meaningful. This is a very inappropriate time to be bothering people. What is it you want?"

Another man appeared in the foyer, a grim look in his

174

eyes. Peso. He had his two Cholos with him, who regarded Lowell with silent menace. They and Lowell had met before. They bristled. He smiled and nodded. They bristled even more.

"Hi," said Lowell. "As you can see, I'm not road kill."

"It's still early," said the bigger one.

"Maybe you didn't hear my brother," Peso said to Lowell.

"You know, I hate to keep bothering you folks, but I really do feel I should complain about you staking out your clowns on me the other night. Fortunately, no harm was done, other than them getting arrested and all," Lowell went on. "But really, if I'd gotten a little more help around here, it wouldn't have happened at all."

The silence was electric. Peso turned bright red. "Fuck you talkin' about?" Roberto gave him a warning look, which Peso brushed aside.

"Alicia was abducted last night," Lowell told them. "From Colorado. Now, either her ex-husband took her or one of you did. I really do hope it was you."

"Fuck's he talkin' about, Robo?" demanded Manny, looking from one son to the other.

"If she's here, I want to talk to her, please. If she's not, I want to know where Lopez is."

Peso stared. "Hey! Only one you're gonna talk to is a ticket agent, about gettin' the fuck out of this town!"

Roberto Sandoval looked at Lowell with an expression of doubt, and something else that could have been genuine concern. But when he looked away, it was enough to convince Lowell that the family was hiding something. "Alicia is not here," he stated. "Where did you get the idea she was?"

"You must be the lawyer," said Lowell.

"We don't know nothin' about it," slurred Manny, half in the tank. "Even if we did, it is family business. Our family business, not yours, gringo! Peso, show this Anglo the door."

Now I know where Peso gets his attitude, thought Lowell, stepping back as Peso and his Cholos closed on him. At that moment, Micaella entered the hallway.

"Wait," she commanded, stepping between them. The men fell back, giving her room. She threw a quick glare at Peso, who hesitated, then put his hand up for the Cholos to back off.

"I'm sorry," she said to Lowell. "This is terrible. We've been so worried about Alicia ever since she moved out. She should never have left home."

"I'm sure she had her reasons."

Her eyes grew hard, and he regretted the comment. "Thank you for your concern, Mr. Lowell," she snapped, "but there is nothing for you to do. She's not seeing anyone."

Lowell looked at her, then at the others. "So she's here?"

"I didn't say that."

"Let me put it this way," said Lowell. "If she isn't with you, that means she's with her former husband. In which case, don't you think you should at least call the police?"

"And say what?" asked Peso. "Tell them some gringo from Florida says my sister's been—" he couldn't even say the word "—bothered? By her rightful husband?"

Lowell was incredulous. His outrage turned to rage. "I don't believe this," he said.

Another voice spoke up from behind him. "You think we don't care about our own flesh and blood? She is my daughter, Señor."

Lowell turned to face Alicia's mother, who had joined the

throng that stood facing him like an impenetrable barrier: a family in unity against the intruding stranger, empowered with righteousness, mistrust, and centuries of insular tradition. The woman was like a movable fortress, filling the kitchen doorway, a large stirring spoon in her hand like the sword of Damocles.

Lowell was overmatched. "I believe you, Señora," he said. "But she has been hurt for a long time and needs help, and if you're not going to provide it for her, then I'm going to have to."

"Why is it so important to you?" cried Micaella.

"Shut up!" Peso ordered her in fury. He glared at Lowell. "She's a big girl, she'll be all right," he insisted. "She's always complaining about Danny this, Danny that. It's between her and him anyway, and nobody else's business. So *ve te.* Beat it. Now." He nodded at the Cholos, one of whom pushed Lowell toward the door, while the other opened it.

Micaella followed them, apologetic. "We take care of our own," she insisted. "She's our family and we love her. You don't even know her. You go back to Florida and take pictures."

Lowell stopped outside the door and looked back at Peso. "What about Danny Lopez?" he asked. "You going to just let this slide as another harmless little macho thing, just boys being boys?"

Micaella's eyes widened and she covered her mouth. Peso glared at her, but seemed to hesitate. Roberto had overheard and stepped outside quickly. "If Danny did anything, I'll see to it he's put in jail," he said, keeping his voice low. "But only when I know the facts. And even then, Alicia won't press charges, I know her. So they'll let him out again right away.

177

When he gets out, he will be very angry. If he finds out you've been meddling in her affairs, he will want to kill you."

Lowell raised his hands, palms upward, in a universal gesture, acknowledging the inevitable. It didn't matter, he now knew, what they said or did. Alicia was in grave danger. He could not abandon her. He would leave this house for the time being because whether or not they would help her, it was obvious that the family was not going to help him. But he wasn't about to give up.

"Call my office if you find out anything more," Roberto told him quietly, slipping him a business card. "Just don't come here again." His eyes looked so sad and wise, Lowell felt that he, if anyone, might be sensible enough to see that justice—not frontier justice—got done.

"Anyway, don't worry about Danny," he heard Peso muttering. "He gets a little wild now and then. But he never hurt anybody."

Lowell stopped once more. "You really believe that?"

"Yeah," said Peso defiantly.

Lowell threw up his hands and walked away.

He heard light footsteps running after him and turned to wait as Micaella caught up to him on the sidewalk. "Peso means well," she told him apologetically. "It's just . . . this is Santa Fe."

"Yeah," said Lowell, nodding. "Santa Fe."

Frustrated, Lowell went back to his hotel, drank a coffee in the coffee shop, then went up to his room to shower and change. He ordered a *huevos rancheros* in the restaurant, and felt revived enough to call Joshua Croft, expecting to get the same taped voice, but needing to complain to someone. He didn't want to call Ariel.

To his surprise, Croft answered. He sounded under the weather. Lowell could relate.

"Used call-forwarding," grumbled Croft. "Big mistake. What's up?"

Lowell gave him a brief version of his encounter with Alicia and of how just when all seemed well, she'd suddenly disappeared.

"I'm worried that Lopez got her," he confessed. "I'm worried about what he'll do to her this time. I have good reason to think he killed his first wife, Amanda Cortez. I think he's going to kill Alicia too, if he hasn't already done so. And nobody around here seems to give a damn!"

"Did you call Hector?"

"Yeah. He thinks she left with family, or on her own."

"And you?"

"I just don't know. I talked to the family and they're protecting something, I don't know what. Probably themselves."

Croft didn't have any kind words of reassurance available for the occasion. Except to say he'd been there. Lowell had never met Rita, though, and couldn't understand.

"There's a bar on the plaza called the Ore House. It's upstairs, looks out over the plaza. Meet me there," Croft told him.

Lowell and Croft sat out on the deck despite the cold, and as Lowell pondered and fretted over the sorry story of Alicia Sandoval and what to do next about her, they got drunk together. Lowell watched the small, unreal world of Santa Fe go by below. People in their Sunday threads, parading in the soft November light. Buying and selling pretty things. Hurrying to the next expensive dinner or support group or arts event. But no Alicia Sandoval. It was almost as though she'd never existed. Trying to wrench his thoughts away from the missing woman, he listened while Croft told him about Rita, the love of his life. Then Lowell spoke about Caitlin, and how he'd never quite been able to shake the ghost of his love for her. Croft shot Lowell one of his more probing looks. "You have any other family left besides that daughter you mentioned?"

"Nope. Just her."

"What about your parents?"

"My mother died when I was young. My father is still living. I think."

Croft smiled. "Real close, are you? Wasn't he the police chief where you grew up?"

"That's right. It was a rich resort town. Maybe like Santa Fe, but the money was a lot more visible and there were no poor people at all, except maybe us. Dad didn't like that and he started making deals. I guess he wanted his own piece of the pie. Maybe I can't blame him. He and my girlfriend's father—Ariel's mother's father—cooked up some scheme out of the war."

"What war?"

" 'Nam. The Admiral had already figured out how to get rich, something about arms sales and procurements. Maybe some other exotic commodities, I don't know, don't want to know. Dad tried to lean on him. The Admiral slapped him down hard. Dad blamed me, for hanging out with the daughter. Accused me of trying to be better than him." Lowell finished his beer—an actual Kirin—and ordered another. "He was right about that part."

Croft smiled and said nothing, his eyes clouded over with

memories of his own. It was close to midnight when the two detectives said good night and headed for the door. Lowell was very careful not to fall over anything, or to walk into any walls.

Determined to stay awake, driven by an increasingly fuzzy sense of urgency to find Alicia before it was too late, he made one more futile sweep of Alto Street past the Salazar residence, saw no sign of her or of Lopez, managed to avoid a DUI arrest by driving with extreme caution, and made it safely back to his hotel room. There he paced until dawn, when he finally drifted off to a bed-tossing, tormented sleep.

SANTA FE
NOVEMBER 22, EARLY MONDAY MORNING

The bedside phone shattered Lowell's disturbed dreams like a hammer thrown through a stained-glass window. "Oh, God," was his first dread-filled thought: that it was Sergeant Ramirez, calling to tell him Alicia had been found with her throat cut in an arroyo. Please let it be Alicia, with some perfectly sensible explanation, he thought, groping for the receiver. Or maybe Croft, with some brilliant insight he'd forgotten to offer last night as to her elusive whereabouts. "Hello?" he growled, finally managing to get hold of the receiver.

It was Ariel, sounding frantic. "Dad!" she shouted. "Are you all right? I've been trying and trying to reach you. Where have you been?"

As guilt-ridden as an unfaithful lover, he crawled out of

bed, only to be staggered by the morning light. "I'm sorry, honey. I just got back last night and haven't checked my messages. What's up?"

"Nothing. I was just worried is all. How's she doing?"

There was no way, he realized, that he could tell Ariel that Alicia had been abducted from under his very nose. Not yet, at least. He felt exactly like a man should feel he'd failed in his mission, fallen to the allure of alcohol, probably abused his body in untold ways, and now had to pay the price. He realized he'd postponed calling Ariel for the express reason that he was terrified of what he would have to say to her, of what she was going to say at the bad news. "Listen," he said, stalling, "I'm only half awake. Can I call you back?"

"All right," she agreed reluctantly. "But hurry."

"I will." He hung up, cursing himself for avoiding the inevitable. He cold-showered himself awake, gulped a cup of instant coffee from the bedside thermos and, out of excuses, called her back. Taking a deep breath, he told her what had happened in Colorado. After she was done yelling at him, he apologized for messing up and allowed himself to commiserate with her for a while. He didn't know what to make of the Website she'd seen, but promised to check it out as soon as he could. He didn't tell her what he was going to have to do this day—there were limits to candor. They said their sorrowful good-byes and hung up. Then he got dressed in his last pair of clean slacks and shirt and went out to face the world. Or rather, he would face it as soon as he could find a decent cup of fresh coffee to purge the rancid aftertaste of the hotel-room instant, plus he wouldn't at all mind some more of those splendid sopapillas he was developing an alarming predilection for, not to mention a morning paper—although he was terribly afraid he was going to find a headline: "Missing Woman Found Murdered."

The weather looked threatening. Leaning against a gusting wind, he walked south along the Trail until he found shelter and sustenance at a nearby establishment called The Old Santa Fe Trail Coffee House and Bookstore. It was a restored Victorian house a few blocks south of the government center, with a great old train-station clock out front. They had the morning newspaper, which revealed nothing other than the standard seaminess of local politics anywhere. There was a sidebar about a planned demonstration by the DeVargas Compadres, the local "activist" group. Good for Peso, he thought. Beats mugging people. The sopapillas were fresh, so was the coffee, and he allowed himself a moment's respite from his troubles, watching the trendy-looking clientele come and go.

Hurrying back to his room, he found Roberto Sandoval's card and called the lawyer's office. Roberto answered in person.

"I have some information for you," said Lowell. "Let's make a trade."

"Trade what?"

"Lopez's first wife for his second."

There was a pause. "What the hell are you talking about?"

"Don't tell me you didn't know he'd been married before, Sandoval."

Another pause. "All right, pal," Roberto said grimly. "You name a place and I'll meet you there after work. Say six o'-clock. But you better have some evidence of what you're talking about."

Lowell named the only place he could think of, aside from Peso's Green Pepper hangout. "El Farol. Do you know it?"

"I know it," Roberto replied distastefully. "Up on Canyon Road."

"See you then."

"What is this—" Roberto began, but Lowell hung up before the lawyer could say anything more.

He had two, maybe three, stops to make before meeting with Roberto. There was a good chance he might not get past the first one.

13

The City Rec Center was open. This being Monday, the older children were in school. But even so, there were several Santa Fe school buses lined up outside and a large, unruly array of children tearing around the grounds, apparently aimlessly, unmindful of the deteriorating weather. Most were of preschool age, but some of them looked like they might be playing hooky.

Several young adults were attempting to maintain order. Apparently they were just setting out on some kind of field trip. Various grown-ups were dropping off their children, admonishing them to behave, tugging at clothing, zipping up rainwear or parkas, making sure they all had their backpacks and lunch boxes. Lowell could hear shouts in English and

Spanish, screams of young children, and a din of horns from cars trapped in the narrow driveway leading from the parking lot in the rear. He parked on the street a block away and walked back, to avoid the fray.

He approached the Rec Center slowly, skirting around the row of buses, keeping the gathered crowd between himself and the building. He didn't want to attract attention to himself, knowing it was possible that Danny Lopez knew him on sight, and kept as close to a group of parents as he could, smiling and nodding and waving as if another parent. He scanned the group of Rec Center employees near the lead bus and recognized Danny almost at once from Alicia's brief description, and realized he'd seen him before somewhere. Danny was standing by the bus door, sharing a joke with the driver. He was short, stocky, and muscular, and wore a cutoff T-shirt with the midriff ripped out. His black eyes were fierce and empty, but there was something about him. Appalled as he was that this man could ever have gotten a job working with children, Lowell could see how he might charm his way into marriage to two bright, lovely women.

"Jorge, Tomas, knock it off!" he heard Danny bellow at two young teens lurking by the side of the building. A freshly lit cigarette was quickly snuffed and the two sheepish boys hurried away.

"That Danny's great with the older boys," Lowell overheard one mother telling her friend. "Girls, too," said the friend. Lowell glanced at her, wondering at the lack of irony in her voice. There was more than parental admiration in her eyes as they swept over Danny's thick arms, his muscular legs.

Danny glanced in their direction, and Lowell stepped

back quickly, behind the nearest bus. Alicia's ex-husband seemed to hesitate, as though uncertain about something. Lowell felt as exposed as a negative to bright sunlight in an open camera. Danny's look moved on past where Lowell had been a moment before and lit on the two mothers. He grinned broadly and waved. They giggled and waved back. Then he was distracted by another parent, with an inquiry regarding the day's events. Lowell moved farther away into the shadows, pondering his next move, worried that Danny would get on board with the other teachers and aides. Sure enough, as the next bus pulled into the loading area, the driver opened the door and called out: "Lopez, you coming?"

Danny grinned and shook his head. "Not today, bro'. Got some work to do."

Lowell let out his breath slowly as the bus pulled out and the crowd of parents and caregivers dissipated. He saw his chance when the last bus pulled away full of waving, shouting kids and Danny Lopez walked alone toward the Rec building.

Grimly, his heart racing, Lowell followed his quarry into the big, vacant clubhouse.

The interior was dim and spacious, intended to accommodate large numbers of kids in a variety of activities. It smelled of sweat and disinfectant. There were banks of fluorescent lights overhead, only a few of which were on. Basketball backboards stood at either end, with gymnastic pads, a volleyball net, and tables laid out with arts-and-crafts supplies in the mid-court area. The hardwood floor was littered with forgotten backpacks, mittens, and other miscellaneous kid gear of every possible color and description.

Lowell couldn't see where Lopez had gone. The building

was semidark, empty, silent and melancholy, like a hollow concrete carcass, drained of life. He entered cautiously, watching all doorways as he approached them.

"Lopez! Danny Lopez?" Lowell shouted out. The great room echoed back at him, as though in mockery. He walked toward a row of offices built into the side of the building.

"You want something?" The voice was low, almost in his ear. Lowell spun, startled. Danny had come up behind him, moving like a raptor. Lowell hadn't even heard him. Danny stood grinning at him, for all the world like an old compadre, a smile devoid of warmth, but full of confidence. It was the voracious grin of a predator, readying for the kill, wielding a Louisville Slugger baseball bat. Lowell ducked just as the blow fell. Lopez had swung for his skull and barely missed— the bat glanced off Lowell's shoulder. But the follow-through threw Lopez off balance.

Despite the shock and pain, Lowell still had the presence of mind to use some of the skills the government had taught him so long ago to keep him alive in battle. He ducked in close before Lopez could recover and grabbed the bat while it was still on the backswing, stuck his foot behind Danny's knee and dropped him hard to the floor.

Lowell was on Lopez's back at once like a wrestler, surprised at the former athlete's softness and lack of basic street savvy. The man had gotten away with using brute force all his life. Intimidation and bullying were his specialties—especially toward women. He hadn't even bothered to keep in shape. Which didn't make him any less dangerous, because any puffy-cheeked little punk could easily blow away Arnold Schwarzenegger *and* Sly Stallone from a nice safe distance with only the slightest exertion applied to the trigger of a cheap gun.

"Where is she?" Lowell demanded, breathing hard in his ear.

"Fuck you," Lopez gasped, suddenly icy calm despite his predicament. He knew who Lowell was from the Cholos. His mistake had been that out of arrogance, he'd considered the interloper from back east no threat at all and had dismissed him altogether until just now.

"I think you know where she is. I want her back."

"Fuck you, man!" Lopez's muscles strained. "She's my wife. She ain't none of your fuckin' business!"

"Your *ex*-wife you mean. There's a huge difference." Lowell tightened his grip, matching Danny's calmness in tone, while feeling anything but calm.

Lopez strained his head to one side to look at him. "Hey, get off, man. I'll fuckin' kill you!"

"Then maybe I'd better stay put."

"You're the guy been lookin' for her. Fuck you want with her?" Danny whined, his voice rising.

"I'm a friend of hers. Unlike you. More to the point is what you want with her. Where is she?"

Danny struggled, his rage building. "Go to hell. I ain't seen her. And if I did, I sure as shit wouldn't tell you, asshole!"

Lowell used his superior weight to increase the pressure, using a hold that worked like Chinese handcuffs—the more Lopez struggled, the tighter it got. "I think you should," he said.

"Look, unless you got a death wish, you better get your ass off me before I kick it all the way to Taos, motherfucker!"

"I'll take that under advisement. Meanwhile, I'm going to ask you one more time what you've done with her."

"Eat shit. I ain't done nothin'. Anyways, my wife don't need you, and she don't need no seminars, and she don't need no trouble."

She's already got plenty of that, thought Lowell. "You mean your ex-wife," he reminded him.

Suddenly Danny twisted in the opposite direction, away from Lowell's weight, catching him off guard. He rolled free and was instantly on his feet. Lowell saw his hands rise and his jaw tighten. He wondered how many times Alicia had seen this same visage just before Danny assaulted her. He rose and moved into a defensive stance, cursing himself for his lack of vigilance. He readied himself, watching Lopez coil like a desert rattler about to strike.

Just then a young female voice called out from across the room: "Danny?"

A young, pretty, harried-looking woman came out of an office and hurried toward them. Danny saw her and dropped his hands quickly, giving Lowell a dark, warning look, his black eyes slits of antipathy. "I'm ready to be taken to lunch like you promis—" the young woman began, then stopped when she saw Lowell. "Oh!" she said.

"Hey, baby. Just tryin' out some aikido moves on this guy." Danny was suddenly loose and easy, his confidence restored. "Ready when you are." He looked at Lowell once more. "See you, man," he said. Then he dropped his voice like a gauntlet. "And when I do, you are road kill." He seized the girl by the waist, none too gently, and marched her to the exit. She smiled up at him admiringly, like she thought herself the luckiest girl in the world.

190

"Hey, Lopez!" Lowell shouted after them. "I thought you were a married man!"

Lopez's look promised death. The girl glanced at him doubtfully. "What's he mean, Danny?"

"Nothin'." Lopez seized her by the elbow and propelled her out the door. "He's just lookin' to get wasted."

The girl giggled.

Lowell watched them go, feeling a sense of apprehension for the young woman and a growing frustration at being stymied once again. Besides which, he was getting tired of being called road kill.

When Micaella Sandoval drove her sister up the canyon that Sunday afternoon, it was a harrowing escape. First that Anglo guy. Then right after he left, Danny had come over twice looking for Alicia, and their father had been much too friendly, even offering Danny a beer over both of his daughters' strenuous objections.

"What harm is there? I don't care what some Anglo's been sayin', he's still her husband in the eyes of Jesus," Manny had insisted. But then Danny had come back and hung out on Alto Street most of the afternoon, shouting Alicia's name drunkenly, ignoring Roberto's polite requests that he move on, while Peso stayed away, sleeping it off somewhere. That was when the two sisters decided they could wait no longer.

They had only a few hours to plan their departure. Just after Danny left the first time, Alicia came down from her room and told her sister she had to get out or she'd go crazy.

Micaella had reluctantly agreed and even suggested a

plan, but it was perilous. She had to make one phone call first . . .

Taking Alicia's single bag, they slipped out the back, cut through the *bosque* and crossed the nearly dry river on foot, finally getting into Micaella's car, which she'd parked on Alameda Street. They drove for a tense ten minutes up to St. Francis and south to the freeway on-ramp, watching the rearview mirror constantly, hearts in their mouths.

It was dusk when they arrived in Pecos and headed north up into the canyon. By the time they reached the cabin, the sun had set and darkness was closing in. The place looked abandoned.

Alicia felt anxious. "There's no one here!" she protested.

"She promised to be here," responded Micaella. "She probably just went into town for supplies." She was referring to their Tia Juanita, who lived down in the village and had been alerted.

Alicia hoped so. The cabin was small and primitive. Her father had built it many years ago for hunting and fishing and almost never used the place. As far as the sisters knew, Danny had never been here and didn't know about it. Far up in Pecos Canyon, it stood on the eastern side of the Sangres, on Federal land that was part of the Pecos Wilderness area of the Santa Fe National Forest. The good part was that it was well away from prying eyes. The bad part was that it was far from help, with no telephone.

At least there would be plenty of firewood available, thanks to the mining and timber companies and their practice of tearing out huge chunks of publicly owned national resources, selling them at an enormous profit, leaving tons of debris in their wake. Whatever else might be said about it, a lot of that debris made good firewood.

Micaella had noted with some concern, however, that the customary cord of split wood usually stacked by the door was nowhere in evidence. She'd have to speak to Tia Juanita about that, as soon as she could find her. She had no intention of allowing her sister to freeze, like the rushing Pecos River outside the door soon would do.

Micaella promised she would bring more food and provisions, and come back for her as soon as it was safe. Meanwhile, she'd go find Tia Juanita down in the village and make sure she came up here, and she'd have one of the Mendoza boys bring over some cut wood and other supplies.

"Cómo esta?" she'd asked her sister, placing her hand on Alicia's almost imperceptibly swollen stomach.

"Bien," Alicia had said. She had not, would not, think about the baby she carried: Danny's baby. She wanted it and hated it at the same time, and was afraid of what she might do. She believed a woman should choose, but shuddered at the thought of having to part with a baby—even Danny Lopez's baby. After all, she had loved him once, she admitted to herself with a certain degree of self-loathing. Micaella would have none of it, she knew. Micaella would insist she go straight to the clinic in Albuquerque. Micaella, above all, was a practical woman.

As Micaella prepared to leave, Alicia had been withdrawn and fatalistic. As though she sensed some impending doom over which she had no control, and could only accept. This was very unlike her, and Micaella couldn't help but feel worried as she drove away. It was bad for a woman to be alone anywhere in rural New Mexico. It was even worse to be pregnant without a man, and determined to have a baby away from her family—if not actually alone. Where was that damned Tia Juanita anyway? If she was out drinking with those lumbermen again—well, she'd teach her a thing or two! Micaella sped on down the canyon as night set in.

Alicia waited with growing apprehension until after dark. There was no sign of Tia Juanita and she began, for the first time, to feel afraid. What had she done? Hiding away like this, with no reliable help. What if something were to go wrong? What if Tia didn't come, and her sister couldn't get back for some time? Micaella had two children of her own. It was going to be difficult for her to help out. It was going to be difficult for them both.

Falling back on the strength and resourcefulness her prepioneer forebears were known for, Alicia resigned herself to her apparent fate and began preparations for the winter that was quickly coming. Because, she now knew, she might have to stay up here indefinitely. Although without Tia Juanita . . . she realized now how foolish it had been to depend on her aunt. Juanita was a notorious drinker, unfortunately much like her brother, Alicia's father. But the thought of going it alone was terrifying.

Her fear of Danny was palpable, although her sister had insisted that he would have no way of knowing she was here. The mountain slopes above her were gorgeous, as always, with brilliant white snow against green forests and a deep blue, sunlit sky. The cool temperatures were refreshing. The sight and sound of the rushing river were soothing, even energizing at times. Her energy was good, and her biggest problem would be finding enough to do. She would have to keep herself occupied.

She knew her parents would be asking for her, and would probably grill Peso and Micaella pretty hard. As for Danny . . . But she trusted her sister. Micaella was strong, she could take the heat. Or feign ignorance with the best of them, and shake them off. Alicia wished she could handle things so easily herself. Before Danny Lopez, she might have been able to. But not now. Not anymore.

Sunday night the temperature in the canyon dropped below freezing, and she hadn't lit the woodstove because the day had been in the sixties and lovely, and the stone fireplace had sufficed. She had fed it dead wood and paper scraps, and had spent the evening reading cozily by the fireside. She had almost felt romantic for a brief moment, which inevitably led to wishing for a companion. A certain person she'd recently met haunted the edges of her consciousness, the surfaces of her skin, all her senses, with a warmth that wasn't entirely external. But she couldn't think about him, or anyone else, just now. Not with what else would soon be stirring inside her, demanding attention.

The next day, Monday, the weather turned dark, cold, and threatening. Alicia found it difficult to get up in the morning, and knew something was wrong.

"Micaella?" she called anxiously. Juanita was still a no-show, and her sister had not returned like she'd promised. There must be trouble at home, something had delayed her. She sighed and got slowly out of bed, feeling very much out of sorts. She touched her stomach. It should be too soon to feel anything yet, other than the nausea and an occasional cramp-

195

ing. But those pains during the night and this morning worried her. She felt them again after she moved about, a little bit worse. She looked out the window, hoping for some sign of Juanita or her sister.

She could see through the gaps in the dirty muslin curtains that the sky was gray and threatening. Another early winter storm might be coming, unusual for this time of year, but then, nothing was as it should be, nothing was normal anymore. In any case, she would have to lay in some provisions. The seasons of Santa Fe were actually not very different from those in the north country, according to what she had read in those impossibly romantic novels she loved, which helped her to forget her troubles. Leaves changed—although mostly they were just the yellow aspens, no red or orange ones—snow fell, then came spring flowers and new leaves, and a hot, tempestuous summer, with sudden storms that came and went: short, fierce storms, like a lover without patience or skill, only brute force and quick, uncaring withdrawal. Like Danny, who never cared for her except as a possession.

The weather troubled her. It was unusual, and darkly portentous, that it should snow so early, and from the way the weather looked, might again soon. This somehow reminded her of her friend Ariel's dad, Tony Lowell, who had fought his way through an unseasonal snowstorm to reach her and gone to such trouble on her behalf, which she still couldn't understand. She thought about his crooked smile, his warm laugh, those flashing eyes that changed colors—she had to stop herself. This was not helping. It had all been so brief and strange, their short time together. What was it about him, then, that troubled her? Or was it her family, their reaction to him that

196

reinforced her fear of actually exercising her freedom of choice? She'd tried it their way, letting others make choices for her, such as with Danny, and look where it had gotten her.

As the cramps subsided, she became aware that she hadn't dressed yet and was shivering in her pink chemise. Why had she worn something like that on a November night, so thin and flimsy? She grabbed her white terry robe from the blue-painted wardrobe that came with the cabin and pulled it tightly around her. Hurrying to the now-diminished woodpile Micaella had left inside the door, she grabbed a couple of piñon logs—she'd have to gather more today—and tossed them into the stove, along with a small bundle of sticks from another pile. This was crazy, she told herself. What am I doing here?

Once more she looked out the window. The clouds were even darker now, sinister black billowing swirls, and she began to feel the canyon closing in on her. The silence was tangible, broken only by the occasional cry of a wild animal, hunting. Or dying. Last night she'd heard a great horned owl, and the piercingly lonesome howl of a coyote up in the forest. It had terrified her, so alone in the mountains like this. It was a double omen—both wild creatures were bad luck in local Indian lore. Especially the owl. She shivered again and lit the fire. Now for water. There was a well, and an electric pump, that provided water for the kitchen and bath. The cabin had power, so she need only worry about the lines coming down. At least this cabin had a real bathroom, with plumbing and everything. Her parents had been raised with no conveniences: a hand pump and an outhouse, and that was it. So this was luxury, and she shouldn't complain.

Once the water was boiling, Alicia whipped up some eggs

and sliced potatoes, put them in a frying pan with a pat of butter, and added the prerequisite red chilies. Then she ground some coffee beans with a hand grinder. The loneliness was palpable. She began to cry softly, tried to busy herself with chores to prepare for the storm that she knew was coming. She made her breakfast and ate it feeling the silence all around, in the canyon, in her soul. Once more she thought briefly of the man who'd come to rescue her, and once again drove such thoughts out of her mind. She didn't want to think about men just now. If ever again.

The pains recurred briefly, then eased up again, and she decided to go out while the weather held and gather some firewood in case Micaella or Tia Juanita were still delayed.

She had seen a number of suitable tree falls down by the river and thought she could manage to cut and gather some of the smaller limbs with the axe her father had left in the woodshed. Bundling up, she headed out into the frigid mountain air and across the empty road to the riverbank. Then, suddenly, she felt the sharp stab of pain again. Gritting her teeth, she cried out. Gasping, fighting off the pain and the fear that came with it, she stumbled back to the cabin, crawled into bed, and wept.

When Alicia Sandoval screamed, far from the hearing of any but the owls, coyotes, and birds, a psychic woman in Santa Fe named Emily Tartikoff heard her and immediately called her friend Christina Taylor, who instructed her to leave a message for Tony Lowell at the Inn at Loretto. Alicia's sister Micaella also felt her sister's distress somehow and knew something was wrong. Very wrong.

Micaella Sandoval had also been having strong second thoughts about the wisdom of her actions. She knew, perhaps better than Alicia, just how vindictive their brothers and father could be—even their mother and cousins—when their long-standing codes of conduct were violated. At least by a woman. They actually violated their own codes of conduct all the time—excepting Roberto—with their drunkenness, unfaithfulness, and tendencies toward violence. Still, when it came down to it, when it came down to what they would call family honor, they were unstoppable in their loyalty. They'd been asking about Alicia, suspicious at her most recent departure. Usually, Micaella was direct and matter-of-fact with them. They'd sensed something was amiss. She deliberated whether to tell at least one of her brothers. Maybe Roberto. He was the oldest and the most sensible. He was also the one most likely to listen. Furthermore, he had a truck, and she had promised to bring Alicia a load of firewood and provisions to Pecos Canyon, even though there was plenty of wood out there. Alicia shouldn't try to do any kind of heavy exercise anymore, and the weather was deteriorating by the hour. Maybe she'd better take her some more blankets, too, and a ski jacket. She hurried to the closet, and then to look for Roberto . . .

SANTA FE
MONDAY, NOVEMBER 22, 1:30 P.M.

Tony Lowell found a pay phone, got out the Yellow Pages and looked up the jewelry resale shop Thomas Royster had told him about, the Santa Fe Jewelry Exchange. He found it and dialed the listed number.

"Santa Fe Jewelry Exchange. How can I help you?" The voice was pleasant, a slightly effete-sounding man with an Hispanic accent.

"Do you buy estate jewelry, that sort of thing?"

"We do indeed, sir. Do you have something you'd care to sell or consign?"

"No, I'm looking for some particular items. Do you keep track of the origins of various pieces?"

"Yes, sir. We do occasionally get people who are looking for specific heirlooms and so forth from certain estates or sources. What did you have in mind?"

"I'll tell you when I get there. Who'm I speaking with?"

"This is Rafael, sir. I'll be glad to—"

But Lowell was already out the door.

Before starting the car, he checked the city map and located Cordova Road. The Jewelry Exchange was a nondescript yellow-block building with a discreet wooden sign mounted on the corner of Cordova Road, just behind a gas station facing St. Francis Street. Lowell parked in front and went in.

The interior looked like a small museum, its shelves lined with mostly Spanish knickknacks, icons, Madonnas, and other bric-a-brac. There was also a large, locked glass case in the back. Rafael met him at the door. He was tall, slender, and wore Buddy Holly horn-rimmed glasses. "Are you the gentleman who called?" he asked.

"That's right. I'm looking for something that might have been sold or consigned a few years ago."

"That's a long time, sir."

"Yes. That was why I was hoping you might keep records and be able to check."

Rafael frowned. "Do you have a name, sir? Or a list? Anything by which to trace—"

"I have both." Lowell handed him the list he'd gotten from Mrs. Cortez.

Rafael glanced at it. "Some of it does look familiar. What was the consignor's name?"

"Lopez. Daniel Lopez."

Rafael frowned slightly and looked at him doubtfully. "Are you a police officer?"

"Not exactly." Lowell had stopped at an ATM and gotten a fresh supply of twenties, delving into deficit financing. He sacrificed one now, along with one of his tattered business cards. "I'm on an investigation. I'd appreciate any help you can provide."

Rafael looked dubious, but working as he did for little more than the minimum wage, he accepted the money. "All right, sir. I'm not the owner, so I have to do this on my own time. But if you'll come back around five, that's when we close, I'll be able then to look into the files."

"I'd appreciate it," said Lowell.

14

The Green Pepper Bar on St. Michael's Drive was the last place Tony Lowell wanted to be just now, especially after his bender the night before with Croft. He stopped at Furr's and bought some aspirin and an antacid, hoping for anything that might distract him from thoughts of Alicia. It didn't work. He could think of little else.

Two blocks away in the Green Pepper, the Cholos were gathering. Their leader, Peso Sandoval, was worried. He'd come here trying to defuse some of the very tensions he himself had recently been stirring up in the community. He cared about his sisters, and brother, and their feelings. He knew he had a tendency to go overboard with righteous anger at times. Which wasn't helped by his alcohol problem. His father had the same problem, and hadn't been a very good influence on him growing up, he realized. Always a six-pack after a haul from the Jemez or Pecos Wilderness. Always a *tinto* during family dinners, from the vineyards up at Pojoaqui, always a whiskey when gathered with the hombres.

Peso was worried about his sister Alicia, who had up and disappeared again. He loved her plenty, but he couldn't understand her. He knew that she, in her own way, was even more a rebel than he was. But she was always making a fuss about women's issues, making a big deal about her personal problems—particularly with Danny—until he'd gotten into the habit of just ignoring her. When she'd complained about that priest touching her, as a child, the family had forgiven her for just being a misguided, mistaken girl; but all that yelling and screaming about Danny was out of line as far as he was concerned. He'd known Danny Lopez since high school. They'd run together, drunk *cervezas* together, hung out, fooled with cars and girls. He couldn't believe Danny would ever hurt anybody—not really. Not even when Danny had tried to convince Los Compadres to buy AK-47s and militia gear. If he lost his temper once in a while, that was one thing. But his sister could be a pain, he knew.

Danny had his own side to their fights, and if Alicia got a black eye once in a while, well, maybe she pushed a little too hard or something. Maybe she deserved it. He, Peso, had had to put a woman back in line himself once or twice. It was necessary sometimes for men to do that when women got too crazy. His own father—but wait, did he remember his father ever actually hitting his mother? No, he decided. If he'd ever seen *that* happen, he'd probably have beaten the old man senseless.

But now, what was Alicia's problem? She'd seemed so

scared when she came home for those brief few hours—scared to be home, scared not to be home. She'd seemed lonely, and afraid, and whatever ill thoughts he'd had toward her over the years had vanished like an Indian summer before a winter storm. For the first time, for reasons he couldn't face up to yet, he felt afraid for her.

Danny had actually called him a couple times last week, asking about Alicia, where she was, when she would be back. Something about it being time for his wife to come home to start a family. That hadn't sat right with Peso. Danny might be his friend, but Alicia had asked for a divorce—no easy thing for a Hispanic woman in New Mexico to do. And it had been on grounds of cruelty. The family had mostly assumed hysteria on her part, except for their mother, Theresa, who had said: "If my daughter says she's been hurt, she's been hurt. And I won't stand for her staying married to a man who hurts her."

Peso, Manny, and Roberto had given up trying to argue. Roberto had finally offered Alicia his legal services, which she had turned down in favor of a woman lawyer, and Manny and Peso had shrugged and returned to their work. Theresa had comforted her daughter as best as she could, and the family had done their best to hold their heads high and go about their business.

As a result of Alicia's disturbing disappearance yesterday, however, Peso announced that for today's meeting he was abstaining from alcohol. This led to much amusement and derision from his friends the Cholos and the younger members of the Compadres, but he let it slide.

Today's meeting was supposed to be about the possibility of creating a disturbance during the next Fiesta. Something to frighten the *turistas* and get the attention of the city fathers.

Peso, who had presented an elaborate plan of the whole thing, was too distracted to lead the discussion, in addition to his having some second thoughts. He still wanted to go ahead with it, but with some precautions. Perhaps they should just stage an event—all show—just to scare people, not to cause any real harm to anybody.

But now, one of the most militant Cholos, Carlos, seemed to want to bring a halt to the whole thing. "Something happened the other night, man, that's gonna put the heat on," he said. "I don't think we should do it." Peso glanced over at him. He'd heard something around town about it, but hadn't paid attention. Maybe he should have. "There was this *turista*, down at the plaza, went to one of those money machines."

"An ATM," corrected Jaime from where he was sucking on a Budweiser over at the bar. Jaime'd had his head shaved and was having second thoughts about that as much as anything.

"Whatever, man," snapped Carlos in annoyance.

"Go on. What happened?" Peso was irritated by the intrusion on his thoughts, but also worried about how his plans were coming apart.

"Somebody shot the dude and took his money, man. The cops been all over the barrio."

"They're blaming us, is that it?" Peso was suddenly alert and apprehensive. Of course the Compadres would get blamed, unless the D.A.s could pin it on one of the gangs.

"The guy who did it was Latino. Some people saw him. The press is gonna make us look like another Miami, with us as the bad guys."

Peso frowned. He wondered who might have done something like that. He didn't like some of the answers that came to mind. One in particular, who had been using inflammatory rhetoric for months about taking back the land, taking back the plaza. The Fiesta "incident" was going to be their first overt political act. This robbery and shooting thing wasn't political, though. It was a crime. Unfortunately, with the press, too often the tactics and motives got blurred. Thin lines were crossed in terms of what was a political act and what wasn't. But he was damned if he was going to take the rap for somebody else's crimes.

"Maybe he had a good reason," suggested Marta, a tough, second-generation low-rider and, as usual, the only woman in attendance. "Maybe he was *pobre*, maybe the guy at the ATM was *rico*, that's justice."

"That kind of talk will get us put in jail," complained Carlos. "The cops are pissed, the mayor is pissed, Chamber of Commerce is pissed, and we're gonna get blamed."

"I agree with Carlos," another Cholo, Mickey, spoke up. Mickey, with green eyes and red hair, claimed direct descent from the Castilians of Conquistador fame, whose coloring he shared. "We gotta cancel the thing at the Fiesta, man. We ain't no Michigan militia, and we don't want another thing like Oklahoma City."

"Most of the Santa Fe cops are our people," pointed out Jaime.

"No matter," snapped Peso. "They work for the city. The city is one big tourist and development economy, fuck what the mayor says. Whatever else, it'll totally undermine our goals of getting Santa Fe back for *los originales*."

"You mean *los Indios*," interjected a gruff voice over by the bar. "They were here first."

"Fuck that too," snapped Peso irritably, lighting a Marl-

206

boro and staring out at the street. He didn't want to get into that issue just now. *"We* conquered this place and built the city, man. DeVargas built this fuckin' city."

"So anyway," said Carlos, "we don't need no fucking riot. And we may need some better fucking lawyers." He gave Peso a meaningful look. "Like, where's that fucking brother of yours, man?"

Peso knew that Carlos was right. His own mother had tried to teach him, and sometimes he'd even listened, that violence only begot violence. His brother Roberto had learned that long before, which was why he'd become a lawyer. Maybe one of these days he'd start listening to his big brother. Maybe. But meanwhile, there was this problem with his sister Alicia. There was something about that girl that stirred up trouble. And now this Anglo. And Danny. He finally had to admit to himself that he was going to have to do something about Danny . . .

His troubled reverie was interrupted by the shrill ringing of his cell phone. He pulled the compact Nokia unit out of his pocket and checked the caller I.D. readout.

"It's my brother," he told Carlos. "Speaking of el Diablo!" He pushed the enter button. *"Qué pasa?"* he demanded, and listened. Peso glanced around the room, and his eyes fell on the stranger at the bar who'd mentioned los Indios. He did a classic double take. The patron was Tony Lowell. "Holy shit!" he shouted. "He's here!" He pointed an accusing finger at Lowell, while trying to listen to his brother at the same time. All heads pivoted in Lowell's direction. "No, bro', I don't think—no, I don't know, man! I'll call you back!" He punched off the phone and faced Lowell in outrage. "You!" he shouted. "Fuck you doing here?"

207

"Hey!" chirped Marta. "It's the crazy gringo photographer dude from Florida."

"Hello," said Lowell, with smiles for one and all. "I'll take a coffee," he told the gaping bartender.

"You are one crazy motherfucker!" Peso shouted at Lowell, striding over to him. "I can't believe you got the gall to show your face in here!"

"It's like the man once said: 'Let us remember that if we suffer tamely a lawless attack upon our liberty, we encourage it, and involve others in our doom.' Samuel Adams."

"Who the fuck's that?"

"Some beer-brewer guy, dick head," cut in Jaime.

"A radical dude, kind of like you all," Lowell told them. "He was one of the fathers of our country."

"You mean *your* country, Anglo."

Lowell shrugged and put a fiver on the bar for the coffee. "Anyway, once again, I'm looking for your sister."

"You don't know when to quit, do you?" snarled Peso.

"Nope," said Lowell. "By the way, I met your brother-in-law."

Peso stared. "You did what?"

"Down at the City Rec Center. Real nice dude."

Peso glared. "Yeah, right." He pulled out a pack of Marlboros and lit one. The other Cholos gathered around, full of curiosity. "He know you were messing with his wife?" He asked this with what Lowell recognized as real menace.

"I really wish people would stop referring to her as his wife. She got a divorce, whether he likes it or not. And I was not 'messing' with her."

"He kick your butt?" Marta wanted to know.

"No," said Lowell. "We had a friendly conversation."

"Sure," said Peso. "Just like you and me now. And I don't know about him, but I'm gonna hurt you, man!"

"You and he must be close," said Lowell. "You think alike."

Peso snorted a stream of smoke out through his nose, like an angry bull, and jumped to his feet, fists raised. "C'mon. Let's go. Right now!"

Ignoring the fists, Lowell glanced at the Compadres as they began to close in. "Quitting time comes when the job is done," he said without moving, inventing the aphorism on the spot. "But the thing of it is, I think I was wrong about your former Compadres buddy Danny abducting Alicia the other night."

"You gonna fight or not?"

"I'll pass. I don't like the odds, plus it's a little juvenile. Have a seat, I'll buy you a beer."

Peso stared at him for a long moment, threw up his hands, shook his head in exasperation, and sat down again. Carlos waved off the troops. Some of them looked like they were getting sick of being waved off. "Man," Peso said, "I don't get you at all." He took a long draw on his Marlboro, trying to regain his cool, and blew the smoke at Lowell, as though in compensation for not getting to hit him.

Lowell ignored the insult. "You know what I think? I think the one who went up there and grabbed her was you."

Peso looked strangely nervous considering that he was flanked by half a dozen of his toughest sidekicks. He tromped out his cigarette on the floor. "Yeah? What makes you think so?"

Lowell looked at the cigarette. "Marlboros, right?"

"Say what?"

"How else would you know I was with her? So where is she? Wherever it is, she's not safe. If it's anywhere near Santa Fe, he's going to find her."

Peso turned away and put his hands to his head, his rage turning to despair. He shook his head like a horse shaking off a fly and let out a loud sigh. "Okay. Fine. You do what you want to, Anglo. But leave me out of it. I don't have a clue where she is, anyways."

"You expect me to believe that? She told me you took the call. You have caller I.D. on your phone there. You picked up the number of where she was and tracked her down, probably by calling the number back. They'd have answered with the name of the motel and been more than happy to give you the location. Am I close? Plus, you left butts lying all over the place. All you smokers litter too much."

Peso glanced at the butt he'd just stomped out on the floor as though he wished it was Lowell, and flushed. He threw his buddies a warning look, took Lowell aside and dropped his voice. Lowell recognized the low whisper. He'd heard it twice before. "Okay, so I went up there. You're lucky I didn't shoot you for messing with my sister, asshole."

"Why didn't you?"

Peso hesitated for a long moment, glanced over his shoulder and looked embarrassed. "She wouldn't come home if I had."

Lowell suddenly understood. Alicia had intervened to protect him from her brother! She might also have given in, just longing for her Mama. That would explain why there was no ruckus, no resistance, only a few harsh whispers, then soft voices speaking in low, reasonable tones. Anything else would surely have awakened him, tired as he was. The realization was humiliating. It also cast Peso in a whole new light.

"Plus," added Peso, "I don't carry a gun. Especially across state lines. Not that I recognize what you call 'states.' "

"So you took her home. Where is she now?"

"That's just it," Peso replied with a look of frustration. "I don't know! She took off the same day, after you came over. She's crazy, man!"

"Danny's the crazy one."

Peso shook his head, unable to deal with it.

"Peso, help me out here. Alicia needs someone she can rely on, someone who will stand by her, and you're supposed to be her family."

Peso lit another cigarette, then stubbed it out at once.

"Yo, Peso," Marta called out from across the room. "You gonna kick his butt or what? He slept with your sister, man!"

"Shut up, Marta. I'm talking here."

Lowell went to the door and looked out. Nobody stopped him. It was getting dark outside, and the wind was starting up again. He glanced at his watch. It was almost five. "I've got to go," he said. "You think it over and let me know."

Suddenly there was a new presence in the room. All heads turned toward a place directly behind Lowell as he reached for the door handle. There was a strange silence, and the room crackled with electricity as Lowell sensed, before he saw, that someone had come up behind him. He turned and found himself once again face-to-face with Danny Lopez.

As before, Lopez moved first, brutally and swiftly, with a low, guttural snarl: "You ain't going nowhere, Anglo!" The quick right caught Lowell off guard and struck him on the side of the head. He reeled, and the Cholos let out a gleeful yell. Peso stepped aside, as though unsure where he stood. Then the knife appeared out of nowhere—a very ugly, serrated switch blade knife. Just as Danny flew at Lowell with murder in his eyes, Peso reached out and knocked the knife from his hand. With a shout of rage at the betrayal, Danny twisted away and cursed him, then resumed his attack on a still-stunned Lowell with his fists. Lowell managed to fend off the first few blows, but several more struck home and he staggered back against the wall.

Just then the tavern door flew open and the dark barroom was flooded by a brilliant flash of light. Everyone froze and all eyes turned to the door. Peter Herrera stood in the entry with a press photographer, who'd caught the action and was still busy snapping away. There were two policemen right behind them, guns drawn.

"All right, nobody move!" shouted the first cop, stepping forward. He was a little slow. Danny Lopez had already moved big time and taken off the way he had come, out through the kitchen, the elusive broken-field runner of yesteryear once again. Everyone else stood dazed into motionlessness by the flashgun.

"Fuck," muttered Peso. "What's this shit?"

"You want to introduce us, Lowell?" Herrera asked. "This might be a good a time."

"I don't think so," said Lowell as the first cop ran into the kitchen after the departed Danny Lopez. The cop was large and lumbering, and it was no contest. Lopez was long gone.

"Next time, try covering the rear," suggested Lowell. The second cop ignored him, turned away and spoke in low tones over his police radio.

Lowell wiped the blood from a cut on his lip, shrugged off the effect of the punches and met Herrera's worried look with a wry grin. "Peso Sandoval, meet Peter Herrera," he said, nodding toward the reporter.

Peso glared at Peter. "I've read your articles. What do you want?"

"Just an autograph," said Herrera. "Then maybe an interview."

"Listen up, you people!" the second cop shouted at the room. "We have a warrant for the arrest of Daniel Lopez. Anybody withholding information or found to be harboring a fugitive will be subject to arrest!"

"We're just along for the ride," explained Herrera.

The first cop returned, shaking his head.

"You're a little slow on the draw there, pardner," said Peso sarcastically. "What you want him for?"

"The ATM," hissed Carlos. "What I been trying to tell you!"

"What are the charges?" Lowell asked.

The second cop, seemingly furious that his quarry had escaped so easily, waited until the uproar subsided. "The murder of his wife, Amanda Cortez!"

The uproar redoubled, until finally the room fell silent as though all shock and surprise had worn off, leaving heads shaking in dismay and disbelief. Peso looked dazed.

Lowell glanced at his watch. "Well, it's been fun, but I've gotta go," he said. The first cop grabbed his shoulder. "Nobody leaves."

"I'm a licensed investigator on the same case. Check with Sergeant Ramirez, he'll vouch for me," Lowell told him optimistically. The second cop squinted at him dubiously, got on his police radio and stepped back outside, leaving an out-matched partner holding the entire room at bay.

The second cop returned in a minute. "All right, beat it," he told Lowell. "But don't—"

"Yeah, I know, don't leave town," Lowell finished for him, and headed out the door.

Outside in the parking lot, he heard footsteps hurrying behind him and turned around. It was Peter Herrera.

"Wait up!" called the reporter. "Where are you going?"

"To see a lawyer," Lowell muttered, ignoring Peso, who glared after him. "I'll call you later." He left Herrera standing on the sidewalk, utterly confused.

Lowell reached the Jewelry Exchange at ten past five. The parking lot was empty but for a single car, an aging brown Toyota Corolla. He went to the door and knocked. There was no answer. He knocked again. "Rafael?" he called. He tried the door and found it unlocked. That worried him. Slowly, cautiously, he pushed the door open and entered the store. The lights were off. The single large room was dark and silent, except for a strange, soft, tapping noise somewhere near the back.

"Hello?" he called once more. Checking the aisles one by one, nerves on full alert, he worked his way to the rear of the building, moving with increasing caution, watchful of the dark corners and hidden spaces behind the display cases, not knowing what to expect. The tapping noise was unnerving. "Rafael? Anybody here?" He finally found the source of the noise—a portable heater with a small piece of paper stuck in the blower, tap-tap-tapping against the wire enclosure that covered the fan blades. He bent down to remove the paper with a sigh of relief.

Then he saw something out of the corner of his eye. He straightened up abruptly, his skin crawling. A file cabinet nearby stood with its drawers wide open, a smattering of yellow file folders strewn across the floor. Just beyond it, a large jewelry case lay overturned near the back wall. "Oh, no," he muttered. Jewelry was scattered helter-skelter everywhere, and from the amount he'd seen earlier, a lot was missing. The intruder had no doubt grabbed what he could and left in a hurry.

Rafael lay on the floor next to the jewelry case in a spreading pool of blood, the remains of old antique necklaces and bracelets strewn around him. He looked peaceful, his sport coat and dress slacks still neat and tidy. But the third eye in his forehead glared at Lowell with a look of eternal rage and betrayal.

"God damn it!" Lowell muttered. Kneeling by the body, he checked for a pulse, knowing there was none. "Shit," he swore. "I'm sorry, man. I'm sorry. I wouldn't have asked you to get involved if I'd known." But he also knew that this wasn't the first time something like this had happened. He had not forgotten his cousin Elliot, the museum curator back in Palm Coast Harbor years before. He'd asked him for a favor that time as well—with dreadfully similar results.

Lowell felt a surge of rage at himself and at the police for once again being one step too slow on the bloody trail of Danny Lopez, which may well have been what cost Rafael his life. Pulling himself together, he quickly searched through the scattered files. They were of various store records: receipts, accounts receivable, and consignments. It was one of the latter that caught his eye, lying some distance from the others, near the back wall. He used a tissue from his pocket to pick up the folder. It was labeled: "Consignments: D. Lopez." It was dated five years back, and then again, a new date, three years ago. The file was empty. Wishing he had his camera, he knew there was no time to go get it. He carefully replaced the file, backed away to the desk, picked up the store telephone with the tissue and called 911.

"I'm calling from the Santa Fe Jewelry Exchange on Cordova Road," he told the dispatch operator. "There's been a robbery and a homicide." He hung up quickly. Taking great care not to touch anything else, he checked the door and street outside for anyone coming. He knew that if he remained on the scene and waited for the cops, they'd have a lot of questions for him. From experience, he knew he wouldn't like the questions and they wouldn't like the answers. Offering Rafael a final and apologetic farewell salute, he wiped the door handle of prints and left the premises.

15

MONDAY, NOVEMBER 22
SANTA FE, 5:45 P.M.

Darkness crept over the crest of the Jemez Mountains, enveloped Los Alamos and poured down into the Rio Grande Valley. Like a relentlessly advancing army, it marched eastward, overtook Santa Fe and climbed swiftly up the mountainsides on the western slopes of the Sangres, allowing one final volley of fire as the setting sun dipped behind the snow-capped peaks and then was gone.

A tired and troubled Micaella Sandoval left the big Furr's supermarket at dusk carrying two large shopping bags. Her children, Alexis and Lupe, whom she knew she'd been neglecting of late because of this business with her sister, had been clamoring for Christmas cookies, and she'd promised to bake them over the weekend, which had come and gone. And now she was late with her promised supplies to Alicia as well, and increasingly worried about the wisdom of the plan she had made for her sister's escape. Plus, her own larder was low on staples.

Micaella loaded the bags in the back of her four-by-four wondering how she'd let the day slip away and how she was going to get out to Pecos Canyon and back in time for dinner. And there was another thing. She'd promised to bring Tia Juanita a couple of cardboard boxes so she could send her annual Christmas packages to relatives farther south. She hesitated and checked her watch. She remembered that the markets usually stacked empty cartons in the alley behind the store. Since she was here, she may as well go around back and pick up a couple. Better now while she thought of it—it would save her a trip later on.

The alley behind the big supermarket was abandoned, but as she drove around back, she saw the pile of boxes in the beam of her headlights, stacked around an overflowing Dumpster. Pulling up next to the Dumpster and leaving the engine running, she got out, braced herself against the wind, and picked through the pile for one or two boxes that weren't wet or damaged. She didn't hear the Camaro as it eased slowly into the alley behind her, headlights off, blocking her exit. So intent was she on getting the job done that she didn't notice either as the car door quietly opened, the man got out and walked up softly behind her.

"Hey, *cunada,* what's happening?" As she spun around with a startled cry, he hit her in the stomach and knocked her breath away before she could scream. Then he began to hit her systematically: sharp blows to her face, her head, and her neck. "Okay, Micaella," he grunted after a while, stopping to catch his breath. "Don't make me work for this. Where is she?"

It was past six o'clock and the holiday "Happy Hour" was already well under way when Lowell managed to park the Buick on Canyon Road and elbow his way into El Farol. He regretted his choice at once: the place was packed and the din was horrendous. Roberto Sandoval sat alone at the best table for four in the restaurant area, despite the line of waiting patrons. He was talking to someone on a cell phone. He spotted Lowell and waved him over, uttered a quick "later" into the phone and ended the call.

Lowell shook Roberto's hand as he sat down, and accepted a menu from the waiter without glancing at it. He and Sandoval faced each other across the table, sizing one another up, both aware of a gap between them as wide as the continent that separated their lives and backgrounds.

Lowell ordered a Santa Fe Ale. "I appreciate your coming up here," he said. "We've got a problem."

Roberto shrugged. "You mean you've got a problem." He turned and gazed out the window. "You should have come at Christmas time." He gestured at the street outside. "The *farolitos* are all lit up. They're these charming little Christmas candles in brown paper bags. Makes the city look like a giant birthday cake."

"I've seen them."

Roberto was visibly uncomfortable as he tried to talk over the din in the room while maintaining a modicum of privacy. "So. You've met Danny Lopez." It was a statement, not a question. He ignored the waiter. "A troubled young man."

"There's a warrant out for his arrest. They're looking for him now."

219

Roberto raised his eyebrows. "What for?"

"Don't you mean 'What for this time?'" Roberto only shrugged. "What for is murder one," Lowell answered. "And I'm worried that he's starting to make it a habit."

Roberto lost his smooth demeanor and put both of his hands on the table in front of him, as though to keep them where he could see them. "You realize the gravity of what you're saying?"

"I think he's just killed a witness who had evidence that might connect him to the murder of his first wife."

Roberto shook his head as though to clear it. He sat forward abruptly. "Would you say all that again?"

"Surely you knew about Danny Lopez's first wife?"

Roberto looked confused by the question. "I don't know where you're getting all this! His first wife ran off, he told us all about it. So what was all that about a witness?"

"I'll get to that, Mr. Sandoval. Since you seemed familiar with Mr. Lopez's activities this morning, maybe you know where he's been this afternoon."

"Not at all. I heard about your running into Lopez from my secretary. She knows the girl he's dating."

"Lucky her," said Lowell sarcastically.

Roberto bristled, then resumed his calm again. "Get to the point, Mr. Lowell."

Lowell dug into his jacket pocket and pulled out a rolled-up manila envelope. He slid it across the table. "Maybe you should have your secretary enter these into your file, if you have one, on the activities of your recent brother-in-law."

Roberto glared at him, then at the envelope. He opened it and shook out freshly made copies of the newspaper articles Lowell and Peter Herrera had dug up. Robert looked at them,

220

then looked again more closely. His face turned dark. "Where did you get these?"

"What difference does that make? They're legitimate. They're about his first wife, Amanda Cortez. As of today, Danny is wanted for her murder."

"How is it I've never heard any of this?"

"Good question, though I'm not surprised. She's been dead for years."

Roberto scowled. "You'd better explain."

"Her remains were found in a cave up in the mountains. With her skull cracked open. So Danny didn't mention that to your sister? Or to you? Funny thing about that."

Roberto pursed his lips. "Tell me about your meeting with Lopez this morning."

Lowell grinned. "I wouldn't say we 'met,' exactly. More like 'encountered.' He tried to knock my head off. He didn't succeed, but I have reason to think he's a bad loser."

Roberto just looked at him and blinked. "Are you implying I'm involved with Daniel Lopez in some way?"

"Not at all, except by former marriage. In any case, I think," Lowell continued, "he had lunch with your secretary's friend, did who knows what-all with or without her, then went and took out all his little frustrations on someone else. Some one who could link him to the death of his wife, Amanda Cortez."

Roberto stared at him for a while, as though processing the information, then took a deep breath and nodded. "You mean this witness you mentioned?"

"Yes. A clerk at the Santa Fe Jewelry Exchange. I called it in fifteen minutes ago."

Roberto flipped open his cell phone. "Excuse me a

minute." He punched a preset number on auto-dial and spoke quickly in low tones, in Spanish. He listened, raised his eyebrows and gave Lowell a look of revised appraisal. Then he hung up and expelled a long, tired sigh. "You are right. I can believe it of him now. Someone did such a thing, and if Danny had a reason, he could do it." He scrutinized Lowell some more. "Mr. Lowell, if you have information crucial to one or more murder investigations here in New Mexico, you may want a lawyer of your own. And it can't be me."

"Can't? Or won't? Assuming I did."

"Can't. I'm a business and government-law attorney. You want a criminal attorney." He offered Lowell a card. "Here's a colleague of mine with an excellent reputation."

Lowell put the card in his pocket without looking at it. "Let's get back to Danny Lopez. One thing that came out of our little discussion is that I got the distinct impression he doesn't know where Alicia is. That's the good news."

Roberto nodded slowly. "I think I've had about enough good news from you for one day," he said.

"I also talked to your brother, who also tried to knock my head off. There's a regular line forming up out there. But I still don't know whether your sister Alicia is alive or dead. Which leaves me about where I started from."

"I thought that was Florida."

Lowell gave him a grudging salute and waved for another beer. He could feel the tension still present around him from his recent encounters with Danny, Peso—and death. "Roberto," he said. "May I call you Roberto?"

"*Por supuesto.* Of course."

"Good. Do you mind if I ask you a question, Roberto?"

"I may or may not answer, but go ahead. Coffee, please," he called to the waiter in a resigned tone of voice.

"Do you or do you not know where your sister Alicia is?"

"I'm not prepared to say."

"So why did you agree to see me, then?"

Roberto laughed. "Just to get you off my back, maybe."

"Sure. You're the lawyer. That's your job, getting people off other people's backs. Unless it's maybe putting them on."

Roberto nodded, acknowledging the nuances. "I'm also Alicia's brother. Believe it or not, Mr. Lowell, we care a lot about her. We were all blinded by Danny's charms, I'll admit that. But he's out of her life now. I have every reason to believe she's safe at this moment."

"Until he finds her again."

Roberto scowled. "If she wants to talk to you, I assume she knows where to find you."

"Maybe she's not free to do so."

Roberto hesitated. With a scowl, he flipped open his cellular phone again and hit another code button. "Peso? *Es* Roberto." He glanced doubtfully at Lowell, then turned half away. "Yes, I'm with him now. What the hell's this about you and Mr. Lowell and Danny Lopez?"

There was some noise on the other end of the line. Roberto listened patiently. Lowell ordered another Santa Fe Ale, changed his mind and switched to coffee. The fatigue was getting to him again. Roberto launched into a long, heated conversation on the cell phone, still in Spanish. He hung up and looked at Lowell.

"You always make this many friends everywhere you go, Mr. Lowell?"

"I usually stay home."

"My brother is under the impression you've been sleeping with our sister." Roberto looked at Lowell, his dark eyes penetrating. "Is that true?"

"Is that what he said?"

"Is it true?"

Lowell shook his head. "Believe what you want, but no. She called me from Colorado and I went up to where she was. We talked most of the night. Sleeping with her, or with any woman in her emotional state, would be the most inappropriate thing I could think of. Attractive though she may be."

Roberto nodded slowly. "I believe you. Sorry I mentioned it, but as I said, Peso has other ideas. Bottom line is, he still wants to kick your butt."

"He's already tried, remember? And how about you?"

"Me, I just don't want to see her get messed over anymore."

"Too bad you didn't feel that way five years ago when she married Lopez."

Roberto's eyes blazed. Then he nodded. "Okay, one for you. My family is still pretty old-fashioned. Especially our parents. The thing is, maybe they know they messed up by throwing her to Danny. I don't think you can blame them for not wanting to make the same mistake again. Now what's this about murder?"

"So they're keeping her prisoner?"

"I didn't say that."

Lowell leaned toward him. "Maybe your family thinks they can protect her from further violence, although the way Peso's acting, I'm not so sure. If you are keeping Alicia against her will, then you are no better than her former husband. As a lawyer, you should know that, Mr. Sandoval."

Roberto looked uncomfortable. "Look, I don't even know where she is at this moment. But I think Micaella does, and maybe Peso. I think they're going to use whatever means necessary to protect her now. Furthermore, if I have to, I will get a doctor's certification to keep her out of harm's way, Mr. Lowell."

"No doctor's going to stop Danny Lopez. He's presumably armed and dangerous, and a wanted man, although he may not know it yet. I saw him before the warrant was issued. He's been wanting to get his hands on Alicia for a long time. My experience with people like him is that when you put their hand in the fire, they tend to react fast. The heat's on, for him. And I think he's going to do everything he possibly can to get to her before they get him. So unless you can guarantee her safety, you'd better hope I find her before he does."

Roberto blinked and looked around the room nervously. "This is crazy. Anyway, they never went after him too hard before."

"Who?"

"The cops." Roberto looked away as he said it, gazing at the fresco on the nearest wall.

"So you knew about all the beatings."

Roberto threw up his hands. "Look, I admit there have been some bad calls for her. But if they're after Danny, they'll get him. I really think she'll be safe now."

"I'd really like to believe you. But she never was safe before. And you just said they never went after him very hard. Tell me something else. What kind of dowry did your family kick in for Alicia's wedding?"

Roberto looked startled. "Dowry?"

"Yes. Isn't that part of an old-fashioned, Old World wedding? The bride gets a dowry—or rather, her family hands one over to the bridegroom?"

Roberto shifted uncomfortably. "I can't answer that. That's private and confidential family business."

"All right. Then I'll tell you something."

"I have a feeling I'm going to wish you wouldn't." Lowell figured the din would cover their conversation pretty well, so he told Roberto about Amanda's missing jewels.

"Sweet Jesus." Lowell could see the wheels turning behind those dark eyes. He could tell that Roberto didn't like the looks of the images that were popping up. Roberto flipped open his cell phone once again and dialed a number. "Get me Sergeant Ramirez," he barked.

This, thought Lowell, ought to be good. Again, the ensuing conversation took place in Spanish, but he recognized a few words. Among them were *"esposa," "joyas" "oro"*—wife, jewelry, gold—and Amanda Cortez's name. Roberto listened for a minute and kept his eyes on Lowell the entire time. He continued in Spanish. "No," he said. *"Yo no se. No lo veo.* I don't know. I haven't seen him."

Roberto hung up, looking visibly shaken. "Son of a bitch," he muttered. "Son of a bitch." He looked at Lowell. "He wanted to know how you knew about that."

"Thanks for not telling him. *Now* can I see your sister?"

Roberto's eyes narrowed as he fought to reach a decision. Just then the cell phone rang, shrill and distinct above the restaurant din. With a doubtful glare at Lowell, he answered. *"¿Sí?* Yes, I'm with him now. *¿Qué pasa?"*

There was an eruption noise over the phone line. Roberto flinched and listened, his expression tense. Lowell could hear a woman's voice over the line, high-pitched and hysterical.

Robert's eyes widened in alarm. "Oh, Christ," he muttered. "Easy, easy. What happened, *hermana*?" Roberto listened some more, his expression making obvious that he didn't want to hear what he was hearing. "Jesus. Micaella, listen to me. You're gonna be okay. But you have to tell me now. How long ago?" He listened briefly. "Fifteen minutes? Shit. Micaella, no more bullshit. Where is she?" Roberto listened as the sobs subsided. "She's in Pecos," he finally repeated, writing it on his notepad, not looking at Lowell, his face pale. "Up in the canyon. At the old hunting lodge. Okay, *querida*. Put Peso on." He waited, his jaw rigid. Lowell waited with him. "Peso," Roberto shouted. "You knew about this?"

He listened, furious. "That's no-man's-land! You let her go alone up *there*?" He shook his head in disbelief. "Those places are just shacks, for God's sake!"

Lowell could hear Peso's protests of denial. Roberto banged the table, his knuckles white. "Forget the cops. You just call Dr. Vigil and meet me up there. I'm leaving now!"

He jumped to his feet. "Lopez beat up Micaella," he told Lowell. "She broke down and told him where Alicia is. Please don't say 'I told you so.' "

"Okay," said Lowell. "But I'm coming with you."

"No way."

"Try to stop me." Lowell was right behind him as Roberto threw a twenty on the table and ran for the door. Out on the street, Roberto hesitated at the curb, looked at Lowell, then threw up his hands. "All right, all right. You win. I have the truck on the next block. Let's go."

Lowell and Roberto sprinted across Canyon Road to the city parking lot, where Roberto's new Chevy S-10 pickup truck was parked. In four minutes, they were speeding south on

Old Pecos Trail, heading for the Interstate. Roberto stomped desperately on the gas. Lowell buckled up and hung onto his seat. They reached the interchange and sped onto I-25.

"How is she?" Lowell asked, finally catching enough breath to speak.

Roberto glanced at him. "Micaella? Or Alicia?"

"Micaella."

"She'll be all right, banged up a little. Just frightened mostly. And ashamed. If he harms Alicia—"

"What are you going to do, assuming we get there in time?"

Roberto looked grim. "I'm going to do what I should have done a long time ago. Kill the son of a bitch." So saying, he let go of the wheel with one hand, reached behind the pickup seat, felt around and pulled out a .12-gauge Winchester.

Lowell looked at the gun and didn't say anything. He felt a knot of fear in his guts, spreading like a forest fire.

16

Danny Lopez saw the flashing lights of the roadblock on St. Francis Drive and cursed to himself. They were out looking for him, he knew. But they wouldn't find him. Not in time to do them any good, anyway. He knew his way in, around, and out of Santa Fe better than anyone, and no fucking roadblocks at the main intersections were going to stop him.

What they would do was slow him down. Fuck! He'd thought he'd had plenty of time to get to that little bitch before she could do anything crazy—and now this shit. Then he'd gotten stuck in the jam on St. Francis from St. Michael's on down to the Interstate for ten minutes before he'd seen what was causing it. Fuck it, he'd decided. Let them sit down there and slow things up. He pulled over onto the shoulder, which offered a broad view of the south end of town, the hills west of Old Pecos Trail, the desert between Eldorado and the state penitentiary, both visible in the distance, and the mountains of Cerillos, farther south. Danny left the engine idling for the heater, lit a cigarette and listened to the radio. Maybe the dumb-ass radio station would tell him what was happening down there. Meanwhile, he'd sit up here and watch their sorry asses until he saw just a little break, and then he was outta here. He leaned back and watched the police strobes flashing down by the Interstate on-ramp, a mile away. That meant they'd be at Old Pecos and Cerillos as well. No matter. There were other ways to kill a coyote.

He had all the information he needed—the files from that fuckhead fool at the Jewelry Exchange, so now nobody could prove he'd sold Amanda and Alicia's crappy little heirlooms. A few crummy gemstones, except that single good one of Amanda's he never did find, and some old Spanish gold. He'd gotten maybe four thousand dollars for the lot, and a lot of fucking good that did him. Paid for a new engine on the Camaro and a paint job—that was about it. Christ, did Alicia really think she'd be able to hide from him up there? He'd have figured it out sooner or later. He knew about that cabin where she was holed up. He hadn't ever been invited to it, which used to piss him off—them being family and all—but he'd heard how Manny used to take the brothers somewhere up the canyon when they were boys to fish, drink beer, shoot rabbits and stray cats—and anything else that moved—and raise hell.

Well, he would raise some hell now.

Thanks to his good old skills of persuasion when the bitch's sister had practically walked into him in the empty parking lot behind the drugstore, he knew where to find her.

But the fucking cops—he knew Micaella would tell them what happened. He should've killed her, too. What's one more at this point? But she'd gotten away. Still, she'd only just be running into the house now, looking for her brothers. Roberto would be at work, the dumb-ass sellout government lawyer. That left Peso. Knowing him, he'd be drunk by now, the shithead. Too drunk to be worth shit. No threat there.

Danny slapped the steering wheel, laughed derisively and yanked up the volume. He'd updated the car stereo with the latest shit, enough fancy sound equipment to make the car rock and roll, literally, where it sat. He knew the thumping of the big speakers in the trunk would jar to the teeth every driver who passed him—the slower the traffic, the better, let 'em suffer! Then he remembered he didn't want to attract any undue attention inasmuch as he was the one the cops'd be looking for.

Grudgingly, he turned the volume back down, to the disappointment of the carload of Cholos that was alongisde him now. Not Peso's Cholos. Somebody else's Cholos. One of them recognized him and waved. Shit! He grimaced, but waved back. Anything the Cholos knew, they weren't about to share with the cops. He was still safe for now.

He put on a Los Lobos CD and tried to figure out how he'd come to this sorry situation. He knew Alicia had gone off to Colorado twice in the past two years after breaking off their marriage—their beautiful marriage—just because she couldn't understand the concept of his God-given rights; still, he would've had her slapped into shape in another year, he figured. Giving her a child should have been enough to do it. For a normal woman. But Alicia wasn't normal, he now knew. Like the way she'd just up and left, for no reason.

He'd been devastated at first, taking to drinking whiskey with his friends, including Peso, who he thought understood. He'd figured that sooner or later she'd come around, come to her senses, come back to her people, her town, her husband. Instead, she'd run off, filed for divorce, and then this final offense—taking up that New Age shit. And to top it all off, this interest from some goddamn Anglo! At least he now knew she was definitely pregnant. With his child—as he'd gotten the bitch sister to admit.

But now Alicia had gone and spoiled everything, trying to hide from him again. She didn't deserve to have no baby of his. Instead, she was going to die. Her, then the Anglo asshole who'd been following her around, messing with his business. It was bad enough being disloyal. Worse to be unfaithful. She'd gone too far. He would be an angel of retribution and punish her for her sins. He'd find her later in Heaven. And she would be repentant then, and contrite. Maybe she'd have to do a little time in Hell first to teach her a lesson. Yeah, that's probably where he'd send her first. But if she came around, maybe she'd be his wife again, in Heaven. He'd probably be joining her there soon enough, the way things were going. Not that he saw beyond the need to kill her. He just sensed he wasn't long for this world. The good ones, he knew, never were.

Taking one last drag on his Camel, Danny tossed the cigarette out the window, drove along the shoulder to Siringo, turned right and kissed the big V-8 over the hill into the neighborhood where he'd grown up, and where the little back road he used to take to Eldorado was. He loved his car—the low-slung, metallic-blue Camaro, with dual four-barrel carbs, dual exhaust and 350 V-8. He put on his beloved Doors' CD and played his all-time favorite song, "The End." "Yeah, baby!" he shouted as Jim Morrison's guttural vocals came on. *"This is the end!"* What could be more appropriate? Stomping on the gas with a defiant roar, he turned onto Camino Carlos Rey and sped south, burning rubber.

"Shit!" he muttered, glancing at his watch. The Sandovals would have mounted a regular posse by now. He knew there was no time to lose. They might even be ahead of him, if Manny or Peso were sober enough. The mama might do it, Theresa. Or Micaella. They could still cause him trouble, bring out some of Peso's compadres, even. He goosed the big eight onto the dirt road hardly anybody else knew about and sped south through Eldorado, where he rejoined I-25 at the Lamy on-ramp. By then, he knew he was in the clear, and floored it.

Danny caught sight of Roberto's pickup on the Interstate, just past Apache Canyon. He recognized it right away by the neat black bed cover. Nobody but a fucking lawyer would keep a truck bed that clean. So they had gotten ahead of him. Fine, he thought. So be it. He'd take care of the whole fucking family if he had to. He could make out Roberto, the driver. But who was the dude in the passenger seat? Then it hit him: the Anglo!

He had the Colt *pistole* ready on the seat next to him. He'd stolen it from a sporting-goods store two years before, right after Alicia had run out on him the first time. He'd kept it for just such an emergency. True, on more than one occasion, he'd been tempted to shoot some rich Anglos he'd had run-ins with around Santa Fe.

He picked up the gun as he bore down on the pickup from the right-side lane. They were slowing on the hill, and he had all the power in more ways than one. No way would Alicia's family or this meddling Anglo outsider stop him. They had an appointment coming with destiny. His destiny. Especially the Anglo.

He chuckled to himself. Boy, would she be surprised to see him. It would be her final, greatest surprise, and a fitting one, since it would come from him, her rightful husband.

The sun was low over the horizon when the Camaro overtook the pickup at the crest of the hill and pulled alongside. Danny raised a pistol and honked at the same time. Lowell looked over at him and saw who it was.

"Look out!" he shouted, and dove for the floor.

Roberto looked over too, and his jaw fell open. "Son of a bitch!" he muttered.

Danny grinned at his expression and squeezed the trigger. But at that moment, a loud horn and flashing lights directly behind him jolted him, and the shot went wild. A pitch-black Pontiac Bonneville had come surging over the crest out of nowhere and was riding his rear bumper. Roberto saw the Pontiac too, and recognized his brother. Danny wavered, swore, and yanked on the wheel to get the Pontiac off his back.

Twisting around to get an angle on the car, Danny squeezed off a shot in its direction. Roberto had dropped back out of range at the same time Peso rammed Danny's rear bumper. Furious, Danny squeezed off a couple more shots in the general direction of the pickup. Suddenly, to his great elation, Roberto spun out of control and skidded toward the meridian.

Peso found himself torn between helping his brother or

heading off Danny. In that moment of hesitation, the fates intervened as his Pontiac hit a patch of ice and he found himself sliding sideways, straight toward a clump of piñons in the middle of the median. With a cry of rage and frustration, he fought to get control of the car, pulled it almost out of the skid, but then hit the trees.

Danny let out a cry of triumph and sped ahead.

Seconds later, Tony Lowell, in Roberto's truck, felt the impact of the first snow drift and looked up just in time to see the pickup hit the ditch, and Roberto slam into the steering wheel. Then he blacked out.

Danny Lopez's Camaro crested the hill up ahead, at Glorieta Junction, and vanished from sight.

Lowell came to, stunned and woozy from the impact, but otherwise unharmed. He tried to collect himself, disoriented, not knowing where he was or what had happened, only that there was something terribly urgent he had to do. The truck was wedged against a row of piñons, and Roberto was pinned behind the wheel, unconscious. He had a gash on his head from striking the dashboard, and he was bleeding—luckily, not too badly. Tearing off the sleeve of his shirt, Lowell managed to stanch the flow. Then he checked Roberto's pulse. It seemed stable.

Painfully, bruised and battered, Lowell pulled himself out through the passenger-side window. Other cars and trucks were skidding to a stop, and he could see Peso's Pontiac a hundred yards away. It had slid sideways into a juniper that straddled the snow-covered center divider. The bushy juniper had prevented Peso from skidding into traffic coming the other way, which most certainly would have killed him. The car looked otherwise undamaged.

235

Lowell dropped to the ground and ran to the Pontiac. Two Indians in a pickup had stopped and were already tending to Peso, who was stumbling out. Lowell caught up to them.

"Peso," he shouted, ignoring the frowns and gesticulations of the two Indians. "How do I get there?"

Peso, sprawled on the ground, blinked. "You keep out of this," he said.

"You can't move, mister," the Indian woman told him firmly. "You're hurt."

"I'm all right," Peso insisted, trying to sit up. They pushed him back down, gently.

Lowell grabbed him by the shirt and yanked him to a half-sitting position, ignoring the Indians' howls of protest. "I'll ask you one more time. How do I get there?"

Peso winced and gasped. "F-first road past Holy Ghost Canyon. You'll see the signs. Only house on the left."

"I'm borrowing your car," Lowell told him, again ignoring the howls of protest. The car appeared basically intact, other than that the driver's-side door was buckled. Lowell crawled through the window and into the driver's seat.

Two truckers had just pulled into the meridian and were running over to assist. "Holy Ghost Canyon," Lowell shouted to the nearest trucker, starting the engine. "How far is it?"

The first trucker stared at him blankly. "Holy what?"

"It's about ten miles up Pecos Canyon," the second trucker yelled back. "Make a left at the intersection when you get to the village!"

Peso's engine was making a noise—probably just a loose manifold, Lowell hoped—but it ran. He spun the battered car back around, and the Indians and truckers scattered, clearing a path.

Moments later, he accelerated north on Interstate 25, with more horses under the hood than were left on some of the ranches thereabouts. The engine screamed with power and fury, and Lowell figured that if any car could overtake the Camaro, Peso's Bonneville was it. Danny had a mile, maybe a two-mile lead, and Lowell knew he could close some of it. The rest would be luck. His head swam, his thoughts were jumbled. The voice that had haunted his dreams at the beginning of all this was now a living presence, almost screaming inside his head. Get to her! Get to her now! He only hoped it was not too late.

He never even stopped to think about the fact that Danny Lopez was armed . . .

Up in the canyon, Alicia Sandoval's cramps subsided as the day wore on, and she finally felt well enough to venture out again for firewood. She struggled with her task, trying to gather enough fuel for several days in case a winter storm came through. Which could happen at any time now. She had nearly wrestled a big dead branch free from the underbrush at the edge of the canyon above the river, tugging with all her might to pull it loose, when another sharp pain tore at her insides, worse than before. She screamed, as much from certain knowledge now of what was happening as from fear and the pain itself. As she doubled over, her foot slipped and she tumbled down the ravine toward the icy river and its freezing torrent. In a few seconds, she would either be drowned or dashed into the rocks in the river, and her chance of survival would be slim. Desperately, she grasped for something to hold onto.

A large tree root jutted out from the riverbank just below, where a once-tall, lightning-struck ponderosa pine was partly upended. The root's sharp ends pointed directly toward her. They could either save her or kill her, she realized, and she had just a split second to react. Kicking hard, she avoided the spikes, grabbed for the root and barely caught it. Freezing though they were, her fingers held. Somehow she clung on, then pulled herself up to a branch, then another higher up the ravine, then to a rock, then a ledge, and slowly she pulled herself up the riverbank, dragged herself to safety at last, and collapsed on the ground gasping.

Then the cramps returned redoubled, and she knew her troubles were not over. Freezing, stiff, shivering, she made her way along through sheer will back toward the cabin—perhaps a hundred impossibly long yards away.

A logging truck roared past her on the road. Alicia cried out and waved feebly, but her voice—weakened by shock—was carried away unheard. She walked as though in a terrible dream. Then she saw the car coming. At first, her heart soared with hope renewed. Then, as the Camaro drew nearer, she recognized it—a blue, nightmarish specter. With a scream, she summoned all her remaining strength and ran for her life . . .

The sun was down by the time Lowell got to the village of Pecos. The weather had turned dark, cold, and threatening. Remembering the directions, he turned left at the center crossroad and headed north along the wild Pecos River. The two-lane highway ran steeply upstream into a heavily forested canyon on the eastern slope of the Sangre de Cristo Mountains. A brown sign informed him he was on Federal land, marked as being part of the Pecos Wilderness area of the Santa Fe National Forest. It began to snow, a light dusting that fell harder as he climbed farther up into the mountains. He reached Holy Ghost Canyon just as darkness closed in.

The dirt road was far up in the canyon, close to the river— just to the east—where a wall of almost sheer rock rose a thousand feet on the other side. Lowell quickly understood why the women had chosen this location for their hideout. The good part was that it was well hidden and away from Santa Fe; the bad part was that it was far from help. His heart sank as he rounded the last bend in the road—and saw the cabin up ahead. Danny Lopez's Camaro was parked right at the front door of the cabin.

Lowell shut off the engine, rolled silently to a stop a hundred paces away and switched off the lights. He hoped Lopez hadn't noticed him as he'd come tearing up the canyon, or heard the roar of Peso Sandoval's big V-8.

He knew with a sick feeling there could be no peaceful resolution to this encounter. He climbed quietly out of the car, leaving the door ajar so as to make no noise. The snow was accumulating fast now, coming down hard. The wind howled, covering his approach. He saw two sets of footprints approaching the door, and signs of a scuffle on the little porch. The cabin was a shack, really—small and primitive. He reached the door and saw a dim light through the uncovered window. Moving cautiously, he stepped close to the wall and peered in.

She was bent backward over a crude wooden table, trying to fend him off. Danny tore at her blouse with one hand, raining blows down on her with the other, and she was fighting back. He was taunting her, and Lowell could hear his words plainly through the thin glass of the window.

"You were with a goddamn Anglo, weren't you! *Puta!*" He screamed. "I'm going to kill you for that! I'm going to kill you, bitch!"

That was when Lowell kicked the door open. Danny jumped up, shock and surprise on his face, and fumbled for his gun.

Alicia moved at once. With a desperate lunge, she found the gun before Lopez did, and grabbed it. Danny knew what she was doing, but his reactions were slowed by the fact that Lowell was charging across the room toward him roaring like a mountain lion. Lowell was almost on him when Alicia got a grip on the pistol. Danny saw her too late and grabbed for a lamp to strike her with. Lowell hit him with a flying tackle, sending Danny to the floor and the lamp skittering.

Just as Danny raised his head, Alicia shot him in the side of the face, just missing Lowell. Howling, Danny reeled like a drunken man, and stumbled to his feet, clutching his mouth. His teeth were gone where the bullet had entered in one cheek and exited out the other. His adrenaline level was so high, he felt more shock than pain. As he tried again to strike Alicia, she fired a second time, hitting him in the shoulder.

Danny let out a scream and spun away, lurching for the door. But first he had to get around Lowell, who blocked his path. Enraged to the point of madness, Danny shrieked and dove for Lowell—the same switchblade knife suddenly appearing in his hand as if from nowhere. Lowell braced himself, dodged the lunge and threw his leg out as Danny rushed at him, tripped over Lowell's foot and fell headlong just as Alicia fired once more, wildly. Danny let out a bellow of terror and clawed his way to his feet. A second later, he was out the door.

Lowell let him go and gathered Alicia in his arms, trying to cover her and stop the violent trembling and bleeding, knowing what it meant, what new horror she had suffered. Neither of them said anything, neither knowing what to say. They heard the Camaro engine roar to life, tires whining in the snow as Danny tore off down the snowy dirt road and out onto the canyon highway.

"You keep showing up," she finally murmured, and collapsed in Lowell's arms.

A mile down Pecos Canyon Road, Roberto Sandoval and his brother Peso saw headlights coming straight at them as the overheating pickup sputtered and crawled its way up the canyon. The Interstate truckers had managed to get them back on the road, with much travail and despite the strong protests of the Indians who had been tending Peso.

"Jesus!" Roberto shouted, seeing the car coming at them. "This guy is crazy."

"Look out! He's heading straight for us!" yelled Peso.

Roberto tugged desperately at the wheel, barely managing to avoid a head-on collision as the Camaro roared past them in the middle of the two-lane road.

"That's Danny's car!" Peso exclaimed. Then he yelled again, like a man who's had a momentary glimpse into hell. "Did you see that?" he shouted. "He got no face, man!"

"What in hell—?" muttered Roberto.

"I don't know what happened to him, but if he's hurt her," Peso snarled, "I'll find him and finish the job."

Suddenly there was the terrible screeching, grinding sound of rubber, a car skidding out of control on the road behind them.

Roberto hit the brakes and looked back as they heard the scream of protesting metal before the full impact of what was happening hit them. Danny, careening down the canyon, had lost control. They just glimpsed the red taillights smashing through the guardrail on the rim of the canyon as the car went over the edge. Then the lights vanished into the abyss. Moments later there was a flash of yellow fire, followed by a deafening explosion from the black depths of the riverbed far below, echoing up and down the high canyon walls like a dozen thunderclaps. Then there was silence.

Roberto pulled the pickup over onto the narrow shoulder climbed out and ran back to look down into the canyon. Peso joined him.

"Jesus," breathed Peso. "What do we do, man?"

"Forget it," said Roberto. "We have to get to Alicia."

"Son of a bitch," muttered Peso as they got back into the truck. "I hope he's dead, man. So I don't have to kill him."

"I think your chances for that are gone," said Roberto, heading on up the canyon.

"That asshole son of a bitch was crazy!"

A mile up the canyon, Tony Lowell heard the explosion and pondered what it meant. He could see a glow in the distance as he carried Alicia to Peso's car. She was wrapped in a blanket and still shocked by what had just happened inside the cabin. He realized he didn't know her at all, other than as a woman who had been overtaken by events until she'd been driven to total desperation. The fear and menace must have long been lurking in her mind. She must have sensed that what had just happened was inevitable.

An odd and wistful thought crossed Lowell's mind as he gently laid her in the front seat, tucked the blanket around her and buckled her in. He couldn't help but wonder what she would have been like had all this not happened to her, had all those crucial life's choices not been made *for* her, but *by* her. He had set out to rescue her, and he had done that, ever the rescuer. But what was he to do with her now—what would *she* do now? She was like a beautiful wild creature in captivity: she would not survive unless she was free. But then she'd be on her own, without the survival skills she'd need . . . or had he underestimated her? It was she, after all, who'd shot the sonovabitch!

Alicia's fear of Danny had been palpable, overwhelming, and plainly for good reason. But she had survived in the end. And if he was right about what had happened down in the canyon, Danny Lopez had terrorized his last woman. So Lowell felt that for better or worse, having done what he could, he had carried out the mission that had brought him to Santa Fe. If not to his satisfaction. But he had no idea of what would happen from this point on, and he began to worry that his very presence might ultimately serve only to make things worse.

As he reached the second switchback below the cabin on the Canyon road, Lowell saw the headlights of Roberto's pickup truck winding its way toward them far below, two switchback turns still to go. Beyond, he could see the flames and smoke of the fire at the bottom of the chasm.

Quickly, he backed out into the road once more. He

turned downhill, cut the engine and rolled to the spot where the fire could be seen still raging below. Alicia opened her eyes, and saw what had happened at once. "I have to see!" she insisted. He helped her out of the car and led her to the edge, holding her tightly. He could see a car door not far down the ravine, glowing metallic-blue in the light from the rising moon.

"Danny's down there," she said, her voice strangely vacant. "That's his car."

Lowell nodded. "With any luck at all," he said softly, "he'll stay there."

"He's dead," she breathed. "I killed him!" She looked at him, wide-eyed.

"Bullshit," snapped Lowell. "You just defended yourself. He's the one drove himself over the cliff."

In a short while, the headlights of Roberto's truck appeared, coming their way. Lowell put on his own lights and a moment later, the truck pulled up. Roberto ran to the car and gently helped his sister out and into the pickup.

"Let's go, *hermana*," he said. "We're going home." He turned to Tony and gave him a long look. "Don't worry," he said. "We'll take care of her this time, I promise. She'll be okay."

Lowell saw her face at the window, and as Roberto pulled the pickup away, she smiled sadly and gave a little wave. Her smile was still bright enough to light up half of Albuquerque—or Tampa Bay.

Deep down, he knew he would never see her again.

Epilogue

MANATEE BAY, FLORIDA
ONE YEAR LATER

Summer had returned to Florida with all its sultry indolence, and in that last week of August, during "Travel Bargain Days," once again a world-weary bevy of life's victims began the trickle that would turn into a torrent, from Canada, and Michigan and Ohio, back south to Florida and the Gulf Coast, and the beaches and waterways of Manatee Bay.

For Tony Lowell, the year had gone better than the one before, but not by much. He'd solved a few cases, done some legwork for Lieutenant Bedrosian as usual, collected a few modest fees.

Not far north of Tony Lowell's hideaway, across the wide expanse of Tampa Bay, a group of New Age devotees had gathered for their third and final Recovery Seminar, this year to be held at the grand old Don Cesar Hotel on St. Pete's

Beach: a bright pink coral Mediterranean vestige of the Roaring Twenties.

Most of the arrivals knew each other, having taken Seminars I and II in the preceding years. Among them were Ariel Schoenkopf-Lowell and her new artist friend from out west, Michael Baca.

Ariel had tried to convince her father to come down for the day and check out the event, having earlier failed to convince him of the wonderful pleasure of seeing Mr. Baca again.

"Who knows, Dad? Maybe you'll even like it and want to sign up. Sometimes they take last-minute attendees. And Mike would love to see you."

"Ariel, this is really kind of out of my league."

"Come on, who knows, Dad? She may even show."

They'd both known who she was talking about.

"Is that psychic person going to be there?" he'd asked, changing the subject. Sometimes he almost, but not quite, had a fond thought for the little blond firebrand.

"Hey!" his friend Perry Garwood had interjected, sitting nearby during one of his regular visits to Lowell's ancient record collection. "I'd like to meet that woman."

"No you wouldn't," Lowell told him.

"Who, Emily Tartikoff? I hate to disappoint you," Ariel chortled. "She had to go to Seattle on business. She sends her love."

"Sorry to hear that."

For reasons unclear even to himself, Lowell had agreed to go. He and Ariel had sailed up the coast, with Perry as semi-trusty crew, in the sometimes-seaworthy schooner *Andromeda* and anchored off Shell Key a day early, just to enjoy the sun and fishing and, in Ariel's case, windsurfing, prior to her plunge into the seminar's demanding schedule. The waters of the Gulf and Tampa Bay were almost uncomfortably warm—too warm for real swimming, but wonderful for dipping at sundown or just floating away the hours, lost in contemplation of where one had gone wrong in life. Lowell still had plenty to contemplate, which is one reason, he told himself, why he'd agreed to tag along.

That first afternoon, he'd spent most of his free time with Ariel, who'd decided to enroll in Recovery III even though she'd taken only the first, in Denver two years before, when she'd made friends with Alicia Sandoval and had missed out on II.

"A lot of people haven't returned," Ariel had reported after checking in at the conference center. One name by tacit mutual agreement was not mentioned. "On the other hand," she went on hopefully, "with all those connections, plus all the traffic out there, they'll be trickling in all day. Probably all night. There's no telling who might still show up."

He'd once again changed the subject. "So how's it going with you and what's-his-name?"

She sighed. "Michael? To tell you the truth, not all that well. It's like he expects something of me, and he's a lot different from the guys I'm used to."

"He's from a different culture, honey. I'm not surprised."

"But he is a fabulous painter," she added.

Lowell had scanned the room as the opening session began. There was no sign of Alicia Sandoval—not that he'd expected, or even held any hope, of seeing her again. Or even wanted to, deep down. But he couldn't help wonder how she was doing, now and then.

"Welcome to Recovery," Facilitator Christina Taylor

opened the afternoon session, with her famed smile. "This year, we are going to work on the true essence of this series of seminars. By the time we leave here, you will truly be on the road to *recovery,* and be fully ready to embrace and rejoin life as it should be lived."

There was the usual collective sigh of hope, mixed with doubt and uncertainty.

Late that afternoon, after Christina's opening session ended, Ariel and Tony walked out together, Ariel effusive on the session's wonderful revelations, which somehow escaped Lowell altogether. She left to take a sauna. Lowell headed for the beach, weighted with an odd sense of loss and disappointment.

There he settled back on his beach towel, applied some Number 30 sunblock and stretched luxuriously on the powdery white sand that reminded him of New Mexico. Perry sat nearby sucking on a Foster's, having decided to crash the party.

"Recovered yet?" teased Perry.

Lowell punched him on the arm—hard—and opened a beer.